Readers Love XENIA MELZER

Arthropoda

"If you like murder mysteries with a paranormal touch, if two tough guys finding ways to admit their vulnerabilities is your thing, and if you're looking for a suspenseful story with a few twists and surprises, then you will probably like this novel as much as I do."

—Rainbow Book Reviews

Eruca

"*Eruca* is a suspenseful, action-packed, fast paced novel with a dark theme…the series just gets better and better."

—Queer Sci Fi

Casto

"I fell in love with Xenia Melzer's writing and I can't wait to see where this story goes."

—Diminishing Thoughts

A Dom and His Writer

"The conflicts are well written, very powerful, and the portrayal of them all allows us to feel everything Richard and Dean go through along the way."

—Love Bytes Reviews

By Xenia Melzer

ARTHROPODA
Arthropoda
Eruca
Apidae

Published by DSP Publications
www.dsppublications.com

CLUB WHISPER
A Dom and His Writer
A Dom and His Artist
A Dom and His Warrior
A Dom and His Gentleman

GODS OF WAR
Casto
Love and the Stubborn
Ummana
Braving the Storm
The Rules of War

Published by Dreamspinner Press
www.dreamspinnerpress.com

APIDAE

XENIA MELZER

DSP PUBLICATIONS

Published by

DSP Publications

5032 Capital Circle SW, Suite 2, PMB# 279, Tallahassee, FL 32305-7886 USA
www.dsppublications.com

Apidae
© 2023 Xenia Melzer

Cover Art
© 2023 L.C. Chase
http://www.lcchase.com
Cover content is for illustrative purposes only and any person depicted on the cover is a model.

Trade Paperback ISBN: 978-1-64108-524-3
Digital ISBN: 978-1-64108-523-6
Trade Paperback published March 2023
v. 1.0.0

Printed in the United States of America
∞
This paper meets the requirements of
ANSI/NISO Z39.48-1992 (Permanence of Paper).

For my daughters – I know you hate the creepy crawlers, but I hope you'll come to see them as the fascinating creatures they are.

And for Parker, who keeps me in an endless supply of inspirational insect TikToks.

APIDAE

XENIA MELZER

1. A Storm is Brewing

His breath was flowing, in and out, like waves on a beach, calm, rhythmical, never-ending, in and out, carrying him from one moment to the next, flooding his blood with oxygen, sweet, wonderful oxygen—it was absolutely necessary when one wanted to live—saturating his cells, keeping his body functioning, in and out; nothing else mattered, just this steady flow of air, back and forth, allowing him to sink deeper into himself, deeper into the safety of his mind, as far as his mind could be safe, even now he felt *them*, a distant scraping at the back of his head, buried in his ears, an insistent hum that never quieted, constantly rising and falling, never evenly, like his breathing, more like tidal waves crashing against rocks, the surf loud and harsh and potentially deadly, threatening to drag him under; he had to concentrate on the soft waves, the ones gently lapping at the sand, leaving wet forms in the sand, like shadows, only more substantial, or not there at all, ephemeral, there and gone again, all the more precious because of it, something to be treasured, running through your hands, not like the sand at the shore line; that was too wet, too clingy, more like the sand farther up, the one that had dried out under the merciless kiss of the sun, in and out; the ants were lethargic today; it was only early spring, after all, about 50 Fahrenheit, in and out; such things didn't matter; only his breathing did, the flow, the steadiness, something reliable, something he could hold on to to keep everything else at bay, and there it was, a second rhythm joining his own, the timing not entirely right, a little off, but George was doing his best, trying to match him, to follow him; he wasn't as used to meditation as Andi, but it was a good idea, George learning it, to be able to help Andi better, to deepen their bond even though it meant inviting disaster once George left him, but not now; now they were finally getting in sync, their breathing the same, rolling effortlessly, like the waves, driven by an unknown force, another layer of protection against the images in his head, the urge to breathe through his flanks, to use his wings, to tuck in his additional legs, to smell through his antennae. George would never truly know what it was like, to sense the world through so many different angles it could make you dizzy just thinking about it. No, it was best if he didn't think about it, if he simply let the pictures flow together, not trying to discern single impressions; that way lay madness, he had to accept it as a whole, but how was he supposed to do that when every second, something new popped up? It was all so damn hard, but there was George, his breathing solid, reliable, like a rock against the wild sea, offering Andi an anchor and a beacon so he could find his way back home. George was there, warm and wonderful. Andi sensed and saw and felt George moving his hands forward, putting them on Andi's, where he had them resting on his knees, palms up, and the connection was there, not only the rise and fall of their chests, also the steady pumping of blood under smooth skin, something else to guide him, another root to keep him in the reality of humans. Andi let the sensations of their connection wash over him, tried to make them his own, to make them part of his very being, just like the arthropods were. Only George was human, like Andi; it was so strange, so unaccustomed, so much what he needed. When he was sure the connection was stable, the anchors strong, Andi opened himself up, dropped his shields, bit by bit, letting the other world in, the one where his perception of everything was completely insignificant—

Soil, so many dead roots, wonderful, a meal, the darkness enveloping him, no need for eyes, he could sense the vibrations in the ground, the air was so clear, not really warm, he was flying between the branches, the leaves offering protection, everything was dampened, it was winter, not the real one with the white stuff, what was that, snow, yes, in some parts of the world, there was snow, rarely seen here, nasty stuff, killed so many, the eggs were hatching, the brood needed feeding, bustling around, countless legs, the rasping of chitin, recognizing the others by their pheromones, telling them where the dead bird was, nourishment, food, it had to be brought in, stored, the brood, it was cozy under the bark, munching away on the liber, getting fat and ready, ready for what, the larvae didn't know, but Andi did, because he was different, not one of them, he was weaving his net between the twigs of the azalea, waiting for prey to fly into it, the praying mantis had caught something, a flower longhorn beetle, it was fighting, Andi could feel it, the strain, then the mantis bit down, severing the head, emptiness, sudden, leaving a hole, filled by the scrambling of a harlequin bug climbing around on the leaf of a southern lady fern over in the next garden, movement everywhere, scrambling and scratching and fluttering and munching and digging, the impressions like the waves on the shore—

Breaking on the rock that was Andi's connection to George, it was okay, he was fine, secure with George's hands on him, his breathing flowing with Andi's own. It was safe, he felt confident, not drowning, at least not as terribly as usual. He could risk it, could afford to stretch his senses a little further, dig a little deeper, like they had discussed, step by step, never rushing, taking his time, because this was new, unfamiliar territory, taking somebody with him who was there and yet not, a weight keeping him grounded on his yoga mat, not letting him dissolve like the foam on the water. Andi thought he had once read a story about a girl who became one with the water, foam on the waves. It wasn't important now, he had a job to do. What had been the first point on their list? Ah, he remembered, all the dead animals in the neighborhood, he had to find them, something specific in the sea of information—

He already knew about the dead bird under the rhododendron bushes of Mrs. Ferris's garden, her cat probably the killer, the tom often caught mice and birds, leaving them everywhere, never eating them because he got so much food from his owner, it didn't matter, he was looking for death, and it was everywhere, the corpse of a mouse, teeming with maggots, the tiny body moving as if still alive, the dried husk of a hedgehog in the grass next to the street three houses below, the water from last night's rain hadn't soaked into it, nothing there to soak into, another bird, too far gone for Andi to recognize what it had been, it wasn't important either, the food was almost gone, only a few scraps left, there was another mouse, buried in the ground with the eggs of a burying beetle, the parents bustling around, getting everything ready for the brood to hatch, for feeding them, a fox, usually too big to go unnoticed by the blobs for so long, the corpse was in a small space under Mr. and Mrs. Sexton's garden shed, it had died only a few days ago, the smell not as heavy and prominent as it would have been in summer, still, strange they hadn't realized it yet, there was a huge ant street leading to and from the shed, flies buzzing around, the heat caused by the friction of the different larvae rubbing at each other in their feeding frenzy made the space cozy, a lot warmer than the outside temperature, ideal for mating, for procreating, what else was there, food, more mice all over the neighborhood, their exact locations like glowing pinpricks in Andi's mind, the map he carried in his head, death everywhere, inescapable, hungry, he needed to feed, this was a race, the slower ones lost, paid with their lives, he wasn't slow, he was—

Back with George, the waves of their breathing lapping gently back and forth, he was secure, again, still, it was a wondrous thing, it made him hope, they had had something else on their list, something more complicated than food, than death, death was always so easy, how sad was that, yes, George had said if Andi felt really confident, he could try to see where all his neighbors were, humans were difficult, so many shapes making up one thing, and it depended on the angle, what he saw or felt or heard or smelled, and putting that together to make sense was so much more than recognizing food, but he could do it, he—

Found Mrs. Ferris in her kitchen, her shape familiar to the arthropods in her house, everything peaceful, an anticipatory hum in the air, she was cooking, meat, it promised nourishment, food again, this time not rotting, blob food, good food, Andi thought he might be hungry, but then again they *were always hungry, always searching, always one meal away from dying, the aroma was heady, pork chops with cheese and gravy, he had to search for all his neighbors, Mr. and Mrs. Sexton, the dead fox under the shed, they weren't home, hadn't been for some time, at least two or three days, maybe on holiday, that was a blob thought, ants didn't care about holidays, all they knew was that the house was quiet, perfect, on to the Muller family house, three kids, it was never quiet there, the youngest child running around with a friend, screeching at the tops of their lungs, the sonic disturbance warping the air, making it hard to navigate, the ground shook from their steps, little crumbs of earth rippling, falling into the tunnel, the oldest daughter was taking a shower, hot, so hot, the air damp, the bathroom a wet hothouse, just like the silverfish loved, there was a car coming along the street, driving too fast, it was heading for Andi's house, never good, the speed promising problems, and there it was, rumbling into his driveway, he knew that car, had seen it before, cars were hard, nothing specific about them, just stinking metal, only when the doors opened, then it was easier, part of the driver spilling out, or rubbing off, Andi wasn't sure, but he knew this one, not just any blob, the door closed with a bang, stress, adrenaline, sharp in the air, mixed with the stench of antifungal nail polish—*

Luke Gelman. What was he doing here? They were on holiday, it had to be urgent, Andi had to get back, warn George, Gelman was at the door, ringing the bell, cursing, there was George, breathing deep, not knowing how things had changed, still so tranquil, holding steady, not allowing Andi to float away, that was good, Gelman started walking around the house,

Andi had to snap out of it now, because George needed to handle whatever Gelman threw at them, he had to, Andi couldn't, he hated people, Gelman wasn't too bad, but he was interrupting something good, and Andi wanted him gone, and George could tell him so in a polite manner, in a way that Gelman would understand, while all Andi had to say to him would make the man so very angry, he focused on George's hands, on their warmth, on the breath flowing in and out and around, and he came back, looked at George, who looked right back, beautiful hazel eyes boring into his own, Gelman had spotted them in the gazebo, he was practically running now, loud enough for George to notice. He turned his head reluctantly, Andi thought, though it could have been because they had done this for so long, been on their mats, breathing, focusing, connecting. Gelman was here now, standing in front of the gazebo, panting and huffing, his hands on his knees, his upper body leaning forward. A picture of urgency, accentuated by his pheromones clogging the air.

Andi was sure he didn't want to hear whatever Gelman had come for.

2. Hitting hard

George wasn't amused by Luke Gelman's arrival for several reasons. The first being that this meditation had been going very well, better than any before, he and Andi finally connecting in a way that really helped Andi. Since the McHill/Portius/Miller case in the fall, life had been hectic. The Castain case had finally found its way into the courtroom, meaning George and Andi had spent a few days under the scrutiny of lawyers who reminded George of bloodhounds eager to rip them apart. He had kept his cool, though, and Andi had rebuffed them so stoically, they had finally given up on getting him to make a mistake. The FBI had called twice for some details on how they had managed to arrest the two assassins from the triple murder, and Chief Norris had kept on assigning them the nastiest cases, always in the hope of tripping them up. Gelman, who was now slowly catching his breath—the man really should work out more—had so far achieved nothing to improve their situation, and George was getting impatient. The chief's constant interfering with them meant they couldn't focus on getting Andi's *geschenk* under control the way George wanted to, and even though it seemed to have settled down a bit in the last weeks, he knew too well how fast things could change. The meditation course they had visited together had given George some ideas how he might be able to play a more active role in supporting Andi when he conferred with his tiny spies. Their one-week holiday that had started the day before was meant for them to practice and experiment, and now Gelman was here ruining it, George just knew it. The man was clearly upset, and it didn't take a detective to know something was up. The way Andi was tensing up next to him wasn't promising either.

"Luke, what brings you here?" They were on a first-name basis since Christmas, though at the moment George was tempted to throw a "Mister Gelman" in to show how annoyed he was.

Gelman took another huge gulp of air before he straightened up. "Hello, George, hello, Andi. I tried to call you. On your phones."

George sighed inwardly. He sometimes forgot that Gelman had a degree in psychology and was able to read a room—or garden in this case.

Their irritation was clear, Andi never bothering to hide it in the first place and George stressed enough to not make the effort.

"We were meditating. We had them off. Plus, we're on vacation."

"I'm sorry, okay?" Gelman held up his hands to placate them.

"What do you want?" Apparently Andi had reached the end of his patience. He stood warm and tense half a foot behind George, his gaze boring into Gelman.

"There's a problem."

"And?" George hated this game of back and forth.

"And we really need your help. Now."

"Again, what do you need?" George could feel Andi's stress levels rising, saw it from the corner of his eye in the way his partner's lips were thinning, the muscles in his jaw bulging.

"Tyler Norris went missing yesterday around 4:00 p.m. It's not the usual twenty-four hours the CPD requires before considering a person missing, but since it's the chief's son we're talking about, the case has priority."

George turned his head to look directly at Andi. His partner seemed resigned. As much as he hated the chief, her son was only fourteen years old. They couldn't turn their backs on that.

"Do you think he was abducted?" He looked back at Gelman.

"To be honest, at this point, we're considering everything an option. He has no history of running away or even acting up against his parents, and as far as I can tell, Tyler's relationship to his father, Aloys Norris, is stable. He was at home with Tyler but in his workshop while Tyler was supposed to study for a test in school. He only realized his son was gone when he called him for dinner at six and he didn't come. He last saw him at four, before he went to work on some kind of sculpture. Tyler's backpack is missing, as well as his favorite stuffed bear, which could suggest he went on his own, even though I don't think a fourteen-year-old would take a stuffed toy with him, but since there are no traces of anything, we just can't say. And the dogs can't follow his scent because of the rain last night."

"And the chief wants us to come?" George did nothing to hide his skepticism.

"No, she doesn't. She's trying to keep this as quiet as possible, hasn't even informed the mayor yet." Gelman sighed. "But I've seen you two work, and I agree with the rest of the precinct that you are the best chance Tyler has at the moment. Miss DuPont is searching the darknet for any hints that this was planned, and the beat officers are getting ready for a wide search. Before they start stomping around the house and destroy what few clues there might be, I want you to take a look. Please."

Andi was already marching toward the house. George followed, talking over his shoulder to Gelman. "We just need to get proper shoes. Meet us out at the driveway."

Inside the house, Andi was already putting on his hiking boots. George followed suit, neither of them bothering to change into different clothes. George's own yoga pants were brand-new, a beautiful dark blue that matched the lighter blue of his long-sleeve, and perfectly fine for being seen in public. And Andi's clothing—Andi's clothing matched his wearer perfectly. He did have some new items; George had taken advantage of his partner's willingness to let George buy his clothes, but budgeting was a thing, and replacing an entire wardrobe took time. He put on his own boots, then followed Andi to the mudroom where he had his weapons safe. They got out their guns and badges, and on their way back to the main entrance, George made a little detour through the kitchen, collecting two bottles of water and the box with the Tylenol. He had done research on pain medication and was adamant that Andi used ibuprofen only when the pain got unbearable and aspirin not at all. He was also looking into teas that could help with mild headaches. Of course, he had no intention of denying Andi the strong drugs when he really needed them, but he also didn't want his partner to have a stroke, heart attack, or internal bleeding.

While Andi closed the door, George went over to Gelman's sedan to get Chief Norris's address. She lived in Fenwick Hills, which was about forty minutes from Andi's house on James Island. The drive via the Maybank Highway was uneventful and silent. George knew Andi was preparing himself to open his connection to the arthropods wide, probably their only chance to find Tyler. He put his hand on Andi's left thigh, a wordless promise that his partner wasn't alone, that George would have his back. First Andi went a little stiff; then he let his own hand rest on George's, accepting his offer of help. George was proud of how good they had gotten at nonverbal conversation.

The chief's house was at the end of Hickory Springs Road, a two-story house in a huge garden bordering on Bloody Dick Swamp. They could see it ahead, as well as the throng of cars parked along the street, meaning there were already too many people at the house, which would make it that much harder for Andi to get a reading on anything. At the very end of that line, Gelman was leaving his boring sedan, waving at them to drive closer. While George was still looking for a parking spot, Andi suddenly grabbed his hand tighter.

"Stop here."

George didn't argue. He set the blinker and parked the Escalade at the side of the road, hoping it wouldn't get any scratches from passing cars. Before he could kill the engine, Andi was already out, his gaze focused on the muddy expanse of grass next to the road. George hurried to lock the car and reach his partner, who was striding away from the road, directly toward the heart of Bloody Dick Swamp, making squishing noises with his boots. When George reached him, he could tell from the way Andi's shoulders had stiffened that he was receiving information in full surround. Without hesitation, George took his partner's hand. They had found out during a cold case some weeks before that having a physical connection to George before he got dragged under helped to stabilize Andi.

"Little boots, *whum, whum, whum,* quick, *splish, splish,* down there, then right, light vibrations, smells sweet, not sharp at all, hunger, prey, *thump,* up, faster, pant, pant, left, so wet, *pit pat, pit pat,* over there—"

They had also realized that Andi could keep it together for longer when he didn't have to translate what he was experiencing. Getting used to the way Andi phrased things, often using onomatopoeia when words failed him, was a work in progress, but George was proud that he understood most of what Andi had just relayed to him. He had found Tyler's trail already; his heart had beat normally, not too fast, which would have indicated some sort of adrenaline, either from fear or excitement, and which Andi would have described with a more guttural, panting "ugh" sound. Tyler seemed to have made his way through the swamp with surprising accuracy, only falling once, then going faster, apparently with a destination in mind because his progress was straightforward, no swaying or detours. He had been alone, so this was probably a runaway case.

They reached a small hill, the flanks slippery from the rain and the general dampness of the swamp, swallowing footprints and scent traces alike. Once they reached the top, they saw a dip with a copse, the trees standing close together, creating a wall against the outside world. Andi was walking toward it, going directly for a gap between two angel oak trees. Inside the copse, they passed more angel oak trees, a few silver maple trees, magnolia trees, and cypress trees with some palmettos and fawn palms mixed in. They were huge, blocking the sun and bathing the ground in shadows. The earth was more solid here, not as wet as on the field beyond the hill. Andi was still marching on, no longer talking, fully focused on following whatever invisible trail the arthropods were providing. George stayed at his side, kept his eyes open to protect his partner from branches in his way and roots he could trip over. They reached some sort of clearing— George wasn't sure if the space of roughly twenty-six feet in diameter could be called a clearing or was just a gap in the vegetation—where Andi stopped. He cocked his head, scanning the area for a moment. George followed his gaze, not sure what he was supposed to find. He certainly couldn't spot Tyler or traces of somebody having passed through.

Andi pointed toward a huge boulder around which another angel oak had slung its gigantic branches. It took George a moment, but then he saw it. Partly hidden by a branch, there was a spot where it was darker, indicating some sort of opening.

"Door, wood, old lock, broken, he's in there, alone, content, careful, it goes deep, structure good, food, so much food, coming and coming and coming, a feast, rotting flesh—" Andi dug his fingers into George's palm. "Fuck, George, he's down there with corpses!"

George felt a curse forming on his lips and managed to suppress it at the last moment. He had a missing kid down there—whatever *there* would turn out to be—and a partner fully open to the barrage of arthropods in a feeding frenzy. It was vital that he kept his cool, as the only person who probably could. "Can Tyler hear us?"

Andi looked at him as if he hadn't understood the question, making George's heart sink. His partner was in too deep, he—

"Yes, I think so. He's down there in a room where the corpses are not. I think this is an old prepper bunker. There's cans and weapons and toilet paper and stuff. Everything to survive the apocalypse."

If the slight sarcasm tinging the last sentence had anything to say, Andi was back home, to George's great relief. "Can we just go down there? Is it safe?"

"It's stable."

"Fine. I'll call Gelman, tell him we found Tyler. Then we go in. Can you call out to Tyler so he doesn't get spooked?" It was a stupid question, asked to mask the one George really wanted answered but didn't dare say out loud in case Andi got his defenses up. His partner raised a brow, telling him silently how ridiculous he was.

"I'm fine. I can talk to a child—well, teenager—while you alert Gelman."

"I'm sorry."

"Don't sweat it. We're both learning, and we both know your concerns are substantiated."

"Don't be all reasonable about it. You know that freaks me out." George squeezed Andi's hand before he fished his cell out of the pocket at the back of his long-sleeve. Andi approached the boulder with the hidden door while George listened to Gelman's phone ring. He took the call after the fourth ring, his voice breathless again.

"Donovan, where are you? You took off so quickly, I had no chance of following you." That Gelman was using his last name meant there was company he wanted to present with a certain front. Probably the chief.

"I'm not sure exactly where we are, but we've found Tyler. He's fine. Can you follow the GPS on my cell? Shireen should be able to put it on a map for you."

"You what? How—? Forget it. I'm calling Shireen. We're on our way."

"Gelman? Tyler is inside an old prepper bunker. Since I don't know how reception's going to be down there, I'll leave my cell out for Shireen to track. If you find the place and we're not up yet, don't come in, call for us. It looks stable enough, but we don't want to take any chances."

"Understood." Gelman ended the call, and George followed Andi toward the boulder.

When he reached it, he saw that it formed a small opening, barely big enough for him to squeeze through, then widened into a round space, like the channel left by a drill, where his feet met planks of wood that were still able to hold his weight but already fraying at the sides. A trapdoor, the iron lock rusted and broken, just like Andi had said. George looked up at the small circle of blue heaven above him. He imagined the boulder, which seemed so massive from where they had come in, resembled a cheerio from a bird's perspective. He bent down to open the trapdoor, tried to lean it against the stone, and realized quickly that it wouldn't stay up. It was too deformed, the hinges creaking ominously. George knew Andi had had no problem closing it because he could find his way in absolute darkness, using the arthropods as his eyes, but George had no such connection and no flashlight either. The wooden stairs leading down into the bunker looked solid enough and were spaced evenly, so he would be able to feel his way down. How he would proceed once he was at the bottom, he didn't know yet, but Andi needed him.

"Andi? Where are you?"

"We're here," came the muffled answer from somewhere deeper inside the earth. "If you go around the corner, there's light. Lamps."

"Thank you! I'm on my way!" George stepped onto the first stair and closed the trapdoor carefully, ducking his head. It wasn't as dark as he had feared. The splintered wood let some light through, and a soft glow from around the corner at the bottom of the stairs beckoned him closer. His eyes quickly adjusted to the gloom, helping him find his way to the first old-fashioned oil lamp Andi had lit for him with the matches placed right next to it. Several burnt matches on the ground around the table where the lamp was placed told George that the bunker was still in use. Considering what Andi had felt down here, George knew he wouldn't like what they were going to find.

He followed the tunnel, which was now high enough for him to stand easily and so broad two adults could pass without touching. The murmur of voices led him around another bend, past two doors, one of them steel, the other normal wood, still in great condition. The air down here wasn't stale; there had to be some sort of ventilation going on. Then he reached a wide-open room with a huge table, several chairs, a sprawling shelf at one side with books, board games, tins with unknown contents, and a sewing machine, and in front of it a sofa that looked like something from the eighties but clearly hadn't been used often. Andi and Tyler were sitting on it, looking up at him. A lamp, bigger than the ones that had led him here, was on the table, throwing flickering shadows at the two. The boy didn't look distressed or harmed, just tired, clutching his teddy to his chest, his long, dark lashes almost touching the dark skin on his cheeks while leaning against Andi. Which was strange. Children usually avoided Andi, somehow sensing that he was different. Then again, Tyler was a fourteen-year-old who had taken his favorite toy with him. He seemed younger than most boys his age and still carried some baby fat with him, which George assumed couldn't be easy for him.

"Hi, Tyler. We've been quite worried about you." George smiled at the boy, who narrowed his eyes at him, a gesture that reminded George so much of the chief he had to blink.

"Andi says you're okay." It sounded as if Tyler was still debating the truth behind that.

"I'm very okay." George took a step forward, and Tyler tensed. Not used to children reacting to him that way, George looked at Andi for help.

His partner sighed; the dark circles under his eyes had deepened since he had entered the bunker. George was immediately alarmed.

"He's like me," Andi said.

George felt his eyes going wide, staring at the chubby boy with the first hints of a jawline, the teddy bear, and the Spider-Man backpack at his side. "He is connected to them?"

"Not to *them*, no."

"Then how is he like you?"

"He talks to ghosts." Andi made a sweeping gesture to encompass the room, probably the entire bunker. "That's the reason he's here. They called him in his dreams, asked him to come and play with them."

George rubbed his face with both palms, trying to wrap his mind around what Andi was saying. If somebody had told him only a year ago that there were people talking to ghosts—mediums, he thought they were called—he would have laughed in that person's face. After everything he had learned since he met Andi, he didn't doubt for a second the truth in his partner's words.

"I thought you talked to ghosts too!" Tyler sounded alarmed when he turned his body to look at Andi.

"Sorry, Tyler. I never explained, did I. The reason I know about the bodies down here is not because their ghosts have told me." Andi looked Tyler fully in the eye. "You can't tell anybody what I'm entrusting to you now, understood?"

That Andi even thought about confiding in a fourteen-year-old worried George deeply. What if Tyler blabbed to his mother about it? The chief would eat them alive. He opened his mouth to object when Tyler beat him to it.

"First of all, who would believe me? I'm still considered a child, a little behind in my development, I've run away, and I have an 'overactive imagination.' Everybody knows that." He huffed, not completely able to hide the depth of his pain. "And secondly, you're not only the first one who believes me, but *knows* I'm not crazy. I wouldn't want to lose that. Never." There was so much longing in his voice, George felt his heart constrict. He also knew why Andi was willing to be open with Tyler. One wounded, lonely soul recognizing and talking to another. The knowledge that Andi had been like Tyler, an outsider in a world that wasn't ready nor willing to accept the uniqueness he embodied, almost brought George to his knees, making his protective instincts flare. He nodded at Andi, showing him he was fine with what he was about to do.

"Fine, Tyler. I'm trusting you."

The boy nodded with absolute sincerity in his eyes. "How do you know?"

"Because the arthropods—bugs and spiders and such, you know—have told me. Are telling me. One of them has died recently, perhaps two weeks ago? They're still feasting on the body."

Tyler's eyes grew wide. "That's Marco. He's the newest. We started playing after New Year's Eve."

George looked at Tyler sharply. "They're children?"

Tyler nodded. "Like in the book. With the other mother."

George didn't understand the reference but had a feeling it wasn't important at the moment. "Andi, can you tell if it's children in there?" If yes, the case would be nasty and brutal, and George started automatically planning in the back of his head how to get Andi and himself through it as emotionally unscathed as possible. He didn't hold out much hope.

Andi shook his head. "No, they are adults." When he saw George's face, he shrugged. "Too much meat, the bones are too big."

"But Marco and the others, they're my age." Tyler seemed confused, a faint tremor in his voice. Andi patted his back awkwardly.

"I'm sure there's a reasonable explanation for it, Tyler. We both agree there's twenty-six of them in here, so we definitely pick up on the same victims. Why they show themselves to you as children, I don't know. Perhaps because you're a child as well? As ghosts, they're not bound to a shape, I would imagine."

Tyler seemed to mull this over, staring at the lamp on the table. He cocked his head. "Izzy thinks it's like Peter Pan."

"Izzy?" George stepped to the sofa. This time, Tyler didn't tense. He looked up at George, full of trust. Apparently seeing that Andi trusted him was enough for the boy.

"She's been here pretty long. Many years. She knows more. Sometimes she speaks like a grown-up because she's older than the rest." Again he cocked his head. "She says being a child is happy. Safe."

George shared a look with Andi, who shrugged. "Fine. You say there's twenty-six victims down here?"

Both Andi and Tyler nodded.

"Where?"

Tyler gestured toward the shelf behind the sofa. "They come from there."

"Secret room. I think I know where it opens." Andi got up, then hesitated. "Tyler, George and I, we have to go in there and take a look. I don't think you should come with us. Can you stay here and promise me not to peek?"

Tyler clutched his teddy to his chest while chewing on his lower lip. "Izzy says I don't want to see what's in there. I'm staying here with the others."

Andi nodded. "Are they all here now?"

Tyler looked around, not randomly but with the gaze of somebody who was assessing his surroundings. George felt a cold shudder racing down his spine.

"Only TJ and Ben are missing. They rarely come to play. I don't know why. TJ knows great games."

"Okay. You stay here." Andi approached the shelf, his eyes already with that faraway look that meant he was conferring with his tiny informants. He lifted his hands, his fingers caressing the section where the sewing machine was placed. There was a soft *click*, and then Andi grabbed the wood and swung part of the shelf toward himself. George stood left of him and had a great view of the darkness behind the shelf-door, and also the doubtful pleasure of getting a lungful of *eau de mort* when the air from the room rushed out. Coughing, he took a lamp from a nearby smaller table before he followed Andi through the door.

The air was not only more pungent, but also damper, the ground not concrete as in the rest of the underground lair but soil that was suspiciously loose for a room in a prepper bunker. The whole space was roughly forty feet long and a little less broad, and judging from the rotting timber holding the ceiling up—which was also hardened soil mixed with long streaks of rock, probably connected to the boulder outside—George was inclined to say this room had been added to the bunker after it was built. If his sense of direction wasn't leading him astray, it was located behind the visible part of the boulder, where the trees were standing closer together. The ground had to be rocky here; otherwise building the bunker would have been impossible to begin with. The swamp was too close to keep it dry.

"Food, food, eat, prey, need more, hatching, changing, *gurgle, tlk, tlk, tlk, ssht, ssht*, so full, pupae, down, just bones, rotting away, *cht, cht, krt*, here, dig here, there's the food, need it, more, more, MORE!"

George saw Andi going down on his knees, and for the first time he really looked at the ground, didn't just register it for the softness beneath his boots, and he cried out. It was moving. Crawling. Like a living carpet, the soil quivering, flashes of silver and brown and white in the gloom of the lamp, his partner down, tiny bodies swarming his hands, hastening up his sleeves, as if they were welcoming him, surging around him, and George knew he had to get him out. Andi was so still, making soft clicking noises, and now that he was listening closely, George could hear it: the scraping of chitin on earth and stone and skin, a low hum that was even more eerie because he knew what it meant, thousands of mandibles tearing away flesh. The scent was there as well, still a solid presence, although he had gotten used to it by now, fate of the detective, George guessed. The corpses were under the earth, the mixture of rotting flesh and soil scraping at the back of his nose, something familiar he would recognize anywhere. This was really bad. George knew a serial killer case this big would make national news, and he and Andi would be smack in the middle of it. Just thinking about the strain this was going to put on Andi made George wish they hadn't found Tyler. It was a fleeting thought—of course finding the boy was important—and he felt bad about being so egoistical, even though he knew it was justified. A small heaving sound brought George back into the here and now, where he had to take care of a partner who was overcome by sensory input.

Shuddering, George fought the urge to just stamp down in order to kill as many arthropods as possible and get the hell out of this chamber of death. Instead he took another step forward, to grab Andi at the scruff of his neck and yank him up. His partner didn't fight back; he was pliant, lifeless, as George dragged him out of the secret room back into the one where Tyler was waiting, watching them with huge eyes.

3. Dancing on Glass

"Is he all right?"

All right... those were words, not sensations, not the hunger gnawing at his insides, not the urge to dig and feed and procreate and spin a cocoon and turn liquid and become something new in the remnants of something dead; the something dead was a human body, important, killed, he knew that, what did "killed" mean, he needed to eat, so delicious, the temperature just right for the eggs to hatch that much faster, though how he knew what faster meant, he didn't know, the word resonated in his head, there were too many of them, too much input, too concentrated, he had to get back, back to the waves on the beach, the breathing, slow and steady, his walls were there, offering protection, he was coming back, crawling out of the turf, clutching at the warmth of the hand offered to him, he needed to be there, it was too important not to be, George, yes, George was here, Andi was back.

"I think I'm fine. Mostly." He forced a smile for Tyler before he turned to George, who *looked* at him, his hazel eyes full of concern. "I'm sorry. There were too many, and when we entered—I thought I could control it, but they're so hungry. It was too overwhelming."

"It wasn't your fault." George was still holding his hands, grounding him, giving him a connection to the reality of the blobs, of humans, of his kind. He looked down where their skin met, saw an ant crawling over his wrist—

Salt and different pheromones, not the way to the nest, not from the colony, far from it, a wide expanse of warmth vibrating under his legs—

And his perception shifted into an endless line of mirrors, each showing him and the ant, the ant and him; he had six legs and two arms, couldn't use either because was he Andi looking at the ant or the ant experiencing the blob it was crawling over, the soft thumping of his pulse indicating unsteady ground even though it was firm, in a way, warm, no prey, though, obstacles, thin and wiry; he had to be careful not to get caught; it tickled, so strange, being tangled up and being the tangling—

George bent forward and blew on the ant, sending it to the ground where it lay stunned for a moment before it went back toward the shelf, the door into that monstrous room where so many were resting, too many for such a small space, really, partly layered, the bones mixing, the fluids of the rotting flesh seeping into the remains of the ones that had come before; this was bad, a serial killer, for sure.

"Izzy says you're all fractured." Tyler, who looked at him with a similar concern in his eyes as what George always showed.

"Izzy is right." That didn't seem to reassure the boy. Andi looked at George, who didn't seem to know what to say either. He wasn't used to dealing with young people. It was tedious, he decided. "There are a lot of arthropods down here. And I'm all of them."

"Ah, I see." Strangely enough, Tyler seemed to understand. Then again, he was seeing ghosts. That surely helped him with perspective.

George put his arm around Andi's shoulders, always so generous with his warmth.

"I think I heard something above. We have to come up with a good explanation as to how we found Tyler so quickly. Not to mention the room." He indicated his chin in the direction of the shelf.

Andi groaned. Plausibility. The bane of his existence.

"The room is easy. The shelf was a little off the wall, and we're detectives and therefore nosy by nature. Hell, the ground in there is practically moving, not to mention the smell. We all know what that means."

"Yes. That fits." George turned to Tyler. "Now how did we know to look for him here?"

"Fuck." Andi rubbed his face with both hands. When he had gotten the first glimpse of Tyler in the minds of the arthropods—it had been easy, the only boy in the vicinity, moving away from the chief's house—all he had thought of was finding him. Now he regretted his eagerness. They should have made a show of inspecting his room and the house, even though he would have had to interact with the chief then.

"Uhm, could I have lost this?" Tyler was holding a lunchbox made of metal in front of them. Andi cocked his head. It showed Harley Quinn in all her mad glory with her pigtails and her baseball bat, and it was shiny, something that could have reflected the sparse sunlight and caught his attention from the car.

"George, what do you think?"

"It's flimsy but better than nothing. Can I see?"

He took the box from Tyler, weighed it in his hands before he opened it. "It's still full. That's good."

"Yes. Makes it believable that Tyler lost it on the way here. But how plausible is it for Tyler to not notice it being gone? Or falling out? And how did we determine which way to go?"

"I often leave my backpack open and lose things. Mother says I'm careless."

Instinctively Andi stepped closer to Tyler. He could not only hear the hurt in the boy's words, he understood it better than he liked. It was his own pain, inflicted by a mother who cared little and a father who abhorred him for his *geschenk*.

"Your carelessness is what's going to save my and George's asses, so I fully approve."

Tyler beamed. "Izzy says you could say that you went up the hill to get a better view and assumed I had gone into the copse because of the rain."

George smiled even if it was a bit strained. "Tell Izzy she's a genius."

"She can hear you." Tyler shrugged, while George shivered. Andi thought he was holding himself together very well, down here in a creepy bunker with a mass grave and two freaks.

"Detective Donovan?" Gelman's voice was muted through the earth and the boulder above them but recognizable all the same.

"We're coming!" George shouted back, motioning for them to start moving. Tyler picked up his backpack, leaving it open.

"Why did you run away, Tyler? Officially?" Andi thought they needed to hear it at least once, in case there were questions.

Tyler stared at the concrete ground for a moment. "I'm fourteen. I guess I could get away with saying I wanted to have an adventure? Like in the books I read?"

"Sounds perfectly reasonable. You went on your adventure, packed your bag, forgot to close it, lost the lunchbox in the swamp, where I spotted it coincidentally when I left the car. We reached it, saw the hill, thought we would have a better view from there, spotted the copse, remembered it had rained last night, not that we could forget, wet as everything is, went down there, found the boulder and the opening, perfect to seek shelter, and there was the trapdoor. Good story. Better than some I've had to concoct before."

"Yeah. As stories go, this one's no too shabby." George sighed. "Let's hope it's enough."

"Andi?" They had started going in the direction of the trapdoor, George in the lead. Tyler held on to the sleeve of Andi's loose sweater, appearing more like a lost child than a boy on the brink of fifteen.

"Yes, Tyler?"

"I know I'm going to be in trouble over this, but when things have calmed down, can I visit you? Or just call?"

Andi felt his insides going tense. What was he supposed to say now? His own inner kid, the boy who knew exactly what Tyler was going through, wanted to reach out to him, tell him he could come or call whenever he wanted, whenever he needed it. The part of him that kept most people at arm's length to protect himself was recoiling, yelling at him that this was a responsibility he didn't need, didn't want, something with the potential for disaster, because this was the chief's son, after all, the same chief he hated with a passion. But there was so much hope in Tyler's eyes, a desperate kind of hope, speaking of all the times he had been disappointed, and knowing what lay ahead of the boy, the loneliness he would taste for all of his life, Andi just couldn't turn his back on him.

"Your mother and I are not on the best of terms, but I'll give you my number, and you can call me anytime. Even visit, if we can manage."

It was as if the sun was dawning on Tyler's face, and Andi just couldn't bring himself to regret letting him into his life. George was the first on the wooden steps, which were illuminated by daylight, no doubt because somebody was holding the trapdoor open. Tyler followed, and Andi heard the chief's voice, sharp and biting, and the voice of a man, softer, full of relief.

"What did you think you were doing?"

"Tyler, I'm so glad you're okay. Come here, champ."

Andi reached the trapdoor last, held open by Gelman, who stared at him wide-eyed, with a speculative expression Andi didn't like. He left through the narrow opening, stepped into the clearing in front of the boulder. The chief was there, glaring at what Andi assumed was her husband, who was hugging Tyler while murmuring with his lips on the boy's head. Two officers he recognized as belonging to the precinct were standing at the edge of the clearing, looking both relieved and uncomfortable, which probably had a lot to do with the chief, who now turned to him and George, her eyes angry slits.

"You found my son." It didn't sound as if she were very grateful.

George nodded. "We did."

"You were quite fast." The suspicion in her voice was blaringly obvious to anybody listening. If Andi hadn't still been too caught up in the feeding frenzy going on in the bunker, he would have given her a piece of his mind. As it was, he left the talking to George.

"I'm sure Detectives Hayes and Donovan have a reasonable explanation as to how they were able to find Tyler so swiftly." Gelman, smooth like a snake, trying to distract the chief.

"We have indeed a reasonable explanation. Unfortunately, Tyler isn't the only one we found in that bunker." George was all detective, serious and respectable, while letting the bomb drop, effectively making their quick finding of Tyler the least interesting piece of information. Smart man. "When we were down there in the main room with Tyler, we spotted a shelf that was slightly off the wall, which struck us as strange. Upon closer inspection, we found it was a concealed door. Of course we opened it and immediately smelled rotting flesh. Plus, the ground was crawling with insects, bugs and maggots. We didn't look further as to not destroy possible evidence, and it could be just some animal carcass rotting underground, though why somebody would bury one inside a prepper bunker is a mystery to me. To be on the safe side, we suggest getting Dr. Melcourt and CSI here to determine if this is a crime scene or not."

The chief stared at them, obviously thinking very hard what her next step should be. The tension was rising until Gelman whipped out his cell. "I'm going to call the precinct and arrange for Dr. Melcourt to come. Detective Hayes, how stable do you think the bunker is? Do we need supports?"

Andi turned to Gelman. He still didn't know what to make of the man. So far, he hadn't been as helpful as Andi had hoped but hadn't proven himself completely useless either. He wasn't sure how much longer they should give him to get things with the chief resolved. The situation was putting too much stress on them at a time when they were trying to find their footing in working with his *geschenk*. So far the progress they'd made was good, but Andi knew it would be much better if George didn't have to worry about shielding him from the chief all the time.

"The bunker looked solid enough to me, but the room with the insects isn't fortified like the rest. It seemed like a later addition. I'd say some supports aren't a bad idea."

"I'll tell them that. You're staying here till they arrive?"

Andi sighed. "We are." He felt George stepping next to him, putting a hand on his lower back, soothing Andi instantly.

"Chief, I guess you're going back with your husband and son? I'm sure you need some family time after this scare. I'll keep you informed about everything that's going on."

Even though Gelman hadn't delivered for them yet, Andi had to admit the man was good. Basically sending the chief away under the pretense of family matters, which she could hardly refute, thus giving George and Andi some breathing space. The angry look Norris was sending their way told Andi she realized what was going on. With a huff she turned to her husband and son, barking at the two beat officers to stay with Andi and George. The two women nodded uneasily in their direction but kept their distance. Gelman was still on the phone, telling the person at the other end to just come to the same coordinates Shireen had sent him and the chief. George took Andi's arm.

"Let's go sit over there," he suggested in a low tone.

There was a small rock with a reasonably flat surface that was cold but better than standing while he felt the headache coming on.

"I'm sorry. I forgot the Tylenol in the car. As well as the water."

The self-incriminating tone in George's voice made Andi shake his head, though only once. Wincing, he put both his hands at his temples. What a rookie mistake he had just made!

"It's fine. Not your fault I took off like some loon."

"We were looking for a boy who had possibly been abducted. It was a good thing you took off like a loon."

"About that, how did you find Tyler?" Gelman had followed them, staring at Andi with a mixture of interest and suspicion. Andi was too tired to deal with the man, so he simply closed his eyes, hoping he would vanish in thin air. He hadn't that much luck, but George came to his rescue as always.

He relayed the story as they had spun it with Tyler down in the bunker, making it short.

Gelman furrowed his brows. It seemed as if he wanted to say something and thought better of it. Their story was plausible enough, at least the way George told it. His partner had gotten very good at it, infusing his voice with just enough no-nonsense to nip objections in the bud, like how they had known to go slightly left toward the bunker instead of choosing a straight line as a wet and probably frightened boy would have most possibly done, and how they had known to go so deep into the copse. Thoughts for another day, or hopefully never. With the pounding in his head increasing, Andi kept his eyes closed, leaving Gelman to George. The hum of their conversation provided the background for all the images washing up against his walls, which had strengthened due to a lot of meditation. Still, completely shutting them out was impossible—

Hungry, hungry, warm, so many, scritching and scratching in the room underground, showing him pictures of a shape, tall, dark, without the usual markers Andi used to distinguish humans; all he could tell was that it was a male, cocooned in oregano, sage, and basil, mixed with smoke; he knew that scent, yes, he did, a beekeeper, they often burned herbs in their bee smoker to get a more pleasant scent; it was everywhere in the bunker, clung to the fabric of the sofa, on the wood of the chairs, saturated the earth, not in a way blobs would realize; their senses were so lacking, so weak, how could one live being blind and deaf and deprived of all sensual input; no, blobs did get input, it was just muted so their brains wouldn't overheat, their minds wouldn't shut down from the onslaught of information; they weren't built for that, poor things; the smoke, it was important, it hung most prominently in the hidden room, even though at the moment it was mixed with sweet decay, mouthwatering, the promise of procreation and sustenance. Andi didn't understand why the blobs thought it despicable, so alluring, with undertones of rotten eggs, hydrogen sulfide, Andi had learned, and then there were dimethyl disulfides and trisulfides, reminding one of old garlic, the blobs anyway; for Andi, for them it only meant food, something to desire; he couldn't dwell on that, couldn't get lost, he needed to get information on the smoke-human, the beekeeper, he was the one, provider of food, bringing it in regularly, making the maggots fat and healthy; he was so good, no, no, he was a killer, it was bad, so many of them, biomass, feeding others, the cycle of life. Andi wanted to puke, his head hurt so much, what was a head, there were—

"Andi?"

4. DIGGING DEEP

GEORGE KEPT his hand on Andi's shoulder, knowing this would help his partner to stay at least partially with them. He was still shocked by what had happened in the bunker, the way the arthropods had swarmed Andi as if they were welcoming him. It was beyond creepy, and yet he found it more natural than the thought of being in the same room with ghosts. Given the choice, George preferred bugs over the spirits of the deceased. If the situation hadn't been so serious, he would have laughed at how much his life had changed in the past few months. Thinking back at the times when deciding the next step for his career had filled entire weeks for him, he pitied and envied himself. Things had been a lot easier back then, firmly grounded in what humans thought of as the real world. Life had been smaller as well. Constricted. Less vibrant. As if he had worn a black veil that muted all colors and blocked out two-thirds of everything. The veil was gone, so to speak, at least partly. He would never be able to and never wanted to be as open as Andi, and even though he had a lot more to worry about now, he realized he wouldn't change it for the world.

Andi gave him a weak smile, silently thanking him for his support and assuring him he would be able to keep it together until Evangeline arrived.

"Is something wrong?" Again Gelman, intruding on them, testing George's patience.

"No, everything's fine." George kept his hand on Andi's shoulder but turned his body, shielding his partner from Gelman's view. "But we really needed that vacation to regenerate after all the stress in recent times. Being thrown back in without warning is a bit much."

George knew he was being passive-aggressive. He didn't care. As much as he had hated it when his mother had treated him and his brothers like this as teenagers, he had learned to appreciate the advantages of that tactic. Venting one's anger without going for the big confrontation that would cost too much energy—perfect as a temporary solution. Gelman furrowed his brows, indicating he realized what was going on. The man did have a degree in psychology, as George and Andi had found out when he joined the precinct for his mediation.

"I understand. And as I said, I'm sorry for having disrupted your vacation." Gelman waved in the direction the chief had left with her family. "I'm not sorry you found Tyler so fast. It was the right call to get you involved."

There were a few answers George had to that, none of which he could give. He settled for a polite smile instead, the one Andi said reminded him of the clown in *It*. "I'm glad Tyler is back with his parents." A socially acceptable response.

"We all are." Gelman hesitated. "What do you think is down there?"

"As I said, something dead for sure."

"You don't think it's an animal." It was a statement, not a question.

George shrugged. "At this point, it's all speculation. But something dead in an underground bunker that is so well hidden from view? It doesn't bode well." There, he had been vague enough, not given away what he already knew. Twenty-six victims. George shuddered inwardly. This case would be a nightmare; he could feel it in his bones. The press would fall on this like vultures on a fresh carcass, no doubt swarming in from all over the country once the news got out. Luckily, he and Andi were on vacation. They would wait till Evangeline came, show her everything, let her do her work, and then return home. This case was somebody else's problem.

George felt a faint stab of guilt for thinking along those lines. There had been a time, less than a year ago, when he would have done everything in his power to get a high-profile case like this. He would have jumped at the chance of getting justice for so many victims and furthering his career at the same time. Now he had more important things to worry about, mainly Andi's mental health. Without being conceited, he knew they were the most likely detectives to solve the case, and not taking it did leave a bitter taste in his mouth. But he and Andi desperately needed the vacation. The meditation techniques they were using worked, which was good. The downside was, meditation of any kind needed practice, something George hadn't been aware of. Naively, he had thought just sitting down and closing his eyes would do the trick. By now he knew why there were courses to learn proper meditation. It was damn hard to do, trying for the mind, and exhausting. If one wanted to get in sync with somebody else? It was like climbing Mount Everest without oxygen tanks.

After the McHill/Portius/Miller case, Andi had stabilized, much to George's relief, though he was very aware that it was only a reprieve. It was vital for them to establish routines that would help George to anchor Andi when things got out of hand again—like in the bunker. And for that, they needed time.

"You're right. It doesn't look good." Gelman seemed unaware of the turmoil going on in George's thoughts. "I think I hear something."

George strained his ears and turned his head at the same time to where he was hiding Andi with his body. His partner was looking into the copse, where George could hear it now: the unmistakable sounds of ATVs hauling equipment. It was impossible to cross Bloody Dick Swamp with cars, the ground being too treacherous, especially after the rain. Patches of solid ground alternated with pure swamp, ready to suck on the wheels of normal vehicles and never let go. A few moments later, the first ATV appeared between the angel oaks, driven by Evangeline herself. The tires were about three times bigger than those on normal ATVs, enabling the vehicle to navigate on practically every ground, be it swamp, snow, ice, or mud. Four more followed the first one, dragging trailers with equipment. The two beat officers rushed to help with unloading, seemingly relieved to finally have something to do that didn't involve trying not to stare openly at Andi and George with a mixture of awe and fear, as if they were about to bite off their heads. Evangeline hopped down from her ATV with a grim expression.

"George!" She craned her neck to see Andi behind George. His partner had gotten up, discreetly using George's lower back to balance himself. Oh yeah, they needed to get out of here ASAP. "Andi! What have you found this time? Agent Gelman." Evangeline greeted the IA man last, not because she was being impolite, but because she was already gearing up for what she knew would be bad.

"Hello, Dr. Melcourt. I'd say it's a pleasure to see you, but the circumstances suggest it's not. I'm going over to see if I can be of help." Gelman nodded at George before making himself scarce. Evangeline lifted a brow.

"How bad is it?" George had gotten used to her suspecting something about Andi, perhaps even knowing, and never saying it out loud. Like Forard, the SWAT team leader Andi usually worked with, and Waters, the DA for Charleston, she just went with the flow, sometimes with a strange glint in her eyes. It was a complicated dance they did, never naming things, relying on body language and facial expressions. Behind him, Andi sighed.

"You're gonna need more trailers."

"*Ta'i.*" Her shoulders slumped. "I guess I better get down there. Anything else?"

George didn't envy her. "Uh, the room's crawling with arthropods."

"Bad sign." Evangeline turned toward the ATVs, starting to give her orders. She sent the two beat officers to rope off the clearing and directed two of her assistants to get the supports into the bunker. Once she reached her vehicle, she put on a protective suit that even covered the soles of her shoes before approaching the boulder without looking back at them. George saw this as their cue to finally leave. After a short wave to Gelman, who thankfully was busy helping Evangeline's staff and therefore couldn't leave with them, George kept his hand on Andi's shoulder until they reached the car. Getting Andi inside and stuffing him with Tylenol was by now muscle memory. As was unconsciously checking him for signs of how bad things were. Andi's skin color wasn't gray yet, just paler than usual, which was saying something—the man gave the term "white" a whole new meaning, especially this time of year when the sun didn't lend his skin at least a semblance of color. His breathing was steady and deep, indicating he was mostly present in his mind, only his glazed-over look suggesting he hadn't muted all his channels to the arthropods.

George got behind the wheel and started the car, not bothering to make a detour to the chief's house. He was fairly sure Tyler was fine, and they could do without her hostility. With some luck, the whole thing would have blown mostly over when they came back after their vacation. Once they were on the highway, George decided to try to talk to Andi. Sometimes it helped to distract him from the sensory input he was getting and also from the pain of his headaches.

"Did you get anything when we were down there?"

"You mean besides the overwhelming urge to mate and lay my eggs in the rotting flesh?"

Ah, sarcasm. Always a good sign in regard to mental stability. If Andi was able to snark, he had managed to distance himself from his creepy informants. "Yeah. Apart from that."

They both chuckled. Then Andi got serious. "It was a lot, what with so many of them." George wasn't sure if Andi meant the arthropods or the corpses. Both would have had an impact. His partner went on. "What I can say for sure is it was a man, tall, bulky, a beekeeper."

That got George's attention. "A beekeeper? How would you know that? Did he smell of honey?"

Andi shook his head. "No. Smoke. Mixed with herbs. Beekeepers use smokers to calm the bees, and they often burn herbs to make it more pleasant. It's very distinctive."

"But?" George knew there was a "but."

"But the smoke is so prominent it overlays everything else. I can't say if the man is healthy, how old he is, if he's taking drugs. I can't *identify* him."

That was a problem. "Please tell me the smoke is unique."

Andi just huffed. "The smoke is unique in the sense that every time somebody fires up a smoker, it produces a kind of smoke that can be distinguished from others. The key phrase here is *every time*. The killer seems to be fond of basil and sage, but there were also hints of rosemary and thyme, and the mixture changes every time because the herbs are not all evenly dried, sometimes you get stronger ones, sometimes he might run out of one herb or decide he doesn't want it in the mixture. Sometimes the wood he uses is wetter. Sometimes the air pressure doesn't allow for a clean burning process. It's impossible to link the smoke to one beekeeper in particular. What we can do is weed out those who don't use wood in their smoker but oil. And those who don't like herbs or who only ever use lavender or just a single herb. Which leaves a lot of people as suspects."

"Good thing we're on vacation."

Andi didn't react, which prompted George to look at him. "You don't want that case, do you?"

Andi put a hand over his eyes, a sure sign he was stressed. "No."

George waited. He was fluent enough in Andi-speak to know his partner was lining up his thoughts.

"Some of the corpses were veterans."

"How do you know?" George wasn't sure what some of the victims having been in the military had to do with anything, but he was always eager to learn about the *geschenk*. It was all about knowing the enemy.

"Certain bone fractures that are more common among soldiers, a leg prothesis, tiny pieces of shrapnel in the earth around one body, certain chemicals I have learned to associate with the military, and of course, the dog tags."

"Ah. You think the military is going to get involved?" Working with other departments of law enforcement could be either enriching or an absolute bitch, totally depending on who one was working with. Unfortunately, it was most often a clusterfuck.

"I'm sure about five of them. Could be more. One veteran they would probably entrust to us, helping us with the papers, claiming it could be coincidence. Three or more in a serial killer case? They'll want to have somebody in. Or at the very least be kept in the loop, probably with daily reports. Not to mention the FBI, who will get involved no matter what. That's a lot of people trudging around the precinct, all of them eager to give their input and make themselves look good."

"Norris is going to love it." George could already see the chief getting all worked up about sharing jurisdiction.

"Let's just hope she forgets about us. I have absolutely no desire to work with another agency."

George shuddered just thinking about it. Shielding Andi from the chief was bad enough. Having other people tag along during their investigation? The stuff of nightmares.

"We've just started our vacation. We're safe."

"Here's to hoping." After that, Andi went quiet. George got them home, where he put his partner right to bed with another shot of Tylenol and two bottles of water. It wasn't that late in the afternoon—only 4:00 p.m.—and he knew a nap would help Andi to recuperate. George took a long shower before he started dinner, a simple vegetable casserole with four different cheeses. Andi tended to avoid meat, except for the occasional chicken stir-fry. Not because he was a confirmed vegetarian, but because apparently meat, especially red meat, made him even more susceptible to the arthropods. George had read enough scientific articles about healthy eating and the impact of food on people's bodies to not dismiss Andi's claim. Anyway, a mostly vegetarian diet was healthier all around and by cooking for two quite easily managed. He put the casserole in the oven and was getting ready to wake Andi when his phone rang. Silently cursing at the sight of Gelman's name, George accepted the call.

"Donovan."

"George. It's me, Luke."

"I know."

A sigh came through the speakers, and George felt a little bad. It wasn't Gelman's fault that this day hadn't gone the way George had envisioned it. "Sorry. I'm a little stressed."

"It's fine. I guess we all are." There was a pause, long enough to tell George he wouldn't like what was coming.

"Luke."

Gelman must have caught the warning in his tone, because there was another sigh, as if the IA agent was carrying the weight of the world.

"So far, Dr. Melcourt has found ten bodies. And we already know there are more. She's back in the morgue to do the autopsy on the most recent one, because whoever did this needs to be stopped as fast as possible. They're going over everything in that bunker with a fine-toothed comb, hoping to find something that will help find the killer. The entire precinct is in uproar, as you can probably imagine."

"Yes. Andi and I are glad we're on vacation."

The wince on the other end of the line was all the confirmation George dreaded.

"Uh, not anymore, I'm afraid. The chief came in after she had brought her son home. She said since you found the bodies, it's your case."

"That's it. I want you to make our complaint official. I want that stupid, ungrateful bitch removed from her post." George was so angry, he thought he felt smoke trailing out of his ears.

"George, please."

"No. We tried this your way, and I dare say Andi and I have shown remarkable patience while you did nothing much at all to improve our situation. It's obvious nothing will change, and we're both done with the chief constantly nagging and annoying us. She's calling us in purely out of spite, as you well know."

"I know." Another sigh. Gelman had obviously seen this coming. "And you're absolutely right."

"I am. So stop trying to convince me otherwise." George knew Gelman was working toward them giving him more time, and George had no inclination whatsoever to do so.

"I know you're angry. I would be too, if I were in your place. Doesn't change the fact that you and Andi have the highest chance of solving this case, which you know."

George gritted his teeth so hard, his molars started to hurt. "I know. I also know that we both need a vacation because we're terribly stressed out due to you not fixing the situation with the chief."

"I'm working on it."

"Not fast enough. Andi and I need this time off."

"And these victims need you."

"That was a low blow. There will always be cases we can't take on, victims we can't bring justice. Our precinct has some very good detectives.

We're not the only ones." George was getting angrier by the second. He hated being manipulated, and he hated it even more when it was done so obviously by somebody who was supposedly on their side.

"I'm sorry, George. It's just…. Everybody can see this case is going to be a hot mess. There's no telling yet how many other agencies are going to be involved. Apparently four of the victims found so far were veterans, including the latest. Dr. Melcourt found the dog tags, which means the military might be knocking on the precinct's door as well, depending on who those veterans turn out to be."

"Even more reason to not take it. We're on vacation, Luke."

"I really hate to do this to you, George, believe me. But—" There was another lengthy pause during which George geared himself up for whatever unpleasantness was coming his way. "You have to take the case. Chief Norris has the right to order her two best detectives to work on a case as huge as this one. By refusing, you're giving her ammunition she's going to use without mercy, you know that."

"I do know! And why does she have the chance to get ammunition against us? Because you're not doing your job, Luke." George was ready to spit nails.

"It's my fault. I apologize. But I can't change the facts at the moment. You need to come in tomorrow."

"Once this is done, I want her removed. I want it all made official. You will get rid of her as quickly as possible. No more 'mediating,' no more 'waiting just another week.' You sack her the moment you get the chance. Have I made myself clear?" George didn't even need to channel his mother to deliver the ultimatum. He and Andi had been backed into a corner, one he needed to get them out of. If it meant stepping on Gelman's toes, so be it. George was beyond caring at this point. Gelman's voice was chagrined enough to soothe George's temper a bit.

"Understood. I will get rid of her, I promise."

"I don't need your promises, Luke. Just deliver." George ended the call.

"What's going on?" Andi stood at the top of the stairs, looking down on George with disheveled hair and dark circles George could see from where he was standing.

"Andi. You shouldn't be up!"

"Sorry. You're so agitated, my roommates threw a hissy fit."

"Fuck. I'm sorry, Andi."

"Don't be. It's fine. Now tell me why you are—" Andi hesitated a moment. "—angry, but also worried, paired with anxiety, the pheromones are never that high, adrenaline flaring, anger, anger, spiking, coming in waves, mounting up, so sweet, more, no, wrong, it hurts, not good, anger is bad, means bad things, what does bad mean? I don't know, it's so loud, too many vibrations, let me...." Andi shook his head as if he was waking from a bad dream. "Uh, all of that."

"Do you want to know right now, or do you want to sleep a bit more? You have about thirty minutes until the casserole is done."

"You made casserole?" Andi perked up visibly. As long as he could be bribed with food, things were... not good—they rarely were—but tolerable. At least he was in working condition.

"Yes, with potatoes and cauliflower and carrots. And four different cheeses."

"I think I want to hear it now. Then I have something good to look forward to."

"Okay, Gelman just phoned me. The chief has assigned us to the case."

"What a bitch!" It was so heartfelt, George had to smile.

"Yeah, that's what I told Gelman. I tried to keep us out of it, but apparently refusing to take the case could result in her having ammunition against us. Our hands are tied, so to speak."

"A problem we wouldn't have if Gelman had done *his* job."

"I agree with you wholeheartedly. I managed to get his promise to get rid of her as soon as the case is closed."

Andi groaned. "Probably the worst incentive to work on a case I ever had." He closed his eyes. "But effective. With that carrot dangling before me, I think I can manage to power through."

"I don't like it, Andi. This time off was supposed to be a much-needed break for both of us and to give us time to experiment so I can help you better. Look at you. If you told me you're an extra on the *Walking Dead*, I'd believe you without question. Please, you need to promise me, if things get too intense, if you can't bear it anymore, you tell me, and I find a way to get us off the case. Your mental and physical health is much more important than solving this crime. Do you hear me?"

"I do. Thank you." Andi started coming down the stairs. The gratitude in his eyes reminded George once again that his partner hadn't had anybody in his corner since his grandmother died. It made the decision he'd been mulling over since the McHill/Portius/Miller case easy. He would stay in Charleston with Andi, taking care of him, watching his back, helping him adjust to the new intensity of his *geschenk*. He wouldn't tell Andi, though, not before everything was sealed. His partner didn't need to worry about George's application going through on top of everything else he was dealing with.

Suddenly, George felt as if a weight had been lifted off his shoulders. Yes, they were still facing a case that sounded like a nightmare; yes, they still had the chief breathing down their necks and making their lives hell; yes, the *geschenk* was still a threatening presence, which likely wouldn't ever change, but the constant back and forth he'd been doing in his mind ever since he had realized how much Andi needed him and how much he needed Andi was finally gone. He would face the future with his partner, whatever it might throw at them.

5. BEAST OF BURDEN

THE PRECINCT was buzzing like a hornets' nest the next morning, making Andi wish he could go back to his bed. His nerves felt like they had been scrubbed with an iron brush; everything was too loud and too much, the chatter of the blobs adding another painful layer to the sensory input battering into him. The spiders in the building were especially agitated; all the hectic running around made them nervous, the pulses racing through their legs like tiny heartbeats on Andi's mind, timed with the movements of his colleagues, telling him where people were going without him wanting to know it, and the hairs on his legs swayed as if in a breeze, but it was the stress, really, of dealing with the thrumming of the ground. He tried to put his sixth leg forward and would have fallen if George hadn't caught him around the waist. His partner's worried gaze forced Andi to get a grip on himself before George did something he couldn't take back, like leaving the precinct and telling the chief to solve the case herself. Andi didn't fully understand the political implications of backing out now—he didn't have to, because George had taken things in hand—but he did understand the sharp tang of worry he had caught from George the day before when he told him about the chief's latest foolery. It was a bad idea for him to be in the precinct and an even worse idea to take this case. Apparently, though, there was no getting out of it.

Gelman approached them, his whole-body language screaming how sorry he was. The nail polish he used to kill his foot fungus was as prominent in the air as it had been the first day they had met him, or perhaps it was just Andi associating him with it, recognizing him through it, just like he always knew George through scent and heartbeat and the calming flood of his pheromones.

"George, Andi, I'm—"

George shook his head. "Not now, Luke. We're going down to Evangeline, see what she's found out so far." He gently guided Andi in the direction of the staircase, Gelman trailing behind them like a lost puppy. Andi was glad he could get out of the bullpen, the stares and the stomping, the whispers and the general agitation making him tense like a live wire. It was much better to go down to Evangeline in her much quieter kingdom, only today even there it was hectic, what with so many corpses and skeletons to be looked at and still so many to come. An assistant told them Evangeline was still in one of the autopsy rooms, working on the latest victim of the serial killer whose lair they had found.

She looked up from the partly decomposed flesh where bones were sticking out like branches from a dead tree in the swamp when they entered. As always when she was working on a body, her thick dark hair was tied in a tight bun at the top of her head, making her look even taller than her six feet. Her smile was tired and sad. "*Talofa lava*, gentlemen."

"Good morning, Evangeline." George made a step forward toward the slab with the remains. Evangeline didn't like people coming too close to her charges without her permission, so he stopped when he was close enough to see all the details but still far enough away to not touch. Andi didn't bother coming closer. He already knew a lot about the man lying on the cold steel, as well as about the others who had accompanied him in the soil. There was no need for him to confuse himself about this delicious source of nutrients just waiting to be consumed. Gelman stayed behind Andi, studiously not looking at what had once been a living, breathing person.

"You found something truly nasty this time." Evangeline glanced in Andi's direction, giving him an imperceptible nod before she focused back on George. Now that he had a partner, it was so much easier for Andi to leave most social interactions to him, even when it was with people he could tolerate or even liked. Evangeline was a smart woman. She understood how Andi worked, not the why but definitely the how, and had no problem accommodating him. "My colleague in the bunker has told me they have found six more skeletons since I left. They suspect even more because the soil is way too loose even in the deeper layers. And some of the bones they've found don't match what they already have." She sighed, glancing at Andi again. He nodded, indicating that, yes, she was right, there were more to come, which made Evangeline shudder.

"Naturally I can't tell you much about the overall situation yet, except that you're looking at the work of a serial killer, which you probably already guessed."

"Not much room for speculation here." George shrugged.

"*Leai*. Not really, no." Evangeline stepped next to the slab with the remains. "I can tell you about this poor soul, though. His name was Marco

Flores, thirty-two, Hispanic. He was military and definitely wounded while serving his country. I can tell you more once I get his medical files from the Army, and I have already forwarded Shireen his social security number. He was killed by asphyxiation with some kind of rope. I found fibers in the area of his neck which will hopefully tell us what kind of rope the killer used. Also, his right pinkie toe was cut off, my guess is before he was killed, because I was able to find traces of LTB4."

"Uh, Evangeline—" George lifted a hand in question.

"That's leukotriene B4, a chemical involved in inflammation. Put simply, if a wound is antemortem, there's LTB4, if it's postmortem there isn't. As there were only miniscule traces of LTB4, I think the amputation was done immediately before the killing. I already have blood and tissue samples in the lab and can hopefully tell you more once they come back. Estimated time of death was roughly two weeks ago. The exact date I can tell you once the etymologist is done with the insect samples we collected at the site."

So delicious, fresh, still warm.

Andi shook his head. Now was not the time to get lost in the regularity with which the arthropods in the bunker had gotten their food or how the tiny eggs Evangeline had yet to clear from the body were racing toward hatching. The steady pulsing of the life forming inside them was like pinpricks on his mind, burrowing in with no rhythm at all; for that there were too many at once.

"Let's go to Shireen, then. Perhaps she has already found something." He turned toward the door, not waiting for George to give his consent.

"A good day to you, too, Andi," Evangeline called out with a hint of amusement in her voice. Both George and Gelman followed Andi, not without bidding the coroner goodbye. Andi simply lifted his hand, acknowledging everything Evangeline did for him and how she put up with his grumpy ways in one gesture.

George quickly reached his side, leaving Gelman behind them when they entered Shireen's lair. This morning she wore her hair in what could only be described as a bird's nest that had fallen into a pot of neon pink and bright blue color, paired with yellow trousers with wide legs and a long-sleeve tunic in black and silver. The agonizing color clash did not distract from the deep circles under her eyes, though, or the worried look she gave them.

"Guys, Agent Gelman."

"Hi, Shireen. You already know?" George nodded at her.

"I didn't leave the precinct once I heard what you found."

"I'm sorry. That's probably not how you wanted to spend last night."

"You have nothing to apologize for, George. It's the asshole who did this I want to see hanging." The fire in Shireen's voice spoke of a long, sleepless night, too much caffeine, probably in the shape of energy drinks, and a sense of justice born of her own abysmal experiences, something only Andi was privy to.

"We're doing our best to find him or her. What do you have about Marco Flores?" George knew how to get Shireen to focus. The flat-screen on the wall woke with a few taps of her fingers on her tablet.

"*Officially* I don't know much, except that he has been homeless for the last two years. He still collected his pension every month from various ATMs in the Goose Creek area here in Charleston. I have video of him doing so two weeks ago on Tuesday; the facial recognition was a match." Shireen showed them a grainy security cam video of a man in several layers of clothing and with two shopping bags stuffed full of various items who got money out of an ATM. The money vanished somewhere in the depth of the huge coat he was wearing, and he looked around nervously before he left the camera's range.

"Okay. What do you know *unofficially*?" George kept his gaze on the flat-screen.

Shireen gave Gelman a nervous glance. The man shrugged. "I'm not really here, Miss DuPont. And even if I were, anything you have that helps us to get to the madman who did this faster is more than fine by me."

For a moment Shireen seemed to weigh Gelman's words until her natural instinct to help overrode her reservations about speaking in front of somebody from IA. "Unofficially I have already hacked his military records, which we will probably get sometime later today, officially anyway."

"Probably." George was still staring at the screen, which came back to life when Shireen opened Marco's file.

"Marco was a staff sergeant with the Army Rangers, did three tours in Afghanistan, was in an explosion during his last stay there. No lasting damage, but he developed serious PTSD and was honorably discharged three years ago. The first year he lived in a group house with other veterans who have suffered trauma in Menriv Park, which is close to the Naval Base, and apparently, he did well. Then one day he vanished, occasionally paying a visit to the group home, but he never returned to stay. According to his medical files, his PTSD was well handled with Paxil, an antidepressant containing paroxetine, but after he left the home, there is no record of further medication, and paroxetine, or Paxil, doesn't exactly grow in the streets, so it's highly probable he didn't take anything, which in turn fueled his PTSD."

The picture Shireen was painting was sad and only too familiar. People who had risked their lives for society slipping through its net once they returned to civilian life—or at least tried to.

"Nobody has asked for him?" George sounded sad.

"No. He was an only child, and his parents died in a car crash while he was in Afghanistan for the second time. No relatives, just the therapists and veterans at the group home who couldn't keep track of him because he didn't want it. The perfect prey for a serial killer," Shireen said grimly.

"You think the other victims will be like him?" Gelman stepped next to George to get a better look at the flat-screen. For somebody who was supposedly only there to see how the precinct worked, he seemed overly interested. Then again, it was a serial killer case, and Gelman had a degree in psychology. Andi shrugged. Not really his concern, certainly not at the moment.

"Chances are high. As soon as it was clear what kind of case this was going to be, I checked the missing persons here in Charleston but couldn't find anything suspicious, which means the killer is either drawing from all over the country or from the part of the populace nobody misses. Since the bodies are all in one place, I'm operating under the assumption that the victims are from Charleston and perhaps a few of the surrounding cities, though it's unlikely the killer transported them far."

"You're right. Long ways of transport are rare in serial killer cases. It's all about opportunity and staying under the radar." Gelman sighed.

"Anything else?" George was tense; Andi could read it in the hard lines of his muscles, as well as in the pheromones he was emitting. Even though the precinct was crowded and in uproar, George's specific taste and scent were by now so familiar to Andi, he could detect them anywhere.

"That's it from me for the moment. I'll tell you as soon as something new pops up."

"Thank you, Shireen." George briefly touched her arm. "Try to get some rest."

"Will do." It was a blatant lie, as they all knew. With Gelman in tow, they headed for their desks, only to be intercepted by a bellow from Chief Norris, who was stalking the bullpen like a starved tiger.

"Hayes, Donovan, my office. Now."

"Let the games begin." Andi was so far past caring, he wasn't even sure if he could keep his composure to let George handle everything. His partner shot him a warning glare, the sudden spike in adrenaline not lost on Andi. With a sigh, he placed his hand on George's lower back for a moment, silently promising he would behave. Anything to have George's pheromones back to something pleasant and relaxed. The change was almost instant, his partner giving him a small smile.

"I will make this right for us, Andi. I will." George spoke softly so nobody but Andi could hear him.

He nodded. "I trust you."

The effect those words had was staggering. A determined gleam entered George's eyes, and the muscles in his back straightened. He was ready for battle.

They entered the office with Gelman still hot on their heels. The chief's eyes narrowed, but there wasn't much she could do, not after she had officially complained about Andi and George. As far as she knew, Luke was at the precinct to assess their work before she could get rid of them. Antagonizing him would be a stupid move. Watching her chew on Gelman's presence was the only satisfaction Andi could get from the situation.

"Detectives, I'm officially handing the serial killer case to you. I'm sure you'll be able to solve it with no problems whatsoever. Make the precinct proud. You may select up to four other detectives or beat officers to assist you. Should you need more, we'll have to discuss it. I don't think I have to remind you not to talk to the press. They haven't found out yet, but we all know that's just a matter of time." The sarcasm in the chief's tone was hard to miss. Andi sensed her agitation, the adrenaline coursing through her veins, the stench of her sweat because she was in fight mode. He knew people weren't receptive to anything in that state, their learning abilities crippled by the body's need to survive a situation it perceived as dangerous. That the chief saw them as a threat by now, one she had to deal with by using underhanded methods such as pulling them out of a much-needed vacation, made Andi wary of the future. He knew they would somehow get through this case, because they hadn't much of a choice except quitting, which would be a last-resort thing. What they needed to do after the case was—hopefully—solved, was to get rid of the chief.

"We're going to do our best, and thank you for your unwavering support." George had his official mask number six on—no emotions detectable, his disapproval oozing from every syllable while his entire body language radiated indifference. Andi liked to compare this mask with a crab spider disguising as a flower and waiting for the prey to come close enough for the attack.

"I hope so." The chief pretended to look at some papers on her desk, playing a game of power that failed to intimidate George because he was made of sterner stuff and was completely wasted on Andi because he didn't care about hierarchies at all. "I already contacted the FBI. For the time being, they're sending an agent, Geena Davis, a former master sergeant in the military, to work with you. Since she has previous ties to the military, she'll also report back to them, which means one person less trudging around in my precinct. I'm sure you're going to welcome her with open arms." The glee with which Norris delivered that news was enough to make Andi wish he could strangle her right on her desk. George stayed outwardly calm, but his cortisol, glucagon, and prolactin levels were flaring like a microphone's sound curves during the drum solo at a metal concert. It agitated the silverfish and spiders in the room, which in turn affected Andi. He shuffled a bit closer to George, silently reassuring him. Working with somebody from a different governmental branch was far from ideal, but they would manage. Either that Davis woman would be of help, or Andi would scare her off with being, well, himself. Easy peasy.

"Oh, we will, Chief. With a case as big as this one, all help is more than welcome." Ah, social mask number seven, basically the same as number six, but with added veiled hostility, packed in polite conversation. The way the chief's eyes narrowed, George had hit the mark. Before she could say anything else, George turned toward the door, still half shielding Andi with his body. "Since it's so early in the case, we'd like to get everything set up. Please do excuse us."

They were out the door without giving the chief a chance to react. Back at their desks, Gelman still with them, George brought their whiteboards into position.

"I'm not sure there's enough room on them."

"We can get another one. I think there's one in storage." Andi sent his senses out without even thinking about it. "Second floor. Pretty dusty. I don't think anybody will miss it."

"Why don't Luke and I get it while you take a look at the files Evangeline and Shireen have sent? Then we can start brainstorming."

Andi knew George was giving him a chance to take a breather, short as it would be, and was grateful for it. He smiled at his partner. "Great idea, George."

They left to retrieve the whiteboard, and Andi switched his PC on. With a sigh, he leaned back in his chair and closed his eyes while he waited for it to boot up. This case was going to be a nightmare.

6. New Partner, New Luck

FBI AGENT Geena Davis—no relation to the actress either in blood or looks—arrived the next morning shortly after Andi and George had discussed possible members of their task force, deciding to take in Detectives Sandra Mescew and Tobias Gentry, whose love for detail and ability to follow even the sparsest leads to the bitter end they would definitely need in a case this big. Also, Sandra was an excellent shot, and having her at their back was a reassuring thought. They hadn't decided yet which beat officers they might ask for help and had shelved this decision until they actually needed them for legwork or other seemingly menial, though nevertheless crucial, tasks that inevitably came up when so many corpses were involved. As no names had immediately come to mind, they would simply choose whoever was available at the moment. It really was a good thing that none of the beat officers at the precinct had a bad reputation. Currently, Andi and George were staring at the whiteboard. The team at the bunker had now found all twenty-six victims, including four more dog tags from military personnel. They were Private Second Class Geoffrey Elstair from the Navy, Corporal Samuel Grand from the Army Rangers, Corporal Hamed Beshara from the Marines, and Staff Sergeant Kesha Raport from the Air Force, which in theory meant four more investigative agencies could get involved. A prospect George was not looking forward to, though he hoped the fact that Geena was ex-military really meant they would only have to deal with her. The unofficial files Shireen had gotten said all four veterans had suffered from PTSD, just like Marco Flores, and had been living on the streets, with the exception of Kesha Raport, who had been treated in House Cusabo, a mental health facility in Cottageville, Colleton County, some four years ago before she went missing. There was even a missing person entry for her issued by House Cusabo, because like the other four, she didn't have any living relatives, or at least none who had been interested in her whereabouts. As Shireen had already mentioned—and George agreed with her—the same would be true for most of the other victims as well, which made the case both sadder and a lot more difficult. Their killer was obviously smart enough to prey on the weak and forgotten, which meant he was organized. George glanced at Andi, who was staring at the screen of his PC, studying the files Shireen had sent them. The first whiteboard was already filling up, almost as fast as his partner was slipping under. The dark circles under Andi's eyes had gotten even deeper overnight, a sure sign he had been busy strengthening his shields. His hair was a tousled mess, and he was wearing the same clothes as the day before. George would have to make sure Andi got a decent dinner this evening, and he would probably also spend the night at Andi's place to get him into fresh clothes.

His thoughts were interrupted by Chief Norris, who marched in their direction with another woman in tow. When Norris arrived, she stopped so abruptly, the other woman, who George suspected was the agent they would be working with, almost ran into her.

"Good morning, Donovan, Hayes." Norris's tone was clipped, all business. She was probably trying to make a stern impression on the agent, who had stepped next to her, eyeing George and Andi openly. The woman brimmed with energy that was barely contained by her five-foot-nine frame. She wore her dark hair short, the silver streaks in it more prominent because of it. Her outfit—blue jeans, heavy biker boots, a green T-shirt, and a tailored jacket in black—was sensible, accentuating her stocky frame with the solid muscles only somebody who worked out regularly gained, her eyes a piercing gray over her round nose. Her FBI badge was clipped unobtrusively to her belt at her left side, barely visible under the open jacket.

"May I introduce Special Agent Geena Davis to you, who will, as I already told you, act as your liaison to the Army and temporary partner."

Chief Norris turned to Agent Davis. "These are Detectives George Donovan and Andrew Hayes, this precinct's best men. I'm sure you will be able to solve this dreadful case together. If you'll excuse me now." She left quickly, not giving Davis or George a chance to get a word in. The FBI agent smirked, which made the laugh lines around her eyes and mouth dance.

"What a charming host your chief is." She held out her hand to George, who took it, winking at her.

"It's one of her better days, actually. She escorted you here instead of just bellowing out directions."

"I feel so honored. And please call me Geena. The way I see it, this case is one huge clusterfuck with the potential to turn into a fucking disaster. No need to be formal."

George grinned. He felt he could like this woman. "Thank you, Geena. I'm George, and this is Andi." He gestured to his partner, who had actually gotten up.

Geena took Andi's hand. "It's my pleasure. No offense to you, George, but I've seen Andi's solving statistics." She winked in George's direction.

"Pft. Am I chopped liver?"

Andi was chuckling, his hand still held by Geena, who pretended to think about it.

"Not chopped liver. More like the Watson to his Sherlock?"

"And we're done. I knew it! Working with other departments is never worth the hassle!"

"I like her."

George shot Andi a wounded look. "*Et tu*, Brutus?"

"It's a snake pit out there." Geena let go of Andi's hand. The smile fled from her lips, leaving a serious expression. "Jokes aside, I'm looking forward to working with both of you. I also want to assure you that I couldn't care less about who gets credit for the solve. All I want is to catch the sick asshole who did this to members of the military and innocent civilians. Also, I assume we're not the only ones working on this case?"

"We're with you on that one. A shining solving statistic is nice, I won't deny that, but neither I nor Andi have problems sharing the fame. And no, we're not alone. Working with us will be Detectives Sandra Mescew and Tobias Gentry, who are at the moment tidying up their current cases to hand them over to other detectives before joining us." George waved in the general direction where Sandra and Tobias were sitting, who were too busy to even realize he was talking about them. Geena nodded, seemingly not offended by this superficial introduction. Then again, as an FBI agent she was probably used to the general madness accompanying serial killer cases and to a certain dose of hostility, even though this wasn't George's—or Sandra's and Tobias's—intention here. "We also have a pool of capable beat officers we can draw from anytime we need them. You've gotten all the CliffsNotes?"

Geena sighed deeply. "Yeah. Doesn't look pretty."

"It never does." Andi sat back down behind his PC.

George gestured to his own chair. "We have this habit of writing down all the information on whiteboards. It's a good way to get our thoughts lined up, especially in cases as big as this one."

"Not a bad idea." Geena sat down, watched as George picked up his red marker. "Let's compare what we have so far."

"After you." George nodded at her.

"Fine. The last update I got was it's twenty-six victims, found in a prepper bunker, in a hidden room. They were buried on top of each other, the latest victim being Staff Sergeant Marco Flores, killed approximately two weeks ago. We don't know yet how long ago the other military members were killed, who we know of because of their dog tags. Staff Sergeant Kesha Raport was probably killed four years ago, when House Cusabo reported her missing. None of the non-military victims have been identified so far, and Dr. Melcourt hasn't been able to match the bones to the dog tags yet."

"Yes. That's about it. Evangeline is working hard to get the identification underway, but it will take at least two more days, probably a week. We are pretty sure we can assume that the other victims are similar to the five from the Army. Homeless, with some kind of mental problems, not missed because there's no family."

"It certainly seems that way. A skilled predator with a predator-prey system that allows him to stay under the radar. Damn." Geena hit her thigh with her fist. "Chances are, some of those victims can't be identified at all."

"Unfortunately true." George was writing down *PTSD* and *mental problems.*

"We may have seven more from House Cusabo." Andi looked up from his screen. "Shireen just sent me an email. Because of Kesha Raport, she checked if there were any other people reported missing from their facility. There were seven in the last ten years. House Cusabo was founded in the early sixties, and until 2013, they only had two other people from their facility going missing, one in the year House Cusabo opened, 1963, the other in 1982. Which means we're probably looking at a time span of ten years in which the killer has been active in the Charleston area, assuming all missing persons from House Cusabo in the last ten years are among the victims."

"Their names?" Geena turned on her chair to face Andi.

"Ten years ago, TJ Ross and Celia Murdoch went missing within a few months. They were both bipolar. Oh, this is interesting. Corporal Samuel Grand was a patient with them, too, treated for his PTSD. He went missing nine years ago, about six months after Celia Murdoch. Shireen didn't find him at first because he wasn't reported missing by House Cusabo. Officially, he was discharged at his own request, but she found his files in their database."

"Which they granted her access to, didn't they?" Geena sounded amused.

"Uh, yeah, of course. Granted access." George shrugged.

"Don't worry. We all have our hackers who help us along in times of need."

"Yes. Times of need." Andi shook his head. "Anyway, six years ago, a girl named Izzy Whitewall went missing, and four years ago Raport and a man named Lucas Mellen, who was also bipolar. Last year Lola Monarch vanished. She was treated for depression." Andi looked at George and Geena. "So far, the only person who didn't suffer from either PTSD, depression, or bipolarity is Izzy. She was admitted for 'overactive imagination, most probably linked to puberty.'" Andi snorted.

George watched him closely. Izzy was the girl Tyler had told them about, the only one who didn't appear to him as a child. Given that she'd obviously been a teenager when she died, it made sense. And the "overactive imagination"—George was willing to bet she had been like Tyler, a medium of some sort. Andi clearly thought along the same lines, the sadness in his gaze like a dagger to George's heart. Being different was never fun. Being in touch with completely different forms of existence? A nightmare.

"What do you say? Are we going to pay House Cusabo a visit?" Geena was pinching her nose with her fingers.

It was a reasonable idea. The mental facility was their first lead, and until Evangeline was able to identify the other victims, it couldn't hurt to have a look. George eyed Andi. He couldn't detect any aversion to the suggestion. All they had to do was be careful around Geena.

"Let me call them." George put on his jacket before he got his cell out. Andi read the number of House Cusabo to him, which no doubt Shireen had included in her report, then put on his own jacket, a thing of undetermined color and age, which George wanted to get rid of as soon as possible. He was still in the process of getting Andi an entire new wardrobe, a feat that required patience because strictly speaking, Andi didn't own a single item of clothing a person with minimal requirements for looks would deem even remotely appropriate. Deciding what to buy him first was a mixture of opportunity—sales for high-quality clothes because Andi clung to his garments forever—and what he needed most. Jeans, T-shirts, socks, and underwear had made the top of the list, a new jacket more at the bottom because the one Andi had was still watertight and warm despite looking as if it had seen the turn of the last century.

Geena looked ready to go, followed them out of the precinct with a determined stride. The other detectives and police officers in the bullpen made room for them, some of them murmuring something encouraging. Sandra and Tobias just waved, still engrossed in their work. George knew their feud with the chief had never been a secret, and he was pleasantly surprised that their colleagues were obviously siding with them. Gelman hadn't shown himself this morning, hopefully working on ways to get rid of Norris as soon as possible. At the car, there was an awkward moment of who should be sitting where. Technically, it would have been polite to offer Geena the passenger seat next to George. Technically. Practically, George liked to have Andi as close as possible to keep an eye on him, especially when under circumstances as stressful as this.

Luckily, Geena was not only empathetic but also laid-back, because she held up her hands while she stepped toward the back door. "Don't worry. I'm not going to disturb your flow. I'm a big girl and can sit in the back without feeling belittled."

George nodded at her in thanks. Andi was already in his seat, his supply of polite social interaction obviously drained by having shaken Geena's hand. "Thank you. He's already in the tunnel, and it's best not to disturb him."

She opened the door and sat down behind Andi, which allowed her to look at George while talking to him. "It's fine. I've worked with somebody like him before. The important thing is to not feel offended by something he has no control over."

"I *am* here, you know." Andi muttered with amusement. "And you're right. You can ask anybody, my social skills are abysmal. I think I can tolerate you, because you're not an idiot like most other people. Doesn't mean you get special treatment, though."

"Just a place in your shriveled heart?" Geena grinned.

"Don't be greedy. In its vicinity."

George started the car with a soft sigh of relief. If Andi was willing to bicker with Geena, and Geena was taking it so well, there was hope they could get through this case without it becoming an absolute catastrophe. Actually, he had to admire Andi's tactic. He was establishing his unapproachability from day one, thus preparing Geena for the situations when he would inevitably push her away. George only hoped their visit to House Cusabo wouldn't be the first time they had to do it. As understanding as Geena tried to be, George didn't want to test her patience on the first day.

The drive to Cottageville was uneventful. Andi was staring out the window, no doubt preparing himself for whatever the arthropods would throw at him once they reached the facility. George made polite conversation with Geena, telling her about his brother Daniel who was currently stationed in Arkansas. When House Cusabo came into view after a long, winding road flanked by angel oaks, all conversation died.

"Wow." Geena leaned forward to look at the mansion through the windshield. "I did have pictures of Arkham in mind when I heard the word mental health facility, but I wouldn't have thought they'd be accurate. This thing is huge!"

"Lots of people, so many drugs, making it all wrong, the stench is terrible, altered, *krrt*, *krrt*, it's…."

"What did you say?" Luckily Geena seemed to have been distracted by the sheer size of House Cusabo, which had once been a typical Southern Belle, as was evident in the huge porch at the entrance, but had been added to, most probably in the late sixties or early seventies, given the ugly rectangular buildings to both sides, connected via tunnel-like constructions with the main house. The garden, as far as George could see from the car, was extensive, several acres surrounded by a six-foot chain-link fence that was more symbolic than anything else. Climbing over it would have been child's play, and as far as George knew, keeping people hospitalized against their will had become a lot more difficult in the last two decades or so. He parked his beautiful Escalade in one of the parking slots marked *Visitors*. Geena was already out of the car, still assessing the huge monster of a building. So far they hadn't seen anybody outside. Given the weather—not really cold but cloudy with a promise of rain later—he wasn't surprised. George opened Andi's door, taking in his partner's complexion. Andi was pale, which made the circles under his eyes even darker. His cheeks were hollow because food had been low on his list of priorities in the last weeks. George suspected his partner didn't eat all that much when he wasn't there to feed him. Another reason they had needed this holiday so badly. His eyes were glazed over, but there was still a certain awareness telling George Andi was present enough to keep it together. For the time being.

Andi left the car and turned toward the building, his mouth in a grim line. George remembered what Andi had told him about how difficult hospitals were for him, not because of the diseases but because of the drugs that altered a person's pheromones. From the little George knew about mental illnesses, many were linked with changes in the body's chemical reactions, which in turn were then treated with drugs that influenced said reactions, which played havoc with Andi's perception. According to his partner, it was like suddenly being forced to think in a language you knew the basics of but without context. And each person in this building who was here for treatment would be like a flip image for Andi. Frayed at the edges, the core a cluster of colors dissolving into each other, making it hard to read them. Luckily, they weren't here to talk to patients. They were here to talk to Dr. Graham Blackton, the director of House Cusabo.

Geena was holding the door open for them when they reached the porch, the short look she gave Andi not lost on George. He knew he had to tread carefully. Geena might come across as friendly, laid-back, and caring, but he didn't know her, and at her heart she was a detective, just like them, even if her title was ex-military and now FBI. You didn't get into this line of work if your curiosity wasn't way above the levels of most civilian people. Keeping one hand at Andi's lower back, George guided him inside, where a man of perhaps fifty years was standing behind a broad reception desk. He wore a green uniform and greeted them with a smile.

"Welcome to House Cusabo. How can I help you?"

Geena stepped forward, showing her badge. "Hello. I'm FBI Agent Geena Davis, and these are Detectives George Donovan and Andrew Hayes from the Charleston PD. We have a meeting with Dr. Blackton."

"Ah yes, I was informed of it. Please, follow me." With his pleasant smile still in place, the man left his spot behind the counter and led them toward a grand staircase that dominated the hall. Everywhere George looked, he saw a disturbing mixture of old and new, of representative and practical. While the floor at the hall had been tiled, they were now walking over green linoleum that had seen better days. For a moment

George felt as if he were in a horror movie, the camera on female legs in flat white sneakers, frayed in some places, following them along a seemingly endless corridor. They were only missing the half-open doors allowing glimpses into rooms where the same linoleum sported smudges of dubious origin. Sometimes he hated his imagination.

Paintings, done by patients, as announced by a note at the entrance of the corridor, hung in regular spaces on the wainscoted walls, the dark of the wood giving the entire floor a gloomy atmosphere. The motifs of the paintings didn't help either. Most were monochromatic or generally done in dark colors with only two lighter ones of sunsets spaced between. How a patient with depression was supposed to find a more positive outlook on life here George didn't know.

Their guide stopped in front of a door made of the same dark wood as was plastered on the walls. He knocked, and after an unfriendly female voice asked them to come in, he opened the door for them, not stepping in himself. Once they were all inside the office, where a middle-aged woman behind a broad desk was glaring at them, the man closed the door and was gone. George couldn't fault him for it. The old saying of dragon secretaries defending the boss's door came to mind. Before George could put on his charming smile reserved for older women, Geena was at the desk, showing the woman her badge. Her brisk attitude clearly rubbed the secretary the wrong way, as she bristled in her seat, taking her time to inspect Geena's badge. Both women radiated animosity and the willingness to fight. A smart man kept his mouth shut when such situations occurred. He used the time to check on Andi, who was standing slightly back and to his right, using George as his shield. His mouth was moving almost imperceptibly. George leaned a bit closer.

"Angry, always angry, spike, *klck*, *klck*, hungry, wobble, wobble, termites in the foundation, *chrt*, *chrt*, *chrt*, eating, gnawing, can't move, so many eggs in my body, cold, close the door, the net is destroyed, *shkr*, need...."

George touched Andi's forearm, which jolted his partner out of whatever stream of information he had been caught in. Termites, spiders, and silverfish was George's guess. The *shkr* sound was typical for silverfish, and net usually meant spiders. It could have been caterpillars, though not at this time of year, and not inside a house.

He lifted one brow, his way of asking Andi if he was okay. Andi rolled his eyes, which was his way of saying George shouldn't be such a mother hen but that he appreciated it nonetheless.

"Dr. Blackton will see you now." The haughty voice of the secretary—Regina Miles, as a discreet sign on her desk announced—commandeered their attention toward a door to her left. Geena's body was tense like an elastic spring. The thunderous look in her eyes promised death to anybody in her way. George let her open the door, deciding to see how this would play out. Andi stayed behind him, assessing quietly.

Dr. Blackton was a good-looking man in his late thirties, with the first streaks of gray at his temples. His dark brown eyes looked kind, with a certain sharpness George expected from somebody in his position. His smile seemed genuine. George hadn't gone into details during their short call, just asking the man if it was okay to swing by. Geena did the introductions a third time with a note of steel in her voice. Mrs. Miles must have really gotten on her nerves. Like the pro he was, Dr. Blackton ignored her thinly veiled hostility and greeted them all with a handshake before inviting them to sit down on the comfy guest chairs in front of his desk.

"I must say, I was surprised when I got your call, Detective Donovan. How can I be of help?"

George glanced at Geena, who nodded, leaving the playing field to him. "First of all, thank you for seeing us on such short notice, Dr. Blackton. We really appreciate it."

The man grinned a little self-deprecatingly. "I'd say it's my pleasure, but to be honest, your visit has given me an excuse to be late for yet another board meeting where I have to explain to the big bosses why treating patients with mental illnesses is not the gold mine they thought it would be."

From the short summary Shireen had sent them, George knew House Cusabo belonged to Green Oaks Group, a company that owned countless hospitals in the US and South America and offered other medical services like eldercare as well. The Green Oaks Group had purchased House Cusabo only two years ago, shortly after the former director, Dr. Silvana Grassen, had died.

"I don't envy you." George gave the man his best polite smile. "We're here because of a former patient in your facility, Staff Sergeant

Kesha Raport, who was reported missing by House Cusabo about four years ago. We wondered if you still have her medical files."

Dr. Blackton furrowed his brows. "I'm afraid that was two years before I took the position as director here. I'll have to ask Mrs. Miles if we have anything about her. Do you have a warrant? Otherwise, I have to get permission from her next of kin to share the files with you, as I assume she's no longer alive?"

"You assume correctly. And there is no next of kin, which means you can show us the files since we represent the state." George was very careful not to put any pressure on Dr. Blackton. The laws regarding the release of the medical files of a deceased person were complicated. Without any next of kin or officially named representatives, they had a theoretical claim on seeing the files, especially since they were investigating a serial killer case, but if Dr. Blackton dug his heels in, he could make their lives miserable. And with potentially six more victims coming from House Cusabo, George wanted to stay on the man's good side. Of course, Shireen had already hacked the files, but they needed them officially in case they found evidence the state attorney needed for court. "We would also appreciate it if we could perhaps talk to some of your staff who knew Kesha Raport."

Dr. Blackton was tapping his desktop with his index finger. "Hmm. You have proof there is no next of kin?"

"Yes. If you wish, I can send you the part of her military file where her family status is noted." Geena already had her cell out, swiping at the screen. It seemed her ties to the military were still tight despite her being now FBI.

Dr. Blackton nodded, obviously relieved. "That would be wonderful. I'm all for helping the police with an investigation, but you understand, I have to keep in mind that House Cusabo is now part of Green Oaks Group. They can get testy when they think they're in legal jeopardy."

"I can assure you everything is above reproach." George smiled reassuringly while Geena typed on her cell. Blackton told her his email address, and after reading whatever Geena had sent him, he used his office phone to tell Mrs. Miles to get him Kesha Raport's file.

"While we're waiting for the file, let me see who of the staff was here when she was our patient." Dr. Blackton typed away on his PC. "I'm afraid the list is rather long. Ten of the people who should have known her are still working here. Our longest working staff members are Thomas

LeClerk, a nurse, and Dr. Healani Aoki, one of our psychiatrists. They've both been here for over ten years and have probably the deepest insights to offer."

"Are they working today?" George was happy about Dr. Blackton's willingness to cooperate and hoped his staff would show the same enthusiasm. Starting with the two longest-serving members was also a good idea.

"Yes, they are both on duty today. In fact, Dr. Aoki should be free at the moment. Mr. LeClerk's lunch break is in an hour." Dr. Blackton got up from his chair. "Let me show you the way to Dr. Aoki's office."

He approached the door, which opened to reveal Mrs. Miles with a file in her hand. It was brown with a huge red stamp declaring the person had been released. Dr. Blackton took the file and handed it to Geena, who clamped it under her right armpit.

"Thank you, Mrs. Miles. I'm showing our guests to Dr. Aoki and will be back afterward." Dr. Blackton passed his secretary, who eyed him with utter disgust. Geena followed Dr. Blackton, ignoring the secretary as if she were air. George nodded at her, while Andi made an effort to evade her as much as possible. The dragon secretary was obviously not defending the boss but the lair.

7. SMOKE EVERYWHERE

DR. AOKI'S office was on the second floor in the original building. The windows looked out into the grounds behind the building, where Andi could see several different gardens. His tiny informants told him one was a vegetable and herb garden, while the others were for different kinds of flowers. There also seemed to be a Zen garden with lots of stones, which the arthropods weren't so happy about because, aside from some decent hiding spots, this garden didn't provide any food.

On their way up, George, always intent on building and maintaining good relationships with people, was asking about House Cusabo.

"It's such a unique name. Where does it come from? Or is it made-up?"

Dr. Blackton looked pleased about the question and cleared his throat, no doubt preparing for a longish explanation. Andi was ready to listen, though, because sometimes people told more than they intended to, especially when it was about a topic they apparently loved. "It's not made-up, oh no. The name Cusabo comes from a Native American language that's not spoken anymore. The Cusabo were a group of American Indian tribes who lived along the coast of the Atlantic Ocean in modern-day South Carolina, most likely between what is now Charleston and south to the Savannah River. We know very little about them, and their language is completely extinct, I'm afraid. Only a few words, mostly town names, were written down in the sixteenth century. Most of the words lack translation, but scholars are sure by now that Cusabo was from a different language family altogether, one we don't have access to anymore." He sighed deeply. "Don't you think it's so sad, all the culture that was lost during colonialization?"

"Yes. It's a shame. You seem to be very interested in the topic." George's tone held just the right amount of awe to make the director feel flattered. Andi could sense it in the pheromones he was emitting, bolstered by the way he swiped some invisible speck of dust from his jacket.

"I am. I love old languages and everything to do with the evolution of them. It's such a fascinating topic. Ah, here we are!" Dr. Blackton knocked at a door on the right side of the hall they had trotted along while he'd held his lecture about ancient language. After the "Come in" from inside, Dr. Blackton introduced them to Dr. Healani Aoki, explaining briefly to her why they were here.

She greeted them with a professional smile, assured Dr. Blackton she would do her best to assist, and closed the door behind him when he left for the meeting they had kept him from. Dr. Aoki gestured to the chairs in front of her.

"Please, have a seat. What do you want to know about Kesha?" She furrowed her brows. "Or should I say Staff Sergeant Raport?"

Geena smiled at the woman. "Kesha is fine. We would like to know why she left House Cusabo. She was honorably discharged because of her PTSD and the leg she had lost, and according to our files, she responded well to the treatment. Do you have any idea why she ended it?"

Dr. Aoki looked thoughtful. She was—

Strange, her body chemistry altered, her sweat too sweet, sickly, Andi knew what that was, diabetes, such a vicious illness, she needed to have her shot of insulin and soon, it was bad, no deeper meaning though, not for the arthropods anyway, this blob wasn't any different than all the others, taking up space, destroying the webs, upsetting the brood, they all did that, all the time, it was of no consequence what her body chemistry did, just made her easier to recognize, which was good, she was calm, their presence didn't upset her, and why should it, after so many years, what was a year anyway, endless pulsing, up and down, in and out, there was something else, though, smoke, beekeeper smoke, that was important, wasn't it, why, he needed to remember, the bodies—

"I wasn't directly involved in her treatment. That was one of my colleagues, Dr. Fulton, who is now retired. We often conferred because we both specialized in PTSD and depression. We even wrote some articles together about which treatments worked best depending on the case. We also conducted a survey of the different antidepressants usually used in cases of PTSD. Kesha had allowed us to use her case in our studies. She was always open to try new therapies, saying if she could help others with it, her trauma wouldn't be a waste of time." Dr. Aoki smiled fondly. "She was a determined, strong-willed woman."

"Then why did she stop the treatment?" Geena sounded as confused as Andi felt. This didn't sound like somebody who just decided they had enough and left.

Dr. Aoki sighed. "I'm not sure. Everything I could tell you would be pure speculation on my part because I was on holiday when she asked to be released from House Cusabo."

"You're saying there was nothing significant leading up to her leaving? Did she have a fight with anybody, or did something happen?" George leaned a bit forward in his seat.

Dr. Aoki shook her head. "As I said, it's all speculation. To me, it came as a surprise, and Dr. Fulton was definitely rattled by her decision. Kesha was either an excellent actor by pretending everything was fine, or whatever made her leave had enough of an impact to force her into making a hasty decision."

"Was she good at pretending?" George glanced at Andi, who subtly shook his head. As far as the spiders were concerned, Dr. Aoki wasn't lying. It was harder for Andi to read things when there were so many drugs around, altering people's chemistry, suppressing or advancing natural reactions. Luckily for him, there were almost no patients in the center of the house, where the doctors had their offices, which made it easier to tune out the constant hum of confusing impressions that were sometimes just slightly off when the drug was working well or the dosage not high enough, or punching him in the face with how different something he thought he knew could be. It was like looking at a picture from Picasso, all those lines still forming a face, some of them even in the way the observer would expect, others so far off, it took a lot of imagination to give them context. Being connected to the arthropods meant he was already stretched thin when it came to imagination, and adjusting to the warped images he was getting because of the drugs was exhausting. Andi shuddered just thinking about all the mental gymnastics he would have to do to form a coherent picture.

"No. She was a very straightforward woman, with no time for nonsense. Which also made me wonder what could have rattled her enough to just leave." Dr. Aoki shook her head. "As I said, none of it made sense, not then, and certainly not now, come to think of it."

"And she never contacted you or Dr. Fulton again?" George gave Dr. Aoki his full attention.

"No. She was just gone."

"How long do you think it took for her medication to wear off completely? And can you tell us how bad her state of mind would have been?" Geena tapped her index finger against her chin.

Dr. Aoki furrowed her brows. "To be honest, I can only guess. PTSD is a bitch with many faces." She started typing on the keypad of her laptop. "She was on a combination of sertraline and venlafaxine and did trauma-focused psychotherapy, as well as EMDR." Geena cleared her throat, and Dr. Aoki looked up from her laptop. "Sorry, that's Eye Movement Desensitization and Reprocessing. Both therapies are aimed at changing unhelpful beliefs about the trauma, as well as processing it and making sense of it. As I already said, Kesha had managed to process her trauma and to find a new meaning in it. She was doing so well, we were starting to lower her medication." She put both hands on the desk in front of the keypad. The rings on her hand made a clinking noise. "Perhaps that was part of the reason she left, though she wasn't that far down on them it should have made an impact."

"What happens when somebody on these drugs goes cold turkey?" Andi could sense George's distress when he asked the question. His partner's time in Narcotics had left its mark, even if George tried to downplay it. *Just like me.*

"Antidepressants are never fun to wean off, and to just stopping taking them? That's a nightmare. You have all the classics: flu-like symptoms, insomnia, nausea, imbalance, sensory disturbances, and anxiety or agitation. Especially the last three get amplified when the PTSD comes back in full force. As I said, Kesha was remarkably stable; her coping mechanisms were solid. My guess would be she was able to keep it together for about a week before she crashed."

"And the basis for this assumption is?" Geena lifted a brow.

"It takes about twenty-four hours for half the dosage you took to leave your system. With women, that time can be even longer. In roughly the next twenty-four hours, another half leaves the body, and so on. For people with a normal metabolism, it would take about five days to have it completely expelled from their system. Considering that Kesha was a woman, which means the half-time for sertraline is usually one point five times longer than for men, seven to nine days make sense."

"Did she know this?" Andi could sense Dr. Aoki's surprise at his question. It was the first time she heard him speak after the introduction. She caught herself quickly, though.

"Yes. As I said, she was very involved with her treatment, tried to learn everything she could about what was going on with her body and mind."

"Why would a well-adjusted woman who was used to military discipline suddenly decide to stop her own treatment, knowing full well what she was getting into?" Geena was now tapping a staccato rhythm on her thigh. She was truly curious, her pheromones painting a sharp picture in Andi's mind.

"My guess is probably a lot more off the mark than yours, Agent Davis." Dr. Aoki shook her head.

"Can you send us Kesha's medical files?" George gave Dr. Aoki his card.

"Of course, since Dr. Blackton said it's fine. I'm sending you the articles Dr. Fulton and I wrote on the subject as well. Since Kesha was one of our test persons, it might give you some additional insight."

"That would be very kind of you, Dr. Aoki." George got up, smiling at the woman. Geena and Andi followed suit. "If you could direct us to the break room for the staff? We were told Thomas LeClerk is off soon."

"Let me show you. Navigating this building is a bit complicated because of all the additions made over the years." Dr. Aoki got up to open the door for them. They filed out of her office and followed her through the maze of corridors to the left wing, where she pointed out a room with a table, several chairs, a comfy-looking sofa, and a huge coffee machine on a smaller table in the corner. A man of perhaps forty years was sitting on the sofa, holding the largest cup of coffee Andi had ever seen. He was exhausted, the dark circles under his eyes talking as loudly as his body's chemistry, even though the signals were diluted. The man had clearly been in close proximity to drugs of all kinds. Andi could detect *antidepressants, all of them kind of hazy, a washed-out pink with swirls of scarlet, pain medication, ibuprofen, like an old, familiar blanket in different hues of blue with an undertone of something metallic on his tongue, benzodiazepines, muddy and cloying, like glue on his antennae, amphetamines, sharp and cutting, black and a color he had no name for, he felt it in the nerves of his feet, rising up through the hair on his legs, repelling, something else, smoke, like he had sensed it on Dr. Aoki, only stronger, but he had smelled it—felt it—experienced it—before, the bees, yes, bees, the bodies in the ground, the man who put them there saturated in it, was it this man, could it be, so hard to tell, the height would fit, the man was calm, but perhaps just too exhausted, how should Andi tell, there was so much, he couldn't—*

"Seems we came just at the right time." Dr. Aoki's voice cut through the images flooding Andi. "Agent, Detectives, this is Thomas LeClerk, one of our senior nurses. Thomas, these are Agent Geena Davis from the FBI and Detectives George Donovan and Andrew Hayes from the CPD. They are here to talk to you about Kesha Raport. You remember her?"

The man got up from the sofa to shake their hands. "Yes, of course. She was part of the research you and Dr. Fulton conducted."

"Thomas was one of the nurses permanently assigned to the study," Dr. Aoki explained. "I need to go back to my office now. Thomas, Dr. Blackton has given permission to tell the agent and the detectives everything about Kesha. I'm sorry to say she's dead, though I guess we all kind of knew deep down." *Pain, sharp like a knife, flaring up like a fire doused in gasoline.*

She sighed deeply before she bid all of them goodbye, promising to send George everything she had about Kesha. When she was gone, Thomas LeClerk gestured toward the chairs around the table. "Why don't we sit down and you can ask your questions?"

8. Confering with Bees

To say George was on pins and needles was putting his current state of mind mildly. Granted, Geena wasn't half as bad as he had feared, but that was only a small consolation considering the overall circumstances. He tried to appear calm while keeping an eye on Andi the entire time. His partner had slipped into his other state two times already, even though nobody seemed to have realized. It was one reason George had no problem with Geena taking the lead during their questioning. It allowed Andi to stay in the background.

They sat down around the table with Thomas LeClerk. The man was clutching his oversized coffee mug like a lifeline. The way Andi was eyeing the nurse made clear there was something going on. Without any pointers from his partner, though, George didn't know what it could be. Which was why he waited and let Geena do the questioning again.

"Mr. LeClerk, can you tell us anything about why Kesha might have left House Cusabo four years ago?"

George kept one eye on Andi while he watched the nurse's reaction. The man was absolutely calm—or so exhausted he just couldn't muster the energy for a reaction; the way he looked, both things were entirely plausible—and whatever Andi was picking up was so unspecific, he didn't give George any clues.

"No, I'm afraid not. One day she was excited about how well the treatment was working for her, the next she demanded to be released."

"Were you there on the day she left?" Geena's tone stayed calm.

"Yes. My shift started when she signed all the papers. I tried to talk to her, but she was… very agitated."

"And that was unusual for her?"

The nurse sighed. "I don't know how much Dr. Aoki has told you about PTSD and all the different faces it has. For some patients, agitation is a common state, while others appear to be calm most of the time and then there's an explosion, depending on which meds they are on and what kind of trauma they have experienced. Kesha was well on her way to getting it under control. We had found the perfect balance for her medication, she was doing all those therapies, successfully, I might add, and she had her coping mechanisms down pat. In fact, we'd talked about starting to get her back out into society in a few months. She was excited about it, talked about maybe starting a self-help group for people with PTSD. And then she just left, didn't want to talk to me or Dr. Fulton, refused to say anything beyond that she wanted out. What a shame." Thomas sighed before he took a huge gulp of his coffee. "This here is not the easiest job, as you can imagine, and we see people being thrown back to zero more often than we see them succeed. The Keshas are the ones that keep us going, that show us we're on the right track. Losing her was a blow."

"Hard enough to kill her?" Geena struck out of nowhere, like a viper waiting patiently in the sand. George was impressed.

Thomas less so. Again, George wasn't sure if it was sheer exhaustion keeping the man from reacting or the fact that he was indeed innocent. He didn't even seem to be angry. The way Andi leaned his body forward told George *something* was going on with the man, though.

"Killing her would have defeated the purpose, don't you think, Agent Davis? A dead patient is hardly a success story. The research Dr. Aoki and Dr. Fulton were doing was aimed at bettering the lives of people suffering from PTSD, not ending them."

"Why did they stop with the research? Because Dr. Fulton retired?" Geena was back to being jovial, all aggressiveness gone from her voice.

"No. Dr. Aoki could have done it alone or found somebody else. They lost the funding. Unfortunately, money is the main reason why research is stopped. While PTSD is an important field, the distribution of the money is not always… plausible."

"When did they lose the funding?" George was the first to admit he didn't know much about the world of science, but he did know that money ruled the world with an iron fist.

"About six months after Kesha left. Shortly before Dr. Fulton retired. And I don't think it was related in any way."

Geena looked at George, silently asking him if he had any more questions. He shook his head. Geena turned back to Thomas. "Thank you for your time, Mr. LeClerk. Here is my card. The number on the back is Detective Donovan's cell. If you remember anything you think can help us, please give us a call. Sometimes it's the small things that can crack a case wide-open."

Thomas took the card and shoved it into the breast pocket of his scrubs. "Will do." He hesitated for a moment. "Do you know if she had to suffer?"

They had already gotten up from their chairs, and George could feel Andi stiffening beside him. Something was definitely up.

"The autopsy report isn't finished yet. I'm sorry, Mr. LeClerk." Geena eyed the man like a hawk. Thomas shrugged, his gaze glued to his coffee mug again.

"I was just wondering. She was such a strong person. I can't imagine she went down easily."

"We'll keep that in mind, Mr. LeClerk." Geena turned toward the door. George followed before he was stopped short by Andi's voice.

"Would it be okay if we took a look at your gardens? They seem lovely."

Thomas looked at Andi as if he was seeing him for the first time. Given how silent his partner could be, it was easy to forget he was there.

"Of course. Though I don't know about lovely at the moment. You should come back in two months when spring is really there. Anyway, turn left and follow the corridor to the very end. The door there should be open and lead you directly into the herb garden. From there, all other gardens are accessible. Take your time. In this weather, nobody is keen to go outside."

"Thank you, Mr. LeClerk." Andi nodded at the man before he turned to George.

They left the break room and strolled down the corridor with its green linoleum floor and the scent of lemon sanitizer hanging in the air. Really, just like a horror movie waiting to happen. Geena pointed to a door to her right.

"That's my cue. I'll find you boys outside." She stopped in front of the bathroom and waved them to go on when they hesitated. "It's fine. As I said, I'm a big girl. I can find you."

Andi started walking immediately, which gave George a chance to throw Geena one more glance before she went through the door. She winked at him. Not knowing if she was just making fun of him or really trying to give him and Andi some space, George decided to let it go for the moment. He had to take his breaks where he could.

Andi was already ahead, in front of the door, opening it with an ominous creak. George jogged up to him, realizing almost instantly what was going on. Andi was buzzing, his lips vibrating, his gaze locked in the distance behind the fence surrounding the grounds of House Cusabo.

The buzzing meant bees, which wasn't so bad because social insects were easier to deal with than the rest. George put his hand on Andi's shoulder, squeezing tight enough to feel his partner's clavicle, which was way too prominent for George's liking. Andi wasn't eating as well as he needed to. It showed in the loss of body mass. The buzzing faltered for a moment, indicating Andi was still present enough to recognize George.

"What it is it, Andi?"

"*Bzz, bzz, shrrt,* close, *bzz,* so many, *bzz,* the smoke, tired, *ssst.*"

Andi started walking toward the low stone wall separating the gardens, as George had seen from Dr. Blackton's office. They passed through what looked like a flower garden and an area with several greenhouses before they reached a part of the garden at the back of the original building. More than a dozen beehives stood there in a semicircle. While George took in the typical square shapes, he saw movement at the entrance of the two closest to them. A few bees were slowly coming outside, vibrating with their wings without taking flight. Andi stepped closer, his fingers outstretched. He wasn't talking, not even really buzzing anymore. There was just this low droning tone coming from him which worried George a lot, especially when he realized the same tone was reverberating out of the hives.

More and more bees appeared at the entrance of the two hives, the hives next to them coming to life as well. Andi held out his hands to the narrow piece of wood that served as some kind of landing strip for the bees before they entered the hive. The first bee crawled onto his hand, followed quickly by her sisters. Before George had a chance to react, Andi's hands were covered in bees. The droning tone was getting louder, thumping against George's sternum, echoing through his rib cage. Not a single bee came close to him; they were all flocking to Andi, landing on his jacket, in his hair, and on his legs, swarming up his arms, giving George's hand a wide berth, climbing up Andi's neck toward his face. George immediately felt thrown back to the bunker and the way the arthropods in the death chamber had swarmed Andi's body like the oversized pill bugs in *The Mummy*.

Everything George knew about bees he had learned from Andi, so he was aware that panicking was not an option. The insects would pick up on it and get agitated themselves. With a strength he didn't know he possessed, George forced his breathing to calm down. What helped was the fact that the bees still ignored him. They were completely fixated on Andi, which was good and bad. George tried to remember what they had learned in their meditation course. It was important to let his breathing flow naturally, until he was able to sync with Andi. His partner's breathing was very slow, his mind deeply interwoven with the bees. Reaching him there would be difficult, because they hadn't established a steady contact before Andi went down, and George had yet to learn to build it on his own. It was one of the things they had wanted to train for during their holidays. *Thank you very much, Chief!*

George closed his eyes, trusting Andi to keep the bees from him. He concentrated on the sound he felt in his chest, coming from the bees and rising through his fingertips where he touched Andi. It was a steady hum, soothing, lulling. And there it was, Andi's breathing, almost drowned out before, and now he had found it like waves in his ears, as if he were standing on the beach. It took him a while to get in tune with it, forcing him to breathe in longer than was natural for him, then hold it for what seemed to be an insane amount of time before exhaling slowly and steadily so he could make it until Andi finally breathed in again. It was as their instructor at the course had said—nothing was more difficult than adapting to somebody else's rhythm. When it finally happened, George wanted to do a happy dance but kept his cool. No way was he risking losing their synchronicity now that he finally had it.

The next task was to gently pry Andi from the grasp the bees had on him. "Andi? Can you hear me?"

"*Ssst, bzz*, getting warmer, they stole the honey, *bzz*, intruders, huge, blobs, they stole the honey, defend the nest, no, tired, smoke, smoke, *ssst*, protect the queen, the honey, hungry, they haven't come in a while, big blob, smoke, smoke, *bzz*, they stole the honey!"

"Yes, Andi, that's what beekeepers do. You remember? Humans? Like you are?"

"Human, blob, stealing, taking, the nest in danger, *bzz*, George, you're here, don't you see? The honey…."

"I'm sure they gave them some sugar water to compensate for the loss of the honey."

"Not as good, not as nourishing, poor substitute."

"Perhaps you can tell them not to take as much next time?" George figured it was worth a shot.

"I could. Because I can talk. I'm a blob. I can stop them. The honey will be safe." Andi shook his head, and the bees started to retreat from his body. Those on his arms scurried back while those farther away, on his shoulders and in his hair, took flight back to the hive. They scrambled over each other to get back into their home. A quick glance at the other hives showed the bees there were retreating as well. After a few minutes, everything was quiet again; even the low drone that had vibrated through George's body was gone. It felt strange, suddenly being without it.

He squeezed Andi's collarbone. "Are you with me?"

"Yes, yes. Thank you. You're getting better at syncing. I could feel you."

"It still took me too long. Those bees were all over you."

"Don't be so hard on yourself. It takes time, you know that. And the bees...." Andi sighed. "I let them take me under in the hope of maybe finding a clue about our killer."

"And was he here?"

"Hard to tell. The arthropods at the bunker see things differently because most of them are earth dwellers. There are similarities, enough to make me think the probability of him having a connection to this place is high. I can't say for sure, though. I was able to sense several males who fit the picture from all the other people working with the bees. I guess they're part of the therapy here."

"Makes sense. Working with bees requires patience and focus. At least that's what you told me. I can see it being beneficial for people who struggle mentally."

"Animal therapy. It's an effective way of treating all kinds of illnesses, mental and otherwise. The bees were furious, though, because they took so much honey." Andi's brows furrowed in anger.

"I'm sure we can drop a hint with Dr. Blackton. How about we find Geena and return to the precinct? Unless you want to tell me something about Thomas LeClerk?"

"I couldn't get a clear read on him. He'd been handling medication before his break, so everything was muddied anyway, and he was so exhausted, it overshadowed everything else."

"But—?"

Andi rubbed his temples. "I don't know yet. Could be nothing, could be something. There was something in the colors... the vibration was off... sorrow, pain, perhaps lying." He gave a frustrated sigh. "We'll see once I've gotten more attuned to the way the arthropods see things around here."

"How do we convince Geena that House Cusabo is the place we need to keep digging?" George mused.

"I don't know yet. But the perk of having five detectives instead of two is we can split work. Not to mention the beat officers we can send out."

"Which will give us space. Good idea." George let go of Andi's shoulder, gently patting the spot he had gripped. When he turned around, he almost froze. Geena was standing at the entrance to the bee garden, about thirty feet from them. The look on her face was unreadable, and George wondered how long she had been there and how much she had seen and heard. They had talked quietly, to not agitate the bees after they had settled back into their hives, but there wasn't much noise out here except for the occasional bird singing. Inwardly cursing his carelessness, George waved at her.

"We're done here, Geena. If you're ready, we can leave."

She smiled at them, her face inscrutable. All George could do was pray she hadn't seen or heard something she shouldn't. And if she had—he hoped she could keep her mouth shut.

THE DRIVE back to the precinct was mostly silent. Andi was recalibrating after his tête-à-tête with the bees, George worried about what and how much Geena had picked up and pondering how he would react to all the different reactions *she* could have. Geena was just sitting at the back of the car, staring out the window. When they reached the city, she was the one to break the silence.

"What did you think about House Cusabo?"

Since Andi's body language telegraphed loud and clear how much he didn't want to interact with anybody at the moment, it was up to George to answer her.

"I think it's definitely a lead. The circumstances of Kesha's disappearance are suspicious, and there is no such thing as coincidence. And let's not forget about Corporal Grand. We don't know yet when exactly he went missing after he left House Cusabo."

"You think them leaving House Cusabo and their deaths are somehow related?"

"I think the pieces fit too well. And then there's the other people Shireen has found who were reported missing by House Cusabo. Even though we don't know yet if they are among the victims, I'm willing to bet on it. That said, I'm keeping an open mind for other explanations, but until we learn more about the other victims, it's surely a good idea to dig deeper into the history of House Cusabo. Now that we have Dr. Blackton's cooperation, we can officially snoop around." He winked at Geena in the rearview mirror.

She snorted. "Where's the fun in that?"

"Granted, it's more fun otherwise, but for reasons I'll never understand, the DA wants a clean chain of evidence."

"Nitpickers, all of them."

"Why did they put Kesha down as a missing person, but not the corporal?" Andi's question made George hesitate. He hadn't even thought about it. Behind them, Geena whistled.

"I get why he's so good. I have to admit, this hasn't crossed my mind."

"Both Dr. Aoki and Thomas LeClerk said that Kesha left in a hurry, and not on good terms. How would they even realize she was missing if she wasn't in contact anymore? Wasn't that the explanation for why they hadn't reported Grand missing?" Andi let the questions hang in the air for a moment. "Because LeClerk knew where she was. I bet you anything he was the one to file the missing person report."

Geena coughed. "Normally I'd say that's a bit farfetched, but in light of what we heard so far, it sounds absolutely plausible. Dr. Blackton didn't know anything about the whole incident because he hadn't been working at House Cusabo at the time, and Dr. Aoki had been on holiday. Neither of them seemed to know about the missing person report either. At least they didn't mention it."

"The only one who was there when she left and who knew her well was Thomas LeClerk. He even asked if she had to suffer. I knew he was hiding something." Andi punched the console in front of him.

In the mirror, George saw the way Geena looked at Andi. They had to tread carefully. The conclusion Andi had just drawn had come naturally to him, a combination of the "hard" information he had from Shireen and the witnesses and the "soft" information he had gained through the arthropods. George had gotten so used to Andi's way of connecting dots he couldn't even see, he hadn't thought of interrupting his partner's train of thought. All Geena saw, though, was Andi making assumptions based on nothing. The good thing was they were still at the beginning of the case, which meant Andi could get away with what outsiders would perceive as guesswork, especially when it was as conclusive as his suspicion regarding

LeClerk. Later on, it would be much harder to claim a gut feeling when there was evidence pointing in another direction entirely.

"Let's not get too excited. We have to see what Shireen can tell us about the report and who filed it." If Andi was right, which was practically a given, Shireen would lend his "hunch" the credibility it needed and hopefully throw Geena off their track. They could play it down as a lucky guess.

"I'm texting her right now. Let's see what she has once we're back." Andi was already looking for his phone, which was in his left back pocket this time. After he sent the text, he fell silent again until they reached the precinct.

Shireen was already waiting for them, her eyes sparkling from what George suspected was a heavy overdose of caffeine.

"If it isn't my favorite detectives. And you brought a guest."

Yes, she should definitely lay off the energy drinks and sugar. Out loud, George greeted Shireen with the smile she deserved.

"Hello, Queen of the Web. This is Agent Geena Davis, from the FBI. She's here to help us with the serial killer, as you probably already know. Geena, this is Shireen, our IT specialist."

"Hi, Shireen, it's very nice to meet you." Geena held out her hand, which Shireen took without hesitation.

"Hi, Geena. Likewise. I see you survived your first outing with these two. If you ever want to rant or need some advice concerning the handling of Andi, my door is open." Shireen winked in Andi's direction. He simply shrugged.

"Thank you for the offer. I have a feeling I'm going to take you up on that sometime. As it is, Andi has already proven that it's worth suffering his unique charm." Now both women looked at Andi, who stared right back, challenging them silently.

"Uh, we better start working. His prickles are already up." Shireen turned toward the flat-screen on the wall, activating it with a sweep of her finger across the tablet that seemed to have grown onto her right hand. George saw the short glance she gave Andi before she started opening pages on the flat-screen. It reminded George that he wasn't the only one protecting his partner and that beneath Shireen's bubbly, amicable surface was a deeply loyal soul. He still didn't know what Andi had done for her to earn such devotion, and he would probably never find out, but he admired how Shireen had deflected Geena by making her feel included.

"After Andi asked me to find out who filed the missing person report for Kesha Raport, I looked at the file logs of all the people who went missing from House Cusabo during the last ten years. Corporal Grand wasn't reported, as you already know. Of the remaining eight, three were reported by one Thomas LeClerk, while the other five were called in by Regina Miles, the secretary of the director."

"Who did Thomas LeClerk call in?" Andi's voice sounded tight.

"TJ Ross and Celia Murdoch, both in 2013, Ross in May, Murdoch in September. Then Kesha Raport in March 2018. That's strange." Shireen furrowed her brows. Her fingers flew over the tablet's screen. "She officially left House Cusabo in January of that year. Why would they report her?"

"You were right." Geena stared at Andi, who lifted his hands.

"It was just a hunch."

For a moment, the words hung in the air. They used this sentence so often, it tasted stale in George's mouth. Shireen's narrowed gaze darted from Andi to Geena, who looked absolutely amazed. It told George the agent hadn't given Andi's theory that much credit, even if her words had conveyed something different. It also meant she wouldn't believe gut feelings as easily as George might have wished for.

"Well, you better get used to it. Andi's hunches are the ones doing all the work." Shireen grinned at Geena. "It's best not to question them, otherwise the magic wears off."

"I'll remember that." Geena nodded.

"Back to the question at hand. Why would LeClerk report Kesha missing?" Shireen was already busy with her tablet again.

"Does House Cusabo have files about their medication? What comes in, what goes out?" George scratched his chin. "Assuming LeClerk and Kesha were still in contact, it wouldn't be too farfetched to think he provided her with her medicine, would it?"

"Certainly not. It says in her medical file she was on sertraline and venlafaxine. Aha!" Shireen did a fist pump. "For February 2018, we have a discrepancy in what was ordered and how much was given out to patients. It wasn't reported, though. Either nobody found out, or they deemed the amount too small. And February was the only month where prescription drugs went missing."

"Which fits with the timeline." Geena cocked her head. "She left House Cusabo late in January, allegedly in a state of agitation. She was fully medicated then. In February, LeClerk got his hands on the drugs she needed, and in March, he reported her missing. Question is, does that make him a witness who lied to us or a suspect?"

"He was with the bees." Andi had just murmured the words, but Geena heard him. She fixed her gaze on Andi.

"The bees in the garden? How do you know? And what have the bees to do with all this?"

Andi ignored her, his tried-and-tested approach when people got on his nerves. Only Geena was their partner, however temporary. George decided it was time to remove Andi from the situation.

"He was just thinking out loud. It's something he does. Free association, you know?" *Bullshit!* "Shireen, if that's all, I'd like to call it a day. Geena, you must be tired as well. Why don't we all head home and start fresh tomorrow?"

He saw Geena opening her mouth to protest, only to be intercepted by Shireen. "That's it from me so far. I had lunch with Evangeline today, and she said she's positive she can tell you more about the victims tomorrow. You could meet with her first thing after a good night's sleep."

While saying this, she gently shooed them toward the door. George nodded his thanks in her direction before he steered Andi away through the bullpen. He knew Geena had left her jacket at his desk, which forced her to go there.

"Bye, Geena. We'll see you tomorrow. Say eight?"

"Eight's fine with me. Bye, George." If Geena was miffed by their sudden departure, she didn't show it. His rudeness was eating at George, sinking its claws into his sense of propriety. His mother's voice admonished him about being such a prick. But he had no choice. If he wanted to protect Andi, other things had to give. Politeness was overrated anyway.

Only when he had his partner safe in the car did George finally breathe more easily.

9. WHAT TO DO?

IN THE car, Andi put his head against the headrest and closed his eyes. George's stress was adding to his own, making it hard to keep the images coming from the arthropods at bay. He needed peace and quiet so badly. George started the engine, not saying anything. It wasn't necessary. Andi bathed in the tranquility of their closeness, of George's unspoken understanding. His partner stopped at the small supermarket on the way to Andi's house on James Island. "Do you need anything specific?"

Andi shook his head. "No, I'm good."

"Do you still have rice? I'm thinking about making that vegetable rice you like so much."

It didn't surprise Andi that George would stay. He did most of the time these days. Dangerous. And oh so wonderful.

"The one with the dried tomatoes and the feta cheese? I could eat that. And I think there's still rice in the pantry."

"Okay. I'll hurry."

"It's fine. You know I like the car."

"Doesn't mean you have to stay here longer than necessary. Plus, it was a strenuous day."

Andi patted his pockets for his cell. "I can entertain myself until you're back."

George threw him one last worried glance, then hurried toward the entrance. Andi knew he would come back with not only vegetables and feta cheese but also with a fresh package of rice, because Andi's ability to keep track of the contents of his pantry was abysmal. Food just wasn't important enough. Not to him anyway. He was also quite sure that anybody who had spent time sensing myriads of maggots gnawing away at a rotting corpse would go on a voluntary fast. George's cooking was great, though, and he wouldn't deny himself, even if it was more out of necessity than an actual desire to eat.

As predicted, George was back twenty minutes later with two huge bags containing a lot more than just the ingredients for tonight's meal.

At home, George went to the kitchen, suggesting none too subtly Andi should take a shower. "I'll do the same as soon as I have the veggies in the oven."

Andi went without protest. He was too exhausted to argue. The hot shower did nothing to revive him, and turning the water cold just wasn't appealing. When he toweled himself dry, he could hear George in the guest bathroom. The heavenly smell of vegetables with lots of garlic roasting in the oven promised a feast he wasn't sure he would be able to stomach. The more intense his *geschenk* became, the harder it was to eat. Andi's theory was that his body was so overtaxed with the sensory input, it shut down the less important functions. He slipped into his sweatpants, a T-shirt he had gotten from George, a sweater of undefined age that once had been green, he was almost sure about it, and his thick woolen socks. Then he padded down to the kitchen to sit on one of the kitchen stools where he could keep an eye on the veggies. The smell was thick and heavy here, the arthropods excited because of George, but not agitated. It was nice. Bearable. All he could wish for these days.

George came out of the shower a short time later, wearing sweatpants and a T-shirt as well, though he looked more like a model from the cover of a magazine. Andi wasn't blind. George Donovan was a good-looking man by anyone's standards. In Andi's humble opinion, he looked even better when he worked in the kitchen, humming softly while cutting the feta cheese and boiling the rice. Andi could watch him like this forever; everything was peaceful, warm, content, the way a house should be.

The buzzing of his cellphone was an unwelcome intrusion into his serene fantasy. He got up to take a look at the screen where the phone was charging next to the fridge. An unknown number. Andi hesitated. Taking the call meant leaving the peace and acknowledging the world outside. Not taking it meant he would wonder for hours who it had been. Sighing, he swiped the green button.

"Hayes."

"Detective Hayes. This is Aloys Norris speaking, Tyler's father. Do you have a moment?"

Andi was so surprised he held the phone away from his ear. George had stopped whatever he was doing at the counter, looking at him with raised brows.

"Uhm, I do have a moment. Is it okay if I put you on speaker? Detective Donovan is with me at the moment."

"Please do that. I want to thank you both for finding Tyler."

Andi put the call on speaker, mouthing "Tyler's father" to George.

"Hello, Mr. Norris. This is George Donovan. It's nice talking to you."

"Hello, Mr. Donovan. It's my pleasure talking to you. I wanted to thank you both for rescuing Tyler from that bunker. I don't know what we would have done if you hadn't found him. Thank you very much. And please forgive that I'm calling only now. The past two days were hectic."

"It's fine, Mr. Norris. We're glad we were able to help." George put two plates on the breakfast counter.

"Yes. I, uh… I know my wife is not the best at expressing her gratitude."

"We're used to it, Mr. Norris. Don't worry." George's tone was jovial, while his face expressed his curiosity. Andi could sense it, too, in the tension of Mr. Norris's voice. He was working up to something.

"I was wondering…."

There it was. Both Andi and George stared at the phone.

"Yes, Mr. Norris?" George was politeness personified.

There was a heavy sigh at the other side. "I got your number from Tyler. He said you gave it to him, saying he could call you anytime?"

"Yes. I said that." Andi thought he knew where this was going. "And I stand by my word."

"Ah, yes, so very kind of you." Aloys Norris sounded unsure. "Did Tyler, by chance, tell you why he went to that bunker?"

Andi shared a look with George, who shrugged. His partner took over again. "Tyler told us he wanted to have an adventure, like the heroes in his books."

"Yes, yes. The heroes. He didn't mention anything else? Like imaginary friends?" Norris's tone suggested he was poking at an open nerve, waiting for the pain to set in. George opened his mouth to answer, but Andi shook his head.

"He did mention his friends, who thought it was a great idea to go on this trip. Reminded me of myself when I was his age."

"You had imaginary friends as well?" Hope blossomed in Norris's voice.

Andi forced himself to stay calm. At least this was a father who was trying. "Yes. Several in fact. They made my childhood special."

He saw George rolling his eyes. His partner could appreciate the— sad—reference to his *geschenk*.

"So you understand what phase he's going through?"

"Absolutely. It's one of the reasons I told him to call me whenever he wants. Talking to him brings back fond memories." That was a blatant lie, but Norris wasn't here, and even if he had been, Andi's face gave nothing away.

The sigh coming through the phone was pure relief. "I keep telling his mother it will go away when he gets older, but she doesn't believe me. She's very strict with Tyler, forbidding him to talk about it. I don't think that's healthy, but he doesn't like talking to me either."

Because he knows you're just humoring him.

"I thought, if it's really okay with you, maybe he could call you now and then, talk about it? I know you're both very busy, and if it's too much—"

"It's fine. As I said, Tyler can call whenever he wants. If I don't have time, I'll just tell him to call later. And I also have no problem talking with him about his imaginary friends. I think it's good he has them." Andi wasn't so sure about the pros of talking to ghosts, but there had to be some, right? And they took Tyler seriously, which was a major bonus point. That his mother lacked the patience to deal with a child who didn't fit the norm came as no surprise. It just made Andi despise her even more.

"You think? Yes, yes, it could be good. He's not very popular in school…." Another sigh. "Anyway, thank you very much. Both for finding Tyler and for talking to him. If there's anything I can do for you, tell me. I'd be more than willing to help."

"Thank you so much, Mr. Norris. We'll keep that in mind. Have a nice evening, and say hello to Tyler from us." George was gently bringing the call to an end.

"Ah yes, I will do that. A good evening to you, Detectives." Aloys Norris ended the call.

Over the phone, Andi and George stared at each other.

"Wow. Didn't see that coming." George went back to the stove, where he'd been mixing the veggies with the rice and the cheese.

"No. At least Tyler has one parent who's trying to understand." Andi couldn't help the bitterness that crept into his tone.

George brought the pot with the food over to the breakfast counter, where he started filling the two plates. "I thought your mother knew about the *geschenk*?"

"Didn't mean she liked it or had any patience for it. She enjoyed the status she got within the family for birthing my *Oma*'s successor, but dealing with it all? She couldn't be bothered too often."

"I'm so sorry you had to endure that shit, Andi." George put one of the plates in front of Andi, briefly touching his wrist. The warmth of his skin seeped into Andi, made the spot almost hot.

"It's in the past. Not a place I like to visit. Not something I can completely forget about."

"I hear you. Let's dig in." George started eating with a healthy appetite, taking the time to chew, because according to one of his books, chewing was the most important part when consuming food. Andi loved watching him, could almost see him counting the bites before swallowing. He looked down at his own plate. The food smelled great, an enticing mixture of garlic and cheese and dried tomatoes interwoven with the flavors from the roasted veggies. He took the first bite, savoring the textures: grainy rice, soft potatoes, the tomatoes a little chewy, the cheese soft. His stomach seemed to be on board with eating because there was no protest after he swallowed. When he had half his plate eaten, Andi took a break. George was on his second helping, watching him intently.

"You're not eating well."

Such a seemingly innocent comment, loaded with so much context. Andi held George's gaze, not to challenge him, to convey without words the chaos inside his mind and body. When he was younger, he had been better with words, with getting meaning across. The deeper his connection with the arthropods became, the more he lost his ability to communicate in the way of the blobs, instead trying to use the pheromones he couldn't emit, or rubbing the hind legs he didn't have, or waving his butt while buzzing his wings, or tapping the ground in a rhythm no human understood. Luckily for him, George had gotten good at reading him.

"The thing with them crawling on you is new."

Sometimes a little too good.

"Yeah." Andi stared back at his plate, rearranging the chunks of cheese around the rice.

"Andi."

He looked up. George's face was tense, the silverfish restless.

"It's new, and I don't know how it's happening or even why. Happy?" He hadn't meant to be so snappish. It was just too much to process: the case, their trouble with the chief, adjusting to Geena.

"I'm sorry. I know you talk about things when you're ready. It's just—" George made a frustrated arch with his fork.

Andi huffed. "*You* have nothing to be sorry for, George. You're perfect. It's not your fault that Chief Norris is an asshole. It's not your fault I was born this way. It's not your fault the *geschenk* is getting out of control." He looked at his partner. "I'm just so tired, and I don't want to talk about it, because then I have to think about it, and then I would have to admit that whatever is happening at the moment is way beyond what I'm able to handle." It hurt, having to admit his weakness. At the same time, it was freeing. He had never before been able to be open with somebody. Even knowing George would never be able to fully grasp what was going on with Andi, it still felt good to be seen. And his partner didn't disappoint. George shoved his plate aside to reach over the breakfast counter for Andi's hand. He took it, squeezing hard.

"You're not alone. Whatever this is, no matter what comes, how bad it gets, I swear to you, I'll be there."

Andi wanted to believe him so much, his chest hurt. A tiny voice at the back of his head still insisted that George would leave him, that he wouldn't stay. At this moment, Andi was too tired to listen to it.

"Thank you. Can we just sit on the couch?"

"Of course. Why don't you go there and get comfortable while I clean up here? Do you want hot chocolate?"

"I should clean. You cooked."

"And normally I would insist on my right as chef to not be bothered with the menial tasks." George grinned. "But I can't make you work in good conscience when the circles under your eyes should have their own address."

"Charming. I'll take the hot chocolate. See you on the couch."

"Find some game, will you?"

Andi lifted his hand to show he understood. George loved his baseball, basketball, and ice hockey. Football did in a pinch. His favorite were college games, and one of those was always on one of the sports channels. Andi didn't have to look long until he found a college hockey match that had just started. He let it play, waiting for George to bring the hot chocolate.

His partner entered the living room the moment six of the players on TV formed a lump of limbs and sticks. Andi could practically feel the testosterone seeping from the screen.

"Oh cool, hockey. And it's live." George sat down, gave Andi a mug with steaming chocolate goodness, and put his own on the coffee table while he grabbed the thick quilt he had brought over from his home and arranged it over their feet. Then he took his own hot chocolate, leaned back against the couch with a sigh, and concentrated on the game.

Andi sipped his chocolate, not really paying attention to what was happening on TV. He had never understood the appeal of team sports, or any sport really. Team sports required an amount of social interaction he was sure he wouldn't have been comfortable with even if he hadn't had to deal with the *geschenk*. Not to mention all the posturing he thought was tedious. Sitting next to George, listening to his heartbeat through the legs of the various spiders on the ceiling and at the windows was soothing. Even though he was receiving input from his tiny housemates, he was content, mostly because a great deal of the input was about George. To his own surprise, Andi found it not only easy but also natural to simply focus on the man sitting next to him.

Whump, whump, whump, *so steady, strong, never wavering, his scent, a delicious combination of sweet and sour, indicating he was healthy, the blood good, his body warmth enticing, promising safety, the electric field surrounding him like a spring, pulsing outward, swirling gently, peacefully, his body chemistry a kaleidoscope of colors, whirling around in a perfect pattern, everything balanced, his breathing soft and cadenced, warm, inviting, a place to rest, to fall into, to lose himself to, a place where he could exist* with *them, where the pictures he got weren't tainted by human depravity, his own Garden of Eden in a man he'd known for barely a year, and yet he gravitated toward him, like moths to a flame, because he needed to, because if he didn't, he would be lost, he could feel everything dragging him down, pulling on his sanity, his humanity, he couldn't go, not yet, he didn't want to, George was here, holding him, so warm, so soft and hard at once, so perfect to rest.*

Andi woke with a start, not knowing what was going on. The arthropods were quiet, not sleeping, never sleeping, something was always scrambling around, the TV was off, the only light coming from the small lamp next to the couch. He heard a low chuckle.

"Sorry, I didn't mean to wake you. Just wanted to get a bit more comfortable."

Andi took stock of his body. His head was close to something solid, George's chest, no doubt, his hands resting on his partner's thighs. His feet were up on the couch, and George's hand was at his back, stroking him in a soothing rhythm.

"What time is it?"

George looked at his wristwatch. "Quarter past ten. Time for bed?"

"It seems I already was in bed, so to speak."

"You slept soundly through one of the best games I've seen in a while."

"Sorry."

"Don't be. We both needed some downtime. Let's get you to bed."

George carefully lifted Andi's head, untangling himself from Andi's clutches and getting him upright. Andi saw the two empty mugs on the coffee table.

"Hot chocolate always makes me tired."

"Yes, I'm sure it was the chocolate, not the clusterfuck of a case we're saddled with." George got up, pulling Andi with him. "Come on."

They headed toward the stairs after George switched off the light, bathing the room in darkness. Only the dim light of the moon was coming through the windows, creating more shadows than showing the way. Andi took over, relying on the arthropods to get himself and George up the stairs, where he switched on the floor light.

In front of his bedroom, he paused. "Thank you, George."

"You're welcome. Sleep tight." George walked on to the guest room that had become his by now. Andi watched him vanish through the door and was relieved to see the small crack, meaning George had left it open just enough to be able to hear Andi. It was childish, really. He was a grown man who was used to sleeping alone in his house, and yet.... And yet it was like a warm blanket, knowing George cared. Andi stepped into his own bedroom, quickly got rid of his hoodie, brushed his teeth, and went to bed. He closed his eyes, sensing for George through every option he had, seeing him through the eyes of a fly caught in the room, through the antennae of the moths dwelling in the box where the blinds were rolled up, heard his breathing through the legs of the spiders, felt his heartbeat as electrical charges through the pill bugs. George was settling down, already breathing deep, lulling Andi to sleep as well.

THE NEXT morning during breakfast, they talked about the case.

"I really hope Evangeline can tell us something helpful." George was back from his morning run, gulping down one of his disgusting green smoothies. The glass standing in front of Andi was filled with something more palatable, a mixture of maracuja juice, pineapple, banana, apple, and lemon, with some of George's magic powder which promised to provide all the minerals a person needed per day. Andi had his doubts, especially concerning the artificiality of the supplements, but he had once read how important belief was when it came to health, so he kept his mouth shut. Plus, the fruit smoothie was an acceptable alternative to not eating anything at all.

"It may take her some time to get all the bones sorted. They were in disarray, especially more to the top. The killer never dug deep to begin with, and every time he buried a new body, he disturbed the ones already resting." Andi shuddered, thinking about the agitation of the earth-dwelling scavengers whenever the killer had brought a fresh kill.

"I'm aware the situation was overwhelming down there, Andi." George looked at him over the rim of his now empty glass. "But can you try to remember any details that might help us?"

Andi closed his eyes. Compared to experiencing something directly through the arthropods, recalling it was a piece of cake. Granted, not the kind of cake he would like to eat, not even when he was starving, but easy. "He only goes there when he has a body. No visits in between. I assume he is with the bees right before he either makes the kill or buries the body, perhaps part of his ritual, because the arthropods recognize him only through the smoke, which is a bit different every time, but combined with the rest, the body, the pheromones they pick up on, it's a coherent picture. There's also a hint of drugs, hard to tell which ones because it's so weak. I'd say he doesn't take them, only has contact. Nobody else comes to that bunker. We need to find out who the owner is. The killer never stays for long. He brings the body, carries it straight into the secret room, where he always stashes it at the wall to the left while he's digging. He brings the shovel, takes it with him after the body is buried. There's—" Andi furrowed his brows, tried to form a picture of what he had glimpsed under the earth. "There's something on the ground, chalk, mixed with the earth. Don't know what it means. He goes back to the bodies, looks at their feet, touches them, then he puts them in the hole he has dug and shovels earth on it. After that, he makes sure the secret door is closed before he leaves."

"He's methodical, with established patterns. Less likely to make a mistake." George sighed in disappointment. "Any chance you might be able to follow his trail outside the bunker?"

"Probably. Until he gets into whatever vehicle he's driving. Worth a shot, though."

"Yeah. We have to go back to the crime scene anyway." George started putting the breakfast dishes into the dishwasher. "Let's get changed." He looked at the monstrous watch at his wrist. "We have roughly forty minutes to get to the precinct if we don't want to make Geena and the others wait."

"I guess that would be rude on her second day. Mescew and Gentry won't care."

"You're right. Considering how we left her yesterday, it would be even worse. She seems nice. We should try to stay on her good side."

Andi got up from the kitchen stool. "I'll do my very best."

George chuckled. "Let's buy her coffee and a croissant to be on the safe side."

Andi had a sharp retort on the tip of his tongue, about how he was very well capable of being nice to people if he wanted to, but George was already on his way upstairs. Knowing his partner wanted him to put on something he hadn't slept in, Andi followed.

At the precinct, Geena was already waiting, together with Sandra and Tobias. They had obviously gotten the introductions out of the way without the help of George and Andi. When George gave Geena his offering of coffee and pastry, her smile, that had been a little strained, loosened considerably, while Tobias murmured loud enough to be heard that he would have appreciated something sweet as well. Sandra cut in by telling him he was getting too fat and should be grateful that George had forgotten him. Geena wasn't really angry, Andi could sense it, just wary, unsure. Usually it didn't bother him too much how people around him reacted; it just wasn't worth the hassle. Geena, though, was a temporary partner, and they needed her. He couldn't forget that.

"Good morning, George, Andi."

"Good morning, Geena." George opened the door that led down to the morgue for her. "Did you sleep well?"

"It was fine. The hotel is better than some I've been in. Wonderfully quiet, and breakfast was good."

"So you're ready to face the morgue?" George gestured for her to follow him.

"On that note, we're going to stay here and see what new reports have come through." Tobias waved at his desk. "Oh, and we could select two beat officers to work with us? Chief Norris wasn't too happy yesterday when I told her you haven't chosen anybody yet."

"Ah, yes. Do that please." George smiled at Sandra and Tobias, who turned back to the bullpen. "Ready?" he asked Geena again.

"The way you say it, no, I'm not ready." She glanced at Andi, who was walking behind her. "But a girl's gotta do what a girl's gotta do."

"You're going to like Evangeline." It was all Andi could come up with. Polite conversation was not his strong suit. The way Geena looked at him, he got the feeling she understood. Perhaps this day wouldn't be too bad after all.

10. MONSTROUS PUZZLE

GEORGE LED the way to the morgue, glad that Geena didn't seem angry with them. Dealing with a pissed-off agent from another government branch, especially the FBI, was at the very bottom of his list of life goals. After an assistant had told them Evangeline was in her office, they went there, entering after a short knock. The coroner was seated behind her desk, the various piles of paperwork shivering precariously when Andi closed the door.

"Good morning, Evangeline."

"*Malo lava i le taeao*, George, Andi." She looked at Geena. "You must be Agent Davis. Shireen told me about you. I'm Evangeline Melcourt, coroner for the Charleston PD."

"Hi, Evangeline. Please, call me Geena. Considering what we're facing, I think a first-name basis is called for."

The women shook hands.

"I like you, Geena." Evangeline winked at Andi. "You're a lot more sociable than a certain someone I know."

George watched as Andi rolled his eyes. George still hadn't figured out his relationship with Evangeline. It was almost like brother and older sister, with a few twists here and there.

"What can you tell us, Evangeline?"

All amusement vanished from her face. She slumped back in her chair, rubbing the bridge of her nose. Her thick black hair was in a messy bun, as almost always, a few ringlets bouncing around her face.

"I have seen my fair share of mass graves, oh yes. But let me say, this makes number three on my Top Five of Things I Never Ever Want to See Again."

George was too experienced to ask for the two top spots. Evangeline was a seasoned coroner, had done excavations in several areas of war, present and past. If she thought their crime scene was bad, he didn't question her. She got up, her movements as graceful as ever, something he deeply admired. It was like watching a cat walking around.

"I have already sent you everything via email, but let me explain what we've found so far." She dug around between the mountains of paper until she held up a remote control with which she activated the screen on her office wall. Further rummaging revealed a tablet with numerous scratches on the surface, a sight that would give Shireen a heart attack. Some brutal stabbing of the poor screen made an image appear. It took George only a moment to realize it was a blueprint of the bunker.

"We're still in the process of identifying all the victims, which can take a few more days. Here you see the bunker. We have measured it with laser technology to get the most precise numbers possible. The whole thing is ten feet underground. The hall leading to the living room, where the secret chamber is located, is six point five feet long. To the left there are two rooms, some kind of pantry with nonperishable food and a shitload of weapons, thirty-two point eight feet long and thirteen point one feet broad. Next to it is a bedroom, sixteen point four feet long and as broad as the pantry. Opposite of the bedroom is a bathroom, also sixtten point four feet long and as broad. Behind the bathroom is a room with a generator and ventilation system. It's as broad as the bathroom and thirteen point one feet long. These rooms haven't been disturbed for a long time. There was dust on the floor, no footprints. All the doors were locked. We found the key for them in the living room, next to the sewing machine, where the opening mechanism for the secret chamber is.

"At the end of the hall is the living room, nineteen point six feet long and twenty-six point two feet broad. Behind the shelf at the far end is the entrance to the secret chamber, which is the same size as the living room. The difference is that the chamber was obviously added later and is not secured like the rest of the bunker, where we find lots of concrete. The ceiling is supported by wooden beams that are in a state of decline. As far as I can tell, no maintenance has been done since the chamber was built."

George stared at the screen. "I assume that was the nice part of the news?"

"*Ioe.*" Evangeline tortured the tablet screen again, and a blueprint of the chamber appeared. "The bodies were in four squares, each four point nine feet broad and six point five feet long."

"Big enough to bury people of all sizes," Geena muttered.

"Exactly. Mixed with the soil we found traces of white chalk, presumably the killer's way of marking the place where he had to dig."

George looked at Andi. His partner had been a little stressed about not knowing what the chalk could be for. Now the mystery was solved.

Evangeline swiped, and the picture on the screen changed, showing bones in each of the squares. "As I said, we haven't identified all of the victims yet, but when Shireen told me about the missing persons reported by House Cusabo, I asked one of my assistants to cross-reference the teeth of each skull with the medical files of the missing people." Her expressions darkened. "We found matches for each."

Geena made a sound of distress followed by a heartfelt "Fuck."

"*Ioe. Ta'i.* The good news is, and I'm using the word 'good' in a very loose sense here, that we were able to determine the order of the squares." She pointed with a pen. "The one at the right side of the door at the back is square number one, followed by number two at the door. Then number three left, and number four left at the far end. We found seven bodies in numbers one and two, six in numbers three and four. TJ Ross and Celia Murdoch, who were both reported missing by House Cusabo in 2013, we found in squares number one and two. With TJ, we identified Lucas Mellen, who went missing in 2018. With Celia, we found Lori Heller, who was reported missing in 2020. In square three were Samuel Grand and Lola Monarch, vanished in 2014 and 2021. Square number four held the remains of Izzy Whitewall, Kesha Raport, and Lydia Bloomenberg, reported missing 2016, 2018, and 2019, respectively. We were also able to match Kesha Raport's bones because of her prosthesis, and those of Samuel Grand and Corporal Hamed Beshora due to the distinct injuries they suffered during their service. It's quite the puzzle, because every time the killer digs anew, he disturbs the bones already in the earth." Evangeline sighed. "We're almost sure we have all the bones matched to the right bodies by now, and identification is underway, as well as the time span. Judging simply from the people we know went missing from House Cusabo and ended up in the chamber, we're looking at an escalating serial killer. And we may or may not have found his single burial ground."

George groaned. A serial killer was bad enough. An escalating one who was as well-organized as this one seemed to be was worse. One who had lost the place of his obsession? A nightmare. The easiest thing would be to just wait until the man appeared at the bunker again and take him then. Unfortunately, that would mean accepting another victim. And even though Andi was sure he only came to the bunker to bury the bodies, they didn't know if he dropped by occasionally without entering. In fact, it would be strange if he didn't visit in-between kills to relive whatever perverted joy he got from murdering other people. No, they had to assume he already knew that his space was compromised.

"There's one more thing." Evangeline had changed the picture on the screen. It now showed an enlarged skeletal foot. "You're looking at the left foot of TJ Ross. As you can see, he's missing his *digitus minimus*, his fifth toe, as are all the other victims, with the exception of Kesha Raport, where he cut of the fifth toe of the right foot, since her left foot was amputated from the knee down."

"He's taking souvenirs." Geena was grim.

"I can think of no other explanation. As soon as I find out more, I'll give you a call." Evangeline carelessly put the tablet on top of a stack of papers built on what looked like a shoebox, which in turn sat on a chair. For a moment, gravity and hope had an intense discussion if such an arrangement should be possible before gravity threw up her arms and left the room in a fit.

"Thank you, Evangeline." George went to open the door.

Geena waved at the coroner, while Andi just grunted. Evangeline grunted back, her eyes sparkling with amusement. *Yes, definitely sibling vibes there.*

On their way back to their desks, George realized suddenly that Geena would need her own. He felt immediately bad for thinking about it only now. Pondering furiously how to broach the subject, George came to an abrupt stop in front of their workspace. Somebody had put a table next to his desk, complete with a laptop and phone. The Post-it with the broad smiley face told him he had to thank Shireen for this. Making a mental note to bring her something sweet as soon as possible, George went to the whiteboards. Tobias and Sandra sauntered over when they saw them. Andi was already sitting on his chair, switching his computer on. Geena whistled.

"My very own desk. Thank you!"

"Don't thank me. I've only thought about it now. It was Shireen. She likes panna cotta," he added helpfully.

"I'll make sure she gets some." Geena sat down and opened her laptop. "Wow, she even wrote the initial passwords down. Talk about nice colleagues."

"Don't be too enamored yet," George warned her. "You have to change those passwords the moment you switch the laptop on. If Shireen gets past them within ten minutes, you'll have to listen to a *very* long speech about password security, how to generate the perfect password, and how important it is to memorize them and never, ever write them down or let some programs save them." He shuddered, remembering the stern telling-off he had gotten after Shireen had given him a new PC.

"I can see you speak from experience." Geena winked. "What about you, Andi? Are your passwords safe?"

"Always."

"Oh. How come?"

There was a pause, during which George debated if he should intervene or give Andi a little more time to answer. His partner didn't show his closed-off face, so he would say something eventually, though when was anyone's guess. George decided it would be safer if he said something just when Andi started talking.

"My mother's family is German, from Bavaria. I had to learn the dialect spoken in the village where most of them live. You wouldn't believe the passwords I can come up with."

Andi started typing on his own PC.

"You wouldn't want to help a colleague out, by any chance?" Geena was trying to sound nonchalant, and she could have probably fooled a civilian. But George could read her intention of getting to know Andi better clearly in her body language, which meant Andi, who had the senses of whatever arthropods dwelt in the vicinity at his disposal, could see right through her. Waiting for the inevitable dismissal that would result in George having to smooth Geena's ruffled feathers, George was again surprised.

"Use Glaache10*. That should do the trick."

"Excuse me, what?" Geena's fingers were hovering above the keyboard.

"G-L-A-A-C-H-E10*."

"Hmm." Gina furrowed her brows in concentration. "Okay, G-L-A… no, wait, let's make the next two lowercase, just to be on the safe side, so a-a-C-H… and the last one lowercase again, -e 10*. Perfect. May I ask what it means?"

"It's a word for phlegm. The kind you produce at the back of your throat. Some people spit it on the ground."

"And I'm not so sure anymore if I should thank you for your kindness."

"It's my pleasure to help out a colleague in need." Andi shrugged.

"I'm going to leave you alone now."

"Thank you."

Geena turned her gaze to George, who held up his arms in a defensive gesture. She rolled her eyes. Tobias and Sandra snickered. They had followed the exchange silently, too experienced to intervene in anything Andi.

"Don't we have to add to the whiteboards?" Geena crossed her arms in front of her chest.

George reached for the black marker. "That we do."

After they had done a rough copy of the detailed burial site Evangeline had sent them, they stared at the whiteboard, silently willing it to tell them who the killer was. George felt a little irritated because he couldn't add the information about the bees, which to him was like folding a shirt knowing there was a crease he hadn't ironed out.

"We need a profiler." Geena was tapping her foot. "I know my basics, as I assume do you, but this is... more than we covered in serial killers 101. I'm not even sure if it's safe to assume this is his only burial ground."

"I think it is." They all turned toward Luke Gelman, who was standing next to Andi's desk, looking hesitant.

"Luke. What are you doing here? I thought you were busy?" George had no qualms reminding the AI agent why he was at the precinct in the first place. Luke winced.

"For the time being, I did everything I could. Don't worry, the situation is under control." He stepped forward, looking directly at Geena. George's mother had raised him too strictly for him not to adhere to social niceties. Apart from that, Geena had nothing to do with the problems they were having with Gelman, and he really wished to stay on civil terms with her.

"Geena, this is Officer Luke Gelman from IA. Luke, this is Agent Geena Davis from the FBI. She's also our liaison to the military."

"It's a pleasure to meet you, Agent Davis."

"Geena, please. As I told George and Andi, this case shapes up to be such a bummer, we can't be expected to stay all super polite and shit. You a profiler?"

"I studied criminal psychology and did enough courses on serial killers to be adept. I don't profile on a regular basis, obviously, like somebody from the BAU would, but I'm proficient, I'm here, and given how overworked the FBI is, the probability is high that I'm all you're going to get."

This little speech was more to convince George and Andi than for Geena, who had arrived here as the only agent the FBI sent, without a profiler of her own, thus knowing firsthand how understaffed her agency was, and George glanced at his partner. Andi wasn't too happy, evidenced in the way his jaw muscles were twitching and the general tension radiating off him, but he was as much a realist as George, and Luke was right. Time was of the essence.

"Then please enlighten us. Or do you need some time to read the files we have so far?" George lifted one of his brows.

"I have to admit I already know what's in the files." Gelman sounded almost apologetic. "It's a huge case."

"We're listening."

"Why do you think this is his only burial ground?" If Geena was picking up on the undercurrent of not yet hostility but definitely growing animosity, she hid it well.

Luke gestured toward the whiteboard. "As you know, the profiling of serial killers is *very* educated guesswork more than anything else. There's always room for surprises." He made a step forward. "That being said, this killer is highly organized, as is evident in his choice of victims. He seems not to be escalating as far as we can tell from what we have— twenty-four bodies in ten years, evenly distributed in four squares in the ground. And even if he's escalating, he's doing it slowly. Otherwise we'd have a lot more bodies."

"Which could be in different graves," George interjected.

"Always a possibility, but unlikely. He's methodical, using chalk to make sure he doesn't accidentally dig at the wrong place. Why would he do that, if he had more places to dump the bodies? No, I'm sure he wants them all in one place, where he can control them. I'd say he's strong-willed enough to keep his killing urges in check, which would fit with the type of victim he chooses. This means the kill itself is not as important to him. Something else is, something he finds in these vics."

"PTSD, depression, bipolarity." Andi listed the medical findings for the victims.

"Except for Izzy Whitewall." Geena pointed to her name. "It sounded as if she was treated for something puberty related."

"Yes." George nodded. "But 'overactive imagination' isn't that far from hallucinations or manic episodes, which are common for PTSD and bipolarity. He could have gotten confused."

"You think he's not somehow medically trained?" Geena looked at Luke, asking for his opinion.

"Could be George is right, could be he's wrong and the killer is trained and thought he knew better than his colleagues. Though chances are he's somebody who knows a good deal about mental illnesses but has never studied to work in the field."

"This is bad. If you're right, we have unearthed his shrine, where part of his fantasy takes place. How fast is he going to escalate now?" The worry in Geena's voice made George antsy.

"Depends on various factors. He could just leave, start over somewhere new."

"You think he's that controlled?" George stared at Luke.

"No." Andi's voice had that faraway quality that meant he was connecting dots, forming a picture from the hard evidence combined with what only he knew. It was also something nobody besides George should hear, because the information came as a mixed-up jumble of bits and pieces. With a sinking heart, George realized there was nothing he could do to stop this, not when Andi was already opening his mouth. "He needs the bunker, important, the soil, mixing the bones, not on purpose, his trophies, tied to the place, can't leave, needs it, not going anywhere, waiting for the next meal, always so hungry, need, hunger, so deep in the earth."

Luke and Geena stared at Andi with open mouths. George's brain was overheating in his attempt at finding a plausible explanation, *any* explanation at this point that would get them out of this situation unscathed. He didn't know if it was the panic or his fear for Andi's safety, but his synapses seemed blocked. There was nothing.

11. WAVES ON THE BEACH

"WOW! YOU'RE already deep in the case, aren't you? I've heard about this method but have never seen it done. This is quite interesting." Geena patted Andi's shoulder, just once. He winced at the unsolicited contact. Sandra and Tobias just shared a look that spoke volumes. They were used to Andi being, well, Andi. Still, George would have preferred to have fewer witnesses to how strange his partner could act.

"It's what he does. Best not to disturb his flow." George had no clue how Geena could see anything Andi had said as coherent, methodical police work. He had no problem grabbing what she was offering and running with it, though.

"I surely won't." Luke made a step back. "What he said is also plausible. The killer is taking souvenirs, perhaps in the bunker before he buries them, and it's all linked to this place. He's not going anywhere."

"Then what's he going to do?" Geena was still staring at Andi with awe.

"That's the big question. Laying low for the moment, which gives us time to find him. Hopefully before he strikes again." Luke cocked his head. "I will think about this, try to give you a more detailed analysis. Things are bound to get clearer the more Dr. Melcourt can find out about the victims."

"I'm going to see who owns the bunker. Perhaps our killer is easier to find than we thought." Hope mixed with fear they probably wouldn't be that lucky vibrated in Geena's tone.

"Good idea. I'm going through the files of the victims we have identified. Perhaps something will pop up. Sandra, Tobias, could you dig a little deeper into the history of House Cusabo? And Dr. Blackton? But first—" George put his hand on Andi's lower back to guide him toward the exit. "—Andi and I are going to the bakery. After the charming morning we just had, I guess we all can use some sugar. Geena, is there anything you can't or won't eat? And how do you take your coffee? Sandra, Tobias, what do you want?"

"If it's sweet, I'm in. Unless there's cherries involved. As for my coffee, as black as the night. The one you brought me this morning was perfect." Geena smiled at him.

"We'll take donuts with chocolate glazing. Two lattes, heavy on the milk. Thank you very much." Sandra saluted lazily before she and Tobias went back to their desks. They were close enough that George saw no need to haul them over. Sometimes a little space between detectives during an investigation was a good thing.

"Noted. No cherries, coffee of doom. Two abominations of coffee accompanied by the policeman's fuel. We're back in fifteen." George followed Andi out of the precinct, where he took the first full breath in what felt like an eternity.

"That was close."

"I'm sorry." Andi was still distracted.

"It's not your fault, Andi."

"But you're worried. It's like acid on my tongue, burning my insides. Your electricity is wavering."

George made a conscious effort to calm himself down. Being with somebody who couldn't be fooled by pretty lies and good acting was strenuous. "I know I'm stressed. You are too. We shouldn't be here, shouldn't be working on this case, shouldn't have to navigate Sandra and Tobias and Geena, who I really like and hate deceiving. We're just lucky our fellow detectives know you at least a bit, and she thinks you're using some creative methods to solve your cases."

"She doesn't. But she wants us to think so."

The words were like a bucket of ice-cold water. "Do we have to worry about her? Should I try and get rid of her?"

"No and no. She thinks fast, which is good for this case. And she's mainly curious. It spills off her in waves. She doesn't understand what's going on, and she feels drawn to us. Pheromones." Andi shrugged as if that explained everything.

"You mean we're compatible with her?" George had learned a thing or two by now. Pheromones didn't just tell Andi what a person was feeling, they also showed him matches, information that could be valuable for dealing with people.

"You are compatible with her. Very much so. She and I, we fit, but in a more… casual way?"

"I understand." And George did. His vocabulary was growing every day, adding new meaning to words he had never given much thought. Like casual in comparison with compatible. The latter meant they clicked on a hormonal level where sex was definitely on the table, should either of them be so inclined, which George wasn't. The former meant there was no sexual tension, no negativity either, just a seamless fit on neutral ground.

Andi's cell started ringing. He fumbled it out of his jacket, furrowing his brows when he saw the caller ID.

"Hayes."

George saw his partner's eyes widening. "Hello, Tyler. It's nice to hear from you, and it's okay, I have time. Would it be okay if I put the phone on speaker? George is standing next to me."

Andi must have gotten an affirmative because he pressed the speaker button, holding the cell between them.

"Hello, Tyler. How are you?"

"I'm fine, George. Can I…. Can we talk about them?" Tyler sounded so insecure it made George's heart clench. No child should experience the feeling of not being taken seriously.

"Always, Tyler. Andi promised, didn't he?"

"Thank you."

"What do you want to tell us, Tyler?" Andi inquired.

"Uhm, the ghosts, they're acting strange. Izzy says it's because the bones were found."

"Define strange, Tyler. Andi and I, we don't know anything about ghosts or what kind of behavior is normal for them."

"Okay. Sorry. It's, you see, normally, they come and ask me to play. Hide and seek, or just strolling around. But now they come and just blabber. They're flickering too. I think I can see their adult forms, like a badly pixelated computer game. Sometimes there's bones." Tyler's voice had gotten quieter at the end.

George looked at Andi over his cell. They were standing on the sidewalk only a few yards from the bakery. Luckily, there weren't many people around. The air was getting warmer, but not enough to invite people to mill around outside. George nodded in the direction of the apartment building next to the bakery, which had an entrance door with a stone arch. It provided them a semblance of privacy.

"Are you frightened by what you see, Tyler?" George dreaded the answer, because if Tyler was, he had no clue how to help him. He didn't know how to help Andi, whose link to the unknown was at least of this world. Tyler was tethered to something else entirely.

"No. Not really. It's not pretty, because I can see glimpses of them rotting, but I know they're not doing it on purpose. They can't help it, and they always apologize."

"And Izzy thinks it's because they were found?" Andi sounded calm, as if he knew where he was going with his questions.

"Yes. She says it's—" There was a moment's pause, during which Tyler probably conferred with his ghost friend. "She says it's part of waking up. And because there are so many, it's all jumbled. Too much energy."

"Does Izzy know anything about the killer? Or any of the others?"

"No. None of them saw him. They all went to sleep and woke up in the bunker when they were already dead. The killer was always gone, and when he comes to bring somebody new, they can't see him either. He wears armor."

George looked at Andi, who was humming very lowly. A fly that must have woken recently landed on his right temple. When his partner didn't shoo it away, didn't even seem to realize it was there, George had to hold back from doing it for him.

"Can you ask Izzy if that armor could be a beekeeper's suit, by any chance?"

"Izzy says yes. He wears the whole thing, white, with a black grid. No, I can't say that to him, Izzy. He'll think I'm crazy."

"You can't say what to me, Tyler?"

"Uhm, Izzy wants me to tell you that you, that the bees…."

"What's with the bees?"

"She says to trust them. Silly, I know. They're insects."

"It's fine, Tyler. I think I know what she means. Was there anything else?" Andi was obviously trying to wrap the call up without being rude to Tyler.

"No. Just…. Thank you, for listening. And for believing. You can't imagine what it means to me."

"You're welcome, Tyler." Andi didn't offer more. The way he was staring at the phone, his gaze glazed over, made George wish he could drag his partner home to the couch so he could rest.

"Tyler, I think your father is doing his best. It's difficult for him to understand, that's all."

A deep sigh came through the line. "I know. Bye, George. Bye, Andi."

"Bye, Tyler." Andi pressed the button to end the call.

"Do you really know what Izzy means? About the bees?"

The fly was now in Andi's hair, rubbing its front legs together. George wanted to kill it.

"No and yes. I think she means the same thing I'm thinking. That the bees are the key."

"Key or not, we need some sugar and caffeine first."

"Amen to that."

They got the fuel they needed to face the rest of the day, which consisted mainly of staring at the screens of their PCs and calling official places to confirm information about House Cusabo and the victims. Geena managed to find the owner of the bunker, one Thomas Cervill, who had died in 2012, one year before the first victims had been brought to his bunker. He had a son, Timothy Cervill, who seemed to like to stay off the grid but had land in his name right next to the grounds of House Cusabo. They agreed to pay him a visit first thing the next morning before they bid Geena, Sandra, and Tobias a nice evening.

On the way to Andi's place, George bought some fresh vegetables to make stir-fry. Andi was silent until they reached the driveway.

"Would you meditate with me?"

George parked the car before he turned to Andi. "How bad is it?"

"Drowning, everything's thick, like syrup, no traction, sinking, too much of everything, hate people, blobs, going under, I can hear everything, I know too much, always too much, you're worried, don't go, please don't go, can't without you, it's suffocating me, like a blanket, but not warm, never warm, oppressing, I need—"

"I know what you need. Don't worry, Andi." George got out of the car and ran around to help Andi while he tried to calm his own breathing at the same time. No need to add fuel to the already blazing fire of Andi's meltdown. If George had thought it would do any good, he would have cursed Chief Norris yet again. For a brief moment he wondered if curses were real, like sensing arthropods and talking to ghosts, and he knew he would wish the chief a bout of diarrhea while attending some important meeting with her higher-ups. Yes. The very detailed picture in his mind soothed his temper a bit.

"Why are you grinning like Jack Nicholson in *The Shining*?"

"I just entertained the idea of curses being real and the chief getting hit by one." George had Andi out of the car, walking beside him toward the house.

"How… very nice." Andi didn't have to explain because George could hear it in his voice—his partner was having similar ideas.

After they had taken off their shoes in the hall and George had deposited the vegetables in the kitchen, they both went to their rooms to have a shower and get changed. Meditation was best done in comfortable clothing. George made sure their cells were off while Andi put their yoga mats on the floor in the living room. He even went so far as to light a candle, which George had only seen their meditation teacher do. Unless the candle was the point of focus, it had no real purpose except for lending some ambience to the room, something Andi didn't need because he was used to meditating, and George's point of focus was Andi, or more precisely, Andi's breathing.

They sat down across from each other. Andi was back in his ratty clothes, the socks especially begging for somebody to end their misery. But they were hand-knitted from sheep's wool, and George had yet to find a suitable replacement. If the socks and trousers looked bad, not to mention the threadbare sweater, Andi himself was even worse. His skin was pale, paler than any white person had a right to be, blue veins starkly visible under what appeared to be more paper than a protective surface for the body.

George held out his hands to Andi. There was no sense in dwelling on how terrible his partner looked. There was also no sense in dwelling on how George now had a list of increments for how bad the visuals could get before he had to put his foot down and Andi in bed. And as sick as Andi appeared, he was still three to four stages from the worst. It made even less sense to think about how there was no list of positive signs— even in his most rested state, Andi still looked like he had just recovered from the flu.

Andi took George's hands. He was cold to the touch, another sign of his exhaustion. Under different circumstances, George would have tried to get food into his partner before they started the meditation. The way Andi had made his need known, though, had told him there was no time for something as mundane as fuel for their bodies. If only he could get Andi to drink his green smoothies more regularly. George was convinced it would help. Unfortunately, Andi had the same views on green smoothies as a toddler had on greens in general—they happened to other people.

They sat close, their knees touching, their hands resting on them. Andi closed his eyes, and George could hear his breathing becoming deeper. He closed his own eyes, concentrated on synchronizing his breath to Andi's. It took some time, forcing his body into another rhythm, but then it was as if a knot of tension had burst in a kaleidoscope of colors. They were in sync now, going deeper. George could feel Andi, each of his fingers a cold point of contact, slowly warming from George's body heat, which was good, something he could provide, a way he could help his partner with his burden, holding his hands, his own resting on where their knees joined, Andi's knees sharp and bony like their owner, George's covered in muscle, reliable, strong, the fabric on the upper half of the back of his hand rough, with fuzz balls from too much washing, the lower half on a smooth surface, the feeling of newness a sharp contrast to the age of the other. It was a strangely accurate representation of their partnership, something so distinctively clear on the surface, ragged and new, smooth and rough, bought and kept, and yet it was just that, surface, because under that, things changed. The new wasn't better, just different, lent another texture, added to the picture instead of painting it from scratch.

In and out, their breathing flowed, like waves on the sand licking back and forth. The meditation teacher had told them to use this picture, as it was easy to imagine and to hold on to. George pictured himself on a beach, something nice, not the overcrowded sunny beaches in Florida or California, no, his beach had some rocks in the sand, around which the waves bubbled and foamed. It was more gray than white or orange, not hot, not cold either; it was a soothing beach where he was alone with Andi, no distractions, no cases, no chief, and most importantly, the arthropods were drowned out by the waves, which were their breathing, their breathing was the waves, all one, peaceful, perfect. He was holding Andi's hand, it had warmed to his touch, like a snake warming its body under the sun, their steps were in sync, no haste, it was all good. He felt a light tremor in Andi's hand, the beach flickered. George's mind knew there was a problem and wanted to go back, but he had to stay, had to keep Andi here, even if he was still not sure what *here* was exactly, the place where he could keep Andi grounded, that was his job right now; he didn't have to take in what Andi was saying because this wasn't a case, they were at home, this was for Andi, to make him relax. George imagined the cool sand between his toes, the soft kiss of the water when it rolled up to them, in and out, back and forth, waves on the beach, eternal, soothing, consistent, an anchor to keep Andi grounded, a wall to fend off whatever was haunting his partner.

Time became meaningless. George fell into the picture, got caught in the rhythm, the places where his and Andi's bodies met like beacons in a darkness that was a jumble of sensory images for Andi and like a room without electricity for George. There were times when he envied his partner his broader sight on everything. George imagined how wonderful it had to be to not be confined by the limitations of his own senses, to be able to step out of the cage every human lived in—until he remembered the price Andi paid. It was a good thing most humans were unable to escape the prison. The human mind wasn't made for the vastness of the world.

Slowly, Andi's voice filtered into the lulling song of the waves, riding on the splattering noises when water met rock.

"Warm, so warm, you smell so good, of home and safety and *chrt, ssst*, they're not as loud when you're here, holding them at bay, the images, it's flowing, fleeting, like a dance, the waves, like music, my rhythm, not theirs, our rhythm, peaceful, your electricity is back to normal, love it, *thump, thump, bluorp*, dance with me, back and forth, in and out, I'm tired and hungry, or is it them, always so hard to tell, no bodies here, your cooking is so good, I want to eat."

George squeezed Andi's hands, enveloped them with his, imagined holding them forever, until they were both old and gray. The image brought contentment, a promise of a life well lived, of a purpose served. Their breathing sped up, in and out, back and forth, slowly coming back, the beach sinking into the waves while they broke through the surface, back in the living room of Andi's house, on their mats, their hands entwined.

Andi looked better, there was some color in his cheeks, and not the unhealthy kind of impending fever or exhaustion. George smiled at him.

"You said you were hungry?"

"Yes. I think I really am."

George got up to cook, and after he had fed Andi, they sat on the sofa, watching a game of basketball. Andi leaned against George's side, a quilt over his legs, dozing away. It was perfect.

12. Preppers and Bees

"THE SON of the owner of the bunker lives next to House Cusabo. Coincidence?" Andi took a sip of his peppermint tea.

"There are no coincidences, as you well know," George replied in his best Gibbs imitation. He was maneuvering the Escalade through the outskirts of Charleston.

Despite the pressure they were under, this morning wasn't too bad. Andi had slept well after the meditation with George, and Geena had sent them out to question Timothy Cervill alone, saying she wanted to work with Gelman on their killer's profile. Tobias and Sandra were still digging deeper into House Cusabo, now taking a closer look at the former director, the late Dr. Silvana Grassen. They had also enlisted the help of two beat officers, Susan Jones and Mark Deville, who were hyped about the opportunity to work on such a huge case. Evangeline had sent more information about the victims, and Shireen would surely add her findings soon, now that she had more names to work with. Even without the input from the silverfish, Andi had easily read from Geena's body language that she wanted to give them some space, which he appreciated. Considering how bad working with other agencies could be, they had drawn the equivalent to a lotto win with Geena. Being alone with George meant he could relax even more without being scrutinized all the time.

Letting some of his iron control loosen just enough to be able to breathe a little easier felt like heaven to Andi. He was just glad most insects were still either hibernating or kind of sluggish due to the weather. But the sun was already getting more potent with each day, and the arthropods felt it as well. Soon they would bury Andi under an avalanche of impressions. He only hoped the case would be solved by then.

"No. Especially not in a case like this." He fumbled for his phone to scroll through the information Shireen had sent them. "Timothy Cervill is a prime example of a true American prepper. There are no medical files of him after his tenth birthday, which is also the year when his mother died. Apparently, she was the one to keep the family at least halfway inside society. After she died of cancer, Thomas Cervill started homeschooling his son. The land where he built the bunker was only partly his. The rest belongs to the city. Back in the eighties when he started building it, nobody gave a damn because who needed swamp land?"

"I can't imagine what it must have cost to get the ground dry enough to dig the hole for the bunker, even if there's more rocks in that area."

"According to Shireen, Thomas inherited money from his grandfather, a healthy trust he dissolved when he started his alternative housing project, also one of the last fiscal traces Shireen could find of him. There is a short blip after his wife's death, when he collected her life insurance, but then he went completely off the grid, taking his son with him."

Andi scrolled on. "Shireen can't say for sure, but she thinks Thomas started building the bunker in 1983, the year Timothy was born. He finished in 1992, a year before his wife died. She bases this estimate on the turnover of the hardware store Thomas used to frequent. For somebody who was adamant about paying all his bills in cash, he was damn neglectful when it came to evading shopping patterns. Anyway, father and son never got to enjoy the bunker, because in 1994 the city realized there was an illegal construction on part of their land and they forced Cervill to give the bunker up. Nothing much happened after that, it being swamp land and all, and by now it's considered part of the recreational area around the city, though practically nobody goes out there because there's more inviting spaces available."

"You mean technically, the bunker belongs to the city?" George was now on the road leading to House Cusabo.

"The legalities are unclear. I guess lawyers would have a field day with it—or more precisely a field year. Or decade. I assume, due to Thomas Cervill's aversion to the government, he gave the bunker up without much fuss. After all, fighting for it would have meant going to court. You can't expose yourself to the authorities more than that. He bought a patch of land next to House Cusabo, which his son, Timothy, inherited after his father's death in 2012."

"Do they have a bunker there as well?"

"I don't know. Their purchases from the hardware shop they used to frequent suggest not, but they could have simply started switching more often."

"Fine. Here we are." George stopped the Escalade in front of a metal gate similar to the one guarding House Cusabo, though this one was definitely less inviting. Several signs warned trespassers from entering, threatening them with the use of firearms. George looked at Andi. "Anybody home?"

Andi concentrated on the information he needed to filter from the mass of sensations swamping him.

The queen laying eggs, going from comb to comb, the larvae so hungry, always, some of them transforming right at the moment, the feeling of being liquefied always terrible, the faint memory of what he'd been mixed with what he would become, these were strong bees, killing the varroa tics, the dismembered bodies of these parasites strewn on the ground of the hives, wings growing out of jelly, he had no real sense in this state, just a frame of mind he couldn't hope to ever comprehend, if he got sucked in, his own body became purely blood, no form except of the shell keeping it inside, though what was inside remained to be seen, pumping and pulsing, he could feel his sisters in the hive, waiting for him to join them, one blob lived here, the smoke, the beekeeper suit, it was all there, but not the same or was it, so hard to tell, the bees knew only this blob, no way to distinguish him from the killer, not yet anyway, he was in the little cabin, there was room underground, not as big as the other bunker with the death chamber, not filled with death, only food and water, paper, the blob knew they were here, hidden cameras, the blob had a weapon, coming toward the gate—

"Mr. Timothy Cervill, we are Detectives George Donovan and Andrew Hayes from the Charleston PD. We have some questions for you!" George was shouting at the man marching toward the gate with his shotgun at the ready. He had opened the driver's door but stayed behind the relative safety of the steel. Andi did the same.

"What do you want?" Timothy Cervill didn't sound very inviting.

"We want to talk to you about the bunker your father built in Bloody Dick Swamp." George showed his badge over the window of the car door. Timothy was now close enough to take a look at it through the gate. He was also close enough for Andi to get a good look at him. The man was roughly George's size, a bit over six feet, with brown hair and a brown beard, both of which could have used a trim. His eyes were rather large in his hard face, a grayish blue that gleamed in anger.

"The fucking city took that from us. What would I know about it?"

George clipped his badge back onto his belt and slowly stepped forward. "We don't know what you might be able to tell us about it, which is the reason we're here. Can we talk?"

It was obvious Timothy was torn. In the end, though, he seemed to come to the conclusion that he might as well talk now and spare all of them the hassle of getting a warrant and pestering him later.

"Fine, come in." He fished out a key and opened the padlock on the gate.

George locked the car, then stepped through the small gap Timothy had made by opening one half of the gate. "Thank you, Mr. Cervill. We will try to not waste your time."

"Too late for that."

Timothy definitely needed to read up on Southern hospitality, Andi decided. Timothy also made no move to invite them deeper onto his land. He remained none too subtly on the path leading between the trees where Andi knew the cabin and the beehives were located.

George, as always, showed no outward signs of annoyance about Timothy's behavior. To Andi's advanced sight, he was practically screaming with rage, close to snapping, but to the world and Timothy especially, he was the picture of calmness. A contradiction that never ceased to fascinate Andi.

"When was the last time you were at the bunker, Mr. Cervill?"

"Don't know how that's any of your fucking business, but it's been a long time. I was still in school. Maybe when I was eleven? Or twelve?"

George nodded. It fit with what they knew about the history of the bunker. He then took out his cell with a slow, careful motion as to not spook Timothy into raising his shotgun again, which was at the moment resting with the butt on the ground next to his right boot. He wore military trousers and a black tank top displaying a lot of hair, which explained why he wasn't freezing, and a growing gut that didn't fit with the prepper stereotype of the muscular guy who could wrestle a grizzly. At least that was how Andi liked to imagine preppers. George was now showing the blueprint of the bunker to Timothy, sans the description of the bodies.

"Mr. Cervill, is this how you remember the bunker?"

Their suspect stared at the screen for some time. "Not exactly. I mean, it's been some time, and I was a kid back then, but I'm pretty sure that room wasn't there."

Andi didn't have to lean over to know he was pointing at the burial chamber.

"Are you absolutely sure?" George insisted.

"What the fuck, man? I told you I was just a kid then. I'm as sure as can be. It's not like we were there that often before the fuckin' government kicked us out. What do you want with it anyway?"

There was a flare in George's pheromones, telling Andi how much his partner wished to clock the prepper. His admirable self-control won, as it did almost every time. "Thank you. And I know you said you were just a kid, but did your father ever mention how hard it was to dig the bunker? I mean, we're talking swamp land here. It couldn't have been easy."

"Nah, it wasn't. Dad had to use special concrete and everything. It helped that the ground there is a little drier than the rest, because of the trees, you know, and because it's higher than the surrounding area, and there's some rocks keeping everything relatively stable. It's the reason he chose that location in the first place."

"How difficult would it be to dig this additional chamber?"

Like before, the question didn't provoke a reaction in Timothy, apart from a general annoyance that seemed to be part of his very being. "The digging itself wouldn't be too hard. The soil is moist, but not packed. Easy to get through as long as you avoid the rocky parts. Securing the chamber would be a lot more difficult for the same reasons."

"So not something everybody could pull off?"

"No. You need some knowledge about building on wet ground. It's not rocket science, mind you, but you need to have experience. What's this about? The government planning some secret underground lab? Using my old man's hard work for their own gain?"

George ignored Timothy's questions and glanced at Andi, silently asking if he had anything to add. Andi thought for a moment, weighing the wisdom of his words. "You keep bees?"

Timothy furrowed his brows. "Don't know how you know or how it's any of your business, but yes. Bees are a good thing to have."

Andi felt George leaning toward him, just a bit, in a protective gesture that warmed Andi more than his woolen socks or a hot water bottle could.

"How long have you had them?"

Timothy shrugged. "Always. My ma liked them for her garden. She always said it wasn't a garden if there wasn't any buzzing."

Andi was surprised how friendly Timothy's voice got when he told them this. He most definitely had good memories of his mother, or he just liked working with bees. Many people did.

"Thank you, Mr. Cervill. That's it for now." Andi was barely done talking when Timothy urged them back through the gate, closed it with a lot of rattling, turned on his heel, and stalked back from where he had come, his shotgun slung over his right shoulder without so much as a goodbye.

"What a charming person. I guess we can count ourselves lucky he didn't kill us and deigned to talk to us instead." George got back in the car.

"Killing us would have meant more involvement with the government. Talking was the easiest way to get rid of us."

"Why do I have the feeling you know exactly what's going on in his head?" A grin was tugging at George's lips.

"It's the math I do every day, with every encounter I have. I weigh the cost of engaging against the consequences of not doing it and act accordingly. It's kind of an automated process at this point." Andi hadn't meant to sound bitter, but something in his tone must have been off because George winced. He had his eyes firmly on the road, backing away from the gate and looking for a spot where he could turn the car around.

"I'm sorry."

"Don't be. It started long before I met you, and I don't think I could stop it now, even if I don't need it as urgently anymore, thanks to you."

"I'm glad I can be of some help." Andi didn't like the self-deprecation those words showed.

"You're a great help to me. The meditation yesterday? That was exactly what I needed."

"Good."

They were silent until George had managed to turn the car around.

"He keeps bees?"

"Yeah."

"Could he be our guy?"

Andi looked out the window. "It's possible. The smoke signature is similar enough. He also lives next to House Cusabo, which means he's close to a portion of our victims, he is a loner who seems to hate people on principle, tries to stay under the radar, is tall and strong enough to haul a corpse around and bury it, and his father built the bunker."

"I sense a but coming."

"I don't think he lied when he said he hasn't set foot in the bunker since he was a kid."

"You don't think, or you know? No moths in the vicinity? Or silverfish?"

George had learned by now which insects provided the most reliable insights in what regard. Detecting liars was something moths and silverfish were best for. Unfortunately, there hadn't been any close enough to get a good read on Timothy Cervill. All Andi had had were a centipede and a few pill bugs under a stone nearby, and they had shown him the picture of a man who was telling the truth. No quickening of his pulse, no flare in the electric field indicating stress, no outburst of pheromones, though those could have been masked by the overwhelming scent of smoke from the bee smoker.

"No. He was pretty calm the whole time we spoke. Of course, if he is the killer, he may not feel guilt over what he's done, and then I wouldn't be able to detect anything."

"So he stays on the list of suspects."

"Definitely. Together with Thomas LeClerk and whoever else we'll dig up."

"At least it isn't as many people as with the triple homicide of Miller, McHill, and Portius."

Andi groaned. "Don't remind me. That was a nightmare." The only positive thing about that case was that the prime suspect—also the person who had planned the murder—had wiggled out of the grasp of the law easily thanks to his excellent planning, which spared them a long trial where they had to come to the witness stand. They avoided talking about this particular case most of the time because their views on it differed quite a bit.

They both stared out the front window onto the road. George was tapping the steering wheel in a rhythm Andi thought he recognized. Probably some song that was popular at the moment. It wasn't Vivaldi's classical piece *The Four Seasons, Spring*, so George was still quite relaxed.

"The killer is a beekeeper. We have bees at House Cusabo, bees on Timothy Cervill's land. And a ghost told us the bees are important." George changed the rhythm. It sounded like salsa.

"Well, historically speaking, bees have always been important. Since before the first pyramids were built. Apis mellifera and Homo sapiens have coexisted for a long time."

"Apis mellifera?"

"The Western honeybee. It's the one best known. The only other domesticated bee is Apis cerana, the Eastern honeybee. They both seem to have originated in Eastern Africa and spread from there to Europe and Asia."

George stopped his tapping. "I'm pretty sure I'm going to reveal the extent of my ignorance here, but when you say domesticated bee, how many others are there?"

"Uhm, roughly 20,000, many of them endangered. And only honeybees build combs. Most other bees are solitary."

"No honey from them?"

"Pollen. They store it for their offspring. There's this one bee in Germany, I forgot the name, it lays an egg in an empty snail shell, fills it with pollen, closes it, and then buries it under little twigs and grass so it won't get blown away or found by predators. Very impressive." Andi smiled at the memory of watching that bee in a TV documentary. It had looked like a little helicopter, moving twigs more than ten times its size through the air.

"Sounds like a lot of work."

"It's always amazing how much effort creatures are willing to put into procreation. And I'm explicitly not excluding humans." Andi understood the compulsion to bring the next generation forth—he sensed it too often to not know how strong it was—but the things humans were willing to do to obey that biological urge puzzled him.

"Why should you? Anybody who's ever spent a night at a bar or in a club knows what you're talking about."

"Do you do that?" Andi felt curiosity. He normally didn't care much what people got up to outside their range of interaction with him. George had been with him for almost a year now, and during that time, Andi hadn't seen him going out. He did his excessive sport, drank his terrible smoothies, tried to coax Andi into doing the same, and solved cases.

"Well, when I was younger, I went out now and then, did the whole clubbing thing. Wasn't my scene, though, and I was too driven to expend much energy on something frivolous that didn't help me with my career. I had some hookups, never anything serious. And since I'm here, I've been busy solving impossible cases, protecting my gifted partner from a vicious chief, and taking care of said partner."

Andi opened his mouth to say something, but George held up as his hand as if he knew what Andi was going to say. "And I enjoy it all. Don't start with there's no need for me to look after you. We both know there is. And don't even think about how you're taking advantage of me. I get more out of this than just a shiny solving statistic, which I hope you'll be getting into your thick skull sometime soon."

"I know." Andi exhaled long and slow. "I'm trying to get used to it."

"You better." They had reached the precinct, where George parked the Escalade in his favorite spot. "Let's see what Geena, Luke, and the others have for us." He furrowed his brow. "Do we mention the bees?"

"Not explicitly until there's some kind of proof from Evangeline. I sent her a text this morning to look for pollen or anything related to beekeeping on either the victims or in the samples from the bunker."

"Good thinking, Andi. I'm just glad Evangeline goes with whatever you ask of her without making a fuss."

"She knows to trust me." Sometimes Andi wondered if Evangeline perhaps knew more than just to trust him. She wasn't overly religious, but Andi knew she closely embraced her Samoan heritage. And the Samoan people knew their stuff about nature. There was no point pondering it. Either she knew and kept her mouth shut, or she had her suspicions and kept her mouth shut. She was a smart woman, a friend even, not a threat.

George opened the back door to the precinct. "Let's see if bees are already on the table."

13. Modus Operandi

As it turned out, Geena and Luke had gotten a lot of new information from Evangeline and Shireen, while Sandra and Tobias had run into a bit of a wall concerning Dr. Grassen, one they were trying to break through at the moment. George did feel his hackles rise a bit when he saw handwriting that wasn't his on the whiteboards, though he tamped the instinct to snap at Geena and Luke. Andi's hand on his lower back helped a great deal. Having a partner who was so in tune with one's emotions wasn't always easy but definitely had its perks. Andi went to his desk, opening the top drawer where his ballpoint pens for destruction were stored. George approached Geena, who was standing at the whiteboard, smiling at him apologetically.

"Hi, Andi. Hi, George. I hope it's okay. Luke and I started adding the new information." She gestured at the whiteboard. It was the usual chaos of colored lines and names, only this time it was only partly *his* chaos, which made it harder for George to orient himself.

"No, no, it's fine. I'm just still getting used to the whole concept of having additional people helping with the case."

Geena lifted a brow. "You mean you're not used to others meddling with your stuff. I get it. I'd be the same if this were my turf. You can say it. I told you, I'm a big girl."

George laughed, somehow soothed by her bluntness. "Which is the reason I'm trying to be chivalrous. You're almost too understanding. I'm waiting for you to snap."

"Believe me, Detective, when I snap, you'll only notice when it's too late." Geena winked. "Although your wunderkind will probably sense it somehow. How was the visit to Timothy Cervill?"

"Well, he didn't greet us with a necklace of severed pinkie toes, so there goes an easy solve." George sighed dramatically. "He claimed very convincingly that he hasn't been to the bunker since he was kid, and when I showed him the chamber where we found the corpses, he was surprised. Or feigned it very well. The jury's still out on that. We didn't tell him this was a murder investigation, and he didn't seem to know. We should keep an eye on him, but he doesn't stand out as a suspect any more than Thomas LeClerk does." George took the black marker from Geena's hand to add Timothy's name to the list of suspects.

"Damn. Why can't they make it easy for us?" Geena threw her hands in the air. "Anything else?"

"No. Unfortunately not. What do you have?"

Geena looked at Luke, who nodded, apparently leaving the talking to her. He looked tired.

"Well, we have something that could be really good and a lot of information we're still trying to put in context. I'll give you the facts first so you know you have something good to look forward to." Geena's voice was grim. Everybody dealt with death differently, and a certain black humor was common among members of the force. To outsiders it might seem disrespectful of the victims sometimes, but the human mind could only take a certain amount of darkness before it broke. Humor, however feeble or uncalled for, protected those who had to dive deep into the worst humanity had to offer. And this serial killer definitely ranked among the top contenders for that title. "Evangeline and Shireen were able to identify most of the remaining victims. There are five they haven't found anything about yet, one woman and four men. Evangeline has written in her report that those are probably people who have never been in the system. None of them is younger than twenty or older than twenty-five, which probably means street kids. The others range from twenty to sixty, the only extreme being Izzy Whitewall at sixteen. From what Shireen could find online, they all had a history of mental problems: depression, PTSD, bipolarity." Geena tapped the names and illnesses with a red pen she had snatched from her own desk. "It matches what we deduced from the patients from House Cusabo, which means our killer has a type."

"Still no signs of him having another lair?" Andi had the ballpen dismantled and the pieces laid out.

"No, thankfully not." Geena turned back to the whiteboard, where she had written the names in clusters. "We have a time frame. Evangeline was able to date the bones, and what Shireen found about the victims is in accord with it. The killing started in 2013 with TJ Ross and Celia Murdoch, who were killed in May and September. We know this because that's when House Cusabo reported them missing. In 2014, we have Samuel Grand and the Jane Doe. 2015, a John Doe and Muriel Shaw, a homeless person from Charleston. 2016, Geoffrey Elstair and Izzy Whitewall, who vanished from House Cusabo in September. Due to the position of their bones in the quadrants, Geoffrey was killed before her. In 2017 our killer escalated for the first time. Three vics, Cedric du Pont, a John Doe, and Alisha Myers, another homeless person. In 2018, it was Kesha Raport in March, Lucas Mellen in July, he was from House Cusabo, and another John Doe. 2019, James Hershen, Lydia Bloomenberg reported missing in June, and Hamed Beshara from the Marines. 2020, we have the next escalation, four people. Lori Heller went missing from House Cusabo in April. Then we have a John Doe, Ben Los Santos, and Joshua Balugot. In 2021 followed Carl Latimer, Lola Monarch from House Cusabo in April, John Doe, and Anton Winchester. This year we have Marco Flores in January."

"Which means at least three more victims to come." George stared glumly at the whiteboard.

"Not necessarily." It was the first time Luke spoke. "If we found the killer's lair, chances are he won't kill anybody until he's found a new one."

"You don't think he has a spare?" Andi had straightened the spring from the ballpen.

"Even if he has a spare, which is a fifty-fifty chance, it's perhaps not one he can use immediately. I asked Shireen to look for other bunkers around Charleston that could qualify."

"At least those that are documented." Andi had started with the grinding of the plastic parts.

"It's a start." Luke shrugged. "Once we have a list, Susan and Mark can begin checking them out."

"Evangeline also found out that Marco Flores was roofied, heavily so. The killer used flunitrazepam, a popular rape drug, as you surely know. It's very likely he didn't feel the severing of the toe and the subsequent strangling." The expression on Geena's face said loud and clear what she thought of such "mercies."

"Since the killer appears to be very predictable and set in his ways, we can assume the other victims were roofied as well." George wrote the word down and circled it in purple. It was a new color in their arsenal, and they were still discussing how to use it best.

"It suggests that he might be unable to kill his victims when they're awake. It means he's probably not a psychopath who can't feel empathy,"

Luke injected. "Of course, it can also mean he's not skilled enough to kill them while they're able to fight back, though I doubt it. He has to be strong to haul them down into the bunker."

"Then what's his angle?" Geena cocked her head.

"They all had mental problems. Perhaps he thinks he's helping them somehow? Freeing them of the burden they carry?" Andi didn't look up from where he was plowing the plastic pieces into neat rows.

"A scary thought. And plausible. Why else would he kill them?" Geena looked at Andi in an assessing way George didn't like. But Andi didn't show any signs of being troubled, meaning Geena wasn't a threat. For now.

"Did Evangeline find out anything else about his MO?" George asked Geena.

"Yes. As I said, the victims were all strangled. We have one inconsistency, though. The first two, TJ Ross and Celia Murdoch, were killed with a leather belt, which they found in the second quadrant with Celia's bones. It was still slung around her neck. The others were killed with a rope made from manila hemp. And here's the kicker. The belt buckle had initials on it. RMD. Shireen found a Reuben McDonald mentioned in the visitor logs of House Cusabo. He saw Celia several times."

"Who was she to him?" George wrote the name in red, drawing a green line to Celia's.

"We don't know. Shireen couldn't find anything that would suggest they were somehow related. Celia was raised by her mother, no father in the picture. Reuben is a trucker. He travels regularly from Florida to West Virginia, passing through North Carolina on the way. As far as Shireen can tell, he was in the vicinity of Charleston for each of the murders. He's based in Florida but has a one bedroom apartment here in Charleston."

"It fits. Quite well." George added Reuben's name to the list of suspects on the other whiteboard as well.

"It could still be coincidence." Andi had a tissue on his desk, blotted in blue. The ballpen's core was history.

"Let's sum up what we can say fairly surely about the killer so far." George hesitated for a moment. He and Andi were aware that it was only one person. Geena and Gelman were not. Was it worth throwing this question in to muddy the waters? Or would it come back to bite him in the ass? George glanced at Andi, who was engrossed in the destruction he had caused on his desk. Deciding to risk it, he looked at Gelman. "How sure are we this is the work of one killer?"

"Eighty percent. All we have learned so far—the method of killing, the profile of the victims, the meticulousness—it all points toward one killer. Incorporating somebody else in what we assume is a highly ritualized procedure is possible, but not likely."

George nodded. Just like that, they had a scientific reason to operate under the assumption of one killer without showing their hand about having already known. It was just a small piece of the puzzle, but the more of those they had sorted, the less likely the few they couldn't explain stood out. Another thing he had learned from Andi—people liked neat stories enough to ignore the occasional hole in the plot. As long as the defense attorney couldn't use those holes as leverage, they were safe. It was a thin rope to walk, like everything connected to Andi's *geschenk*. There were days when George enjoyed the challenge and weeks like this one when he was glad for everything he didn't have to make up.

"Okay, so we have one very organized, very meticulous male killer who seems to be capable of empathy and who probably feels pity for his victims, hence the reason they're roofied before he kills them. He has a type, people who won't be missed, homeless people, the weak and defenseless, which means he's also calculating and cold."

"Again, we have one inconsistency." Geena held up her hand. "Izzy Whitewall had a family who was quite frantic in their search for her, according to the information Shireen has found. They even offered a reward of two thousand dollars for any information leading to her being found."

"Was there anything that stood out?" George circled Izzy's name with yellow, as he had done with TJ and Celia, indicating they didn't fit the MO as seamlessly as the other victims.

"No. It was the usual avalanche of useless speculation, people claiming they had seen her at a bus station down in Florida or suggesting that she had just run away, given her mental state. Nobody mentioned murder or even hinted at it."

"Hmm. Andi, can you ask Shireen to do a check of the calls that came in?"

"On it." Andi started patting his pockets for his phone.

"Izzy was also the youngest. Perhaps something about her triggered him?" George wrote *trigger* next to Izzy's name.

"Now for the fun part. What makes Timothy Cervill, Thomas LeClerk, and Reuben McDonald plausible suspects?" He tapped at each name.

Geena pointed at LeClerk's name. "He's working at House Cusabo, had direct access to some of the victims, is skilled in recognizing different conditions, has easy access to all kinds of prescriptive drugs, and had a personal connection to Kesha."

"He also reported her and three of the other victims missing," Luke added.

"But why not all? Sure, it could have been a way of staying under the radar, but if the reporting is part of his ritual, I would assume he did it with all the victims." Geena's brows were creased. "And why would he kill somebody he had a relationship with? Kesha was the twelfth victim. I can't imagine he suddenly changed his MO, and we're fairly sure the victims either didn't know the killer or only in passing."

"Good objections." George wrote both in prompts on the whiteboard. "Do we have anything to add to Timothy Cervill?"

Geena, Luke, and Andi stared at the clues already written down. Finally, Andi shook his head. "Nothing. Though if I had to make a ranking of the most likely suspect, I would put him before Thomas."

"I second that." Luke made a vague gesture with his hand. "There are no inconsistencies we know of with him."

"What about Reuben McDonald?" George brought up their latest suspect.

"We don't really know much about him. Celia was the second victim, and according to Shireen's report, she was close to TJ. Perhaps these two were close in a way Reuben didn't like. If we assume killing them was the trigger that sent him on his killing spree, we could also explain the switch from leather belt to rope." Luke seemed only half convinced.

"In the ranking I would put him in the second spot. Thomas comes last." Andi's cell vibrated. He did some swiping, then looked up. "Shireen says she has her new assistant, Timmy, looking into the tips about Izzy's disappearance. And she says Reuben is currently staying in his apartment in Charleston. He's waiting for his next load."

George looked at his watch. "It's already late. How about we call it a day and visit him first thing tomorrow? Geena, do you want to come along?"

She nodded. "If nothing new comes up regarding the killings, I'd like to be there. Let's meet here at eight?"

"Eight is fine by us." George capped his pen. "Luke, thank you for your help today."

"It was my pleasure." Luke waved at them. "I still have some work. See you tomorrow, and don't hesitate to call me if you need help with further profiling."

Geena packed her things as well, leaving George and Andi alone.

"What do you think?"

Andi swept the remains of the ballpen into the trash can. "That this is getting more complicated by the minute."

"Accurate. Let's get home and eat."

They shrugged on their jackets, ready to leave the precinct, when Chief Norris's voice bellowed through the bullpen. "Hayes, Donovan. My office."

George looked at Andi, who rolled his eyes. Exactly George's sentiment.

"Let's get it over with." He put his hand on the small of Andi's back, taking as much comfort from the touch as he hoped to give.

Chief Norris didn't waste time on pleasantries. She hadn't for quite some time. To say the relationship between them was strained was saying it could get a bit nippy in Antarctica.

"Where are you with the investigation?"

"At the beginning." George could be an asshole with the best of them. Andi chuckled, earning him a dark glare from the chief.

"I'm aware. Any suspects?"

"A few. Nobody's standing out yet."

"You're walking on thin ice, Detective Donovan."

George shrugged. When it came to the chief, he had no fucks left to give. "What can I say? You reap what you sow. Anything else?"

The chief started tapping her fingers on her desk, a nervous staccato that didn't help to impress George or Andi. She had to be under a lot of pressure regarding the case, and had their relationship been better, George would have sympathized with her. The way things were, he couldn't care less if she were eaten alive by the mayor or dragged over hot coals.

"I could bring somebody else in."

"To mess with your best detectives? Who you brought back from a well-earned holiday to work this case? An unwise move, as you surely know."

"Don't think this is over, Donovan." She was glaring at him. At the moment, she had nothing, and they all knew it. "You can go."

George and Andi got up, leaving the chief's office as quickly as they had entered it.

Once they were in the car, Andi huffed, the first verbalized sign of his annoyance since she had summoned them. "I can't wait till Gelman gets rid of her."

"Amen to that. How about ratatouille for dinner?"

Andi groaned happily. "I'll help cutting the vegetables."

"It's a deal."

14. WRONG TREE

THE VEGETABLES for the ratatouille were grilling in the oven, giving Andi and George time to have a shower. Strictly speaking it wasn't original ratatouille the way George made it, but it tasted a lot more intense when the ingredients were grilled before they entered their union with the tomato sauce and the cheese. Standing in front of the mirror, Andi stared at his reflection, trying to get himself together before he walked back into the kitchen. George was stressed enough as it was. He didn't need the added worry of Andi sinking deeper into the world of arthropods again. They were waking, more quickly each day, swamping him again, and he was just so tired all the time. If only he could lie down and sleep for a year, everything would surely be better. He couldn't give in to these thoughts, though. They led into dangerous territory, as he well knew. One reason this case was battering him so much—apart from it being a serial killer case, and him being on his last leg—was that depression was an old acquaintance of his. It had been only mild episodes so far; in the beginning he hadn't even realized this wasn't something inherent to the *geschenk*. Once he did, he read up on depression, watched himself adamantly for the first signs to be able to counteract them immediately. Nothing George needed to know. Nothing that had occurred since he'd met George. His partner was his shield in more than one regard. If only his exhaustion hadn't already reached those ink-black depths where coming back to the light seemed like an impossible task, so impossible that attempting it was fruitless. He had never fully recovered from the Castain case, his flanks wide-open to attacks from this other world that wasn't his and yet filled his life so completely. He sighed and dried his hair with the towel, then put on some of the hydrating lotion George had bought him. It was organic, vegan, purely from plants, no animal cruelty. Pure like the man who had gifted it to him. After he had slipped on his pajamas, Andi stared longingly at his bed. Sleep would come so easily; he felt it, knew it. His bones seemed to weigh tons, dragging him to the ground. A low grumble from his stomach reminded him how important sustenance was, especially for somebody who tended to forget to eat regularly. He was too tired to try for grace when he stomped down the stairs, surrounded by a familiar blanket of impressions—

Food, warm, stress, sharp, unpleasant, worry, worry, worry, the blobs too loud, moving, restless, hunger, always hunger, gnawing at everything, filling all space, hunger for warmth, for food, for companionship, no, that was him, not them, they didn't understand such concepts, they understood that both blobs were unbalanced, their chemistry all over the place, the scents agitating, no rest, like bees before swarming, where was the queen, it smelled of tomatoes, he needed to feed—

"What's wrong?"

Andi had entered the kitchen without noticing it, too caught up in the jumble of images from them and thoughts of his own. Too late now, George was worried, staring at him with that glint in his eyes, determined to not let it go. *Wasn't there a song about that?* Andi sat down at the kitchen island, holding George's gaze for a moment before his partner went back to putting the finishing touches on their meal. It didn't mean Andi was off the hook. It just meant George was giving him time to craft one of those half lies Andi had been relying on more and more in the past weeks, torn between confiding in his partner and sparing him the strain. Only there were no more half lies left in him. He felt drained, in every sense of the word. Just one step and he could fall over the precipice, down and down and down until he hit the ground so hard it all vanished.

A clinking sound and George put a plate full of food in front of him. His hand, big and strong and warm, touched Andi's, just a brush, nothing more, breaking the dam. He'd been strong for so long, he just needed a short reprieve, one night where somebody else shouldered all his burdens. He ignored the guilt at doing this to George, he just….

Andi felt tears staining his cheeks. "I'm so tired." The words came out as a whispered sob, his armor cracking into pieces, his hands shaking so badly he couldn't take the spoon.

George was at his side immediately, slinging his arms around him, absorbing the shock waves of his violent heaving with his strength. Andi leaned in, took the support he needed for the first time ever, because there had never been anybody he could lean on, and just having George made him realize how close to breaking he had been before, all the time holding it together by sheer will, but his will was running out and George was here.

Andi didn't know how long they stayed that way, him shaking in George's arms, George making soothing sounds that reminded him of purring. Perhaps he should get a cat, no, animals needed caring, and Andi wasn't a caregiver, he was more like a cat himself; it was so nice to be enveloped by George's warmth.

A spoonful of food appeared in front of his face. George had sat down on the stool next to his, both their plates in front of him. Andi took the bite, started chewing. It was good, as always.

"Yum."

"Wonderful." George took some from his own plate, ate it, offered another spoon to Andi. They took their time, enjoying the slightly cold meal while Andi felt himself calming down. He wasn't fine, not by a long shot, but the hysteria of everything being too much, of drowning in a wave of sheer exhaustion, had given way to simply being empty. Even the images from the arthropods were muted, his brain too tired to compute anything properly, with the exception of how wonderful George felt next to him, how good the food tasted. It was his body's last defense—shutting down to within an inch of complete oblivion for a chance to regroup.

"I think we better get you to bed *pronto*. What do you think?" Bless George for not prying when Andi was so obviously down.

"Yes."

"You go up and brush your teeth. I'll take care of the kitchen and make sure everything's locked."

"Are you coming, then?" Andi would have hated how needy he sounded if he'd had the energy.

"Of course." Calm, steady, reliable. A rock on the beach, breaking the waves.

A few minutes later, George entered Andi's bedroom after a short knock that was more a nod to politeness than the act itself. It wasn't needed between them, something Andi loved. He was done brushing his teeth and had put on his woolen sleeping socks.

"Hold me?" This was new. The most he had asked of George until now was to sit with him until he could sleep. Not tonight, though. Tonight, he needed a connection, as close and intense as possible. He needed another's warmth. No. Wrong. He needed George's warmth, the only person who *accepted* what he was. And George, saint that he was, didn't even flinch, didn't hesitate.

"Gladly. Just let me brush my teeth real quick."

Andi waited until his partner was back, lifting the comforter. They both slipped in, Andi now a bit hesitant. Overcome by his own boldness. What man asked another to snuggle him like he was a child who had had a nightmare? *A man at the end of his rope.*

George didn't seem to suffer from insecurities. He slipped into the bed, grabbed the edge of the comforter to drag it over both of them, pulled Andi against his body, and held him there by putting his arm over his waist. It was perfect.

"Sleep now. We'll talk tomorrow." The low rumble of George's voice showed Andi the way to sleep, his partner's warmth surrounding him like a shield, keeping everything—the world, the kaleidoscope of images it was made of, the troubles of the blobs—out. Peace at last.

"I KNOW it's bad, Andi, but I need you to give me an honest estimate of how bad."

They were in the Escalade, driving to the precinct. After a night of blissful, uninterrupted sleep, they had spent the morning in amicable silence, George respecting Andi's need to absorb as much of the tranquility as possible. Now that they were about to interact with the harsh world again, George demanded information—rightfully so.

"Last night helped. Thank you for that."

George grunted. "It was nothing. Now tell me, do we need to give this case to somebody else?"

"Honestly? I'm not sure. I've never been so tempted to say yes. I-I feel like I'm drowning." Andi hated sounding so helpless, hated not being able to rely on himself anymore, hated how little he hated that he needed George.

"What do you want me to do?" So simple, so straightforward. Andi knew George would protect him at all costs. Which was the reason he would try to power through this case, because he didn't want this man—his partner, his friend, his confidant—to pay the price for Andi's curse.

"I think I can keep it together long enough to solve this case. If… if you could stay with me?"

"Whatever you wish." They stopped at a red light, and George turned to him. "You know you just have to say the word and it'll be my pleasure to tell Norris off."

Andi simply nodded.

"Promise me, Andi. Promise you won't suffer in silence. I can't help you if I don't know what's going on. I hate to say it, but you're so good at hiding your condition, sometimes it's hard for me to pinpoint when to take you out. You *must* communicate, understood?"

Placing a hand on George's thigh, Andi nodded.

"I promise. And—I do better the closer you are. It's difficult when we're in public, I get that. But at home—"

"As if I care what other people think." George snorted. "We're both single. You're my partner. Whatever people want to think, they'll think. That's at the very bottom of our concerns."

Squeezing George's thigh, Andi silently conveyed his gratitude.

"Are you still okay with Geena coming with us? I can find an excuse for her to stay at the precinct."

"No, it's fine. I like her humor. And she's just curious, not mean."

"You would know."

"Actually, the silverfish in the precinct do."

"That's the same."

HALF AN hour later, they were on their way to Reuben McDonald's apartment in Upper King, north of the Historic District. Reuben lived on Woolfe Street in a very nice, freshly renovated ground-floor apartment. According to Shireen he had inherited this place from a distant relative who had bought it back in the '60s, when housing in this area had been cheap. Now the apartment was worth quite a lot, and just staying there occasionally when Reuben was driving through seemed like a waste to Andi. Reuben McDonald had paid with his credit card at a restaurant in the area just the other day, so they were positive they would find him at home. His tour back to Florida was scheduled for the following day, information courtesy of Shireen as well.

"How do you want to do this?" Geena was leaning between the driver's and passenger's seats. She didn't wear any perfume, and the soap she used was neutral, two things Andi appreciated very much. George set the blinker to turn right into Woolfe Street.

"Since we had the pleasure of talking to Timothy Cervill, you can have Reuben if you want."

"And here I thought chivalry was dead." Geena fanned herself.

"Don't get used to it. I'm just having a good day."

"As opposed to your genius yet super grumpy partner, you mean?" Geena winked at Andi.

"I hate people. Suspects are people. You can have them all."

"I can see why you love working with him." If Geena's tone had been any drier, the words would have crumbled.

"It does have its perks." George parked the Escalade at the sidewalk in front of the apartment building. "Beguile him with your feminine charms."

"I can sense a sarcastic note somewhere in there. Luckily for you, I like using my charm."

They got out, and Geena rang the bell. George stood next to her while Andi kept in the background, slightly to George's left, where he could see him in the corner of his eyes, the way he liked it. Reuben McDonald opened the door, and several things became clear at once. First, names could be misleading, because Reuben looked about as Scottish as a mealworm looked like a peacock butterfly. His skin was dark, his hair was in neat locks, and he was a lot smaller than the Highlander type Andi had imagined. He also appeared younger than the fifty-five he was. Secondly, he wasn't their killer. No trace of bees at all. His apartment was filled with the usual suspects, mainly silverfish, spiders, mites, and a few moths in a crack above one of his windows. Andi immediately relaxed, which got him a sharp glance from George. He shook his head subtly, which in turn made George relax as well. Geena held up her badge.

"Good morning, Mr. McDonald. I'm Agent Geena Davis from the FBI, and these are my colleagues, Detectives George Donovan and Andrew Hayes from the CPD. Do you have a minute?"

Reuben didn't seem nervous in the least, even though he was approached by three officers at his home. Maybe it had something to do with George. Andi wouldn't know without asking, which was out of the question. The topic was sensitive, and he was not subtle.

"Of course. How can I help?"

Geena gestured toward the apartment. "Is it okay if we come in?"

Reuben seemed to mull this over for a moment; then he stepped aside, inviting them in. "I'm afraid I can't offer you anything except water. My coffee maker died yesterday."

"That's no problem, Mr. McDonald. We will only take a minute of your time." Geena waited till Reuben led the way into a spacious living room with an open-plan kitchen. It was all very nice, framed pictures of landscapes on the walls, with a few snapshots of Reuben with what Andi assumed were friends. They sat down where Reuben indicated. Geena didn't waste time.

"Mr. McDonald, we're here because the remains of Celia Murdoch were found recently. She was murdered, and we know you visited her a few times while she was in House Cusabo."

Reuben's face fell. "Oh, Celia. Damn. I always suspected she was dead, you know, because she wasn't the type to just vanish. But having it confirmed...." He sighed and rubbed his face with his hand. "Fuck. Pardon my language. I'm just glad Chloe doesn't have to hear this."

"Chloe?" Geena's voice was soft, understanding. Perfect for coaxing information without the person being questioned even realizing it.

"Celia's mother. We were friends. Went to high school together."

"Was that why you visited Celia in House Cusabo?"

Again, Reuben sighed. "Yes. You know, she had her out of wedlock. She was a wild thing, Chloe. Never knew who the father was. Or never told, hard to say with her." He smiled fondly. "A stubborn beast she was."

"We found no hints that she ever visited her daughter."

"She couldn't. At the time Celia was brought to House Cusabo, Chloe was already very sick. Breast cancer. She died half a year before Celia went missing."

"Oh. That would explain why we couldn't find any next of kin." Geena was talking to George, who nodded.

"Yeah. Chloe was all Celia had." Reuben sounded so sad.

"I'm so sorry to ask you this, Mr. McDonald, but did you have an argument with Celia before she died?"

Reuben looked at Geena with a sharp expression. "Depends on how you define argument. She was seeing this guy, TJ, I think his name was, who was also a patient at House Cusabo. She was terribly in love, and they wanted to marry. I tried to talk some sense into her, cautioned her to wait until they were both more stable. Just like her mother, she wasn't very good at listening when what was said didn't fit with what she wanted." Again, there was a certain fondness in his voice. Andi was sure Reuben had loved the women's stubbornness.

"So you weren't angry at her?" Geena insisted.

"Angry? No. Annoyed? Worried? Definitely."

"It's just, we found a belt with your initials with Celia's remains. She was strangled with it."

They all were waiting for a reaction. Reuben shook his head.

"I've never worn a belt in my life, Agent. Can't stand them. And surely not one with my initials. Not my style."

Which was obvious. Reuben was more the loose, worn jeans and colorful T-shirt type of guy. True to his words, he wasn't wearing a belt at the moment. Geena got her cell out, and Andi knew she was looking for the picture of the belt buckle in the hopes of shaking Reuben up. When she found it and showed it to him, he started laughing.

"Oh man, I didn't think I'd ever see one of those again." Then he seemed to remember that he was looking at Celia's murder weapon and sobered up instantly. "Sorry. I'm just shaken. That," he gestured toward the belt buckle, "stands for Ronny, Manny, Danny. They were a local country band back in the late eighties who rightfully never made it past Charleston's city limits. They were so bad, it was cult to go to their concerts. I think it was Manny's dad who ordered a thousand of those buckles and sold them as fan merch."

"You never owned one?" Geena hid her disappointment—a sharp flare that ended in a smooth undertone—quite well.

"As I said, no belts for me. Plus, I'm more into Dragonforce and the likes."

"Pardon me?" Geena looked as puzzled as Andi felt.

"Speed Metal." Reuben shrugged. "The guitar solos help me to stay sharp on the road."

"Ah, I see. Well, thank you for your help, Mr. McDonald. If you remember anything you think might be helpful, please don't hesitate to contact us. Even the smallest things can help." Geena handed him her card, and George followed her example. Reuben took both and put them on the coffee table.

"Will do." He hesitated. "Please find whoever did this. Celia didn't deserve to be murdered. She may not have been perfect, but nobody is, and she had so much to look forward to."

"I promise we'll do our best to catch the killer, Mr. McDonald." Geena led the way out of the apartment, back to the car. Once they were all seated again, she looked at them.

"Not our guy?"

Andi shook his head. "I'm pretty sure he had nothing to do with it. Apart from the fact that he wasn't even remotely nervous, he's also too small to have done it." He held up his hand to stop Geena from interrupting him. "I know height can be deceiving, but believe me, there is no way Reuben was able to get a man the size of Marco Flores down the ladder into the bunker without letting him fall, which according to Evangeline, he didn't. We're looking for somebody who is taller. Roughly George's height and build."

Geena cocked her head to the left, in George's direction. "Or we're really looking at two killers." She didn't sound convinced by her own idea.

"We should definitely keep that possibility in mind." George, ever the diplomat. "Until then, let's ask Shireen about this country band." He hesitated. "Or perhaps google it first. That might spare her some work." Staying on Shireen's good side was important.

Andi found his cell at the third try in his right back pocket. Before he could start typing, George's phone started to ring. Luke's name flashed on the screen in the middle console of the Escalade. George pressed one of the thousand buttons on the steering wheel.

"Hello, Luke. You're on speaker. Andi and Geena are here."

"Hi, guys." Luke sounded haunted. "Just a warning, the press has gotten wind of the serial killer case. Norris is on the warpath, as you can imagine. The leak seems to have come from House Cusabo. Perhaps you can go there, since you're already on the road? Talk to the director?"

In other words, Luke was offering them an excuse to stay away from the precinct for the time being.

"When is the press conference?" The resignation in George's tone was what Andi felt. They wouldn't be able to escape this forever.

"In an hour. The mayor will be there. You don't have to make an appearance because that would hinder your investigation, or so I convinced the chief. Go to House Cusabo and take your time."

"Thank you, Luke."

There was no answer, the unspoken *it's the least you could do* hanging in the air, palpable only for Andi and George.

"One of these days you guys have to tell me what Luke did to piss you off so royally," Geena said conversationally. "Not now, obviously." She held up her hands when both Andi and George turned toward her. "Geez, it was just a joke."

"An accurate if inappropriate one," George answered. "Let's stop and get some sandwiches on the way, okay?"

They reached House Cusabo shortly before lunch. Several vans from different TV stations were parked along the curb in front of the closed gate. Because Geena had called ahead, they were let through the moment the security camera caught their plate number and ushered into Dr. Blackton's office after they had parked close to the main entrance. The director was not a happy man. He had the phone unplugged on his desk, and Andi was sure he had silenced his cell as well.

"Please, sit." Blackton gestured nervously at the three chairs in front of his desk. Sighing, he sank back into his own chair, dragging his right hand over his face. "What a mess."

"We were told you already know who the leak was?" George asked gently. There was no reason to agitate the poor man even further.

Blackton snorted. "Yes. My own secretary, can you imagine? I mean, I knew Regina wasn't happy that I replaced her beloved former boss, but it wasn't like I had anything to do with it. The woman died, for fuck's sake. Pardon my language," he added, throwing Geena an apologetic look.

She grinned. "No problem, Dr. Blackton. I've heard far worse, and I know how good it feels to let loose in situations like these."

He nodded at her. "Regina didn't even try to hide it. I'm not sure if she honestly thought I wouldn't find out because I'm such a useless waste of space—her words, not mine, obviously—or if she just didn't care. She sent an anonymous email to all the news channels in the area and even to some international ones, as well as to my bosses. Needless to say, they want the situation contained as quickly as possible. Until then, I thank the gods every day for the huge property House Cusabo was built on. It keeps those vultures away from the patients. Small mercies and all that."

"I assure you, we're doing everything in our power to find the person responsible for the killings. Can you perhaps send us the email Regina wrote? For our report." George smiled reassuringly.

Blackton nodded. "I'm going to send it right away. Is there anything else I can help you with?"

Andi watched as Geena and George shared a look, both shaking their heads almost imperceptibly. He leaned forward. "Actually, yes. Could you tell us who is responsible for the bees? You've got quite a few hives."

"Ah, the bees. One of our best ideas, even if I say so myself. I have to give my predecessor credit for installing them. They are wonderful therapists. Dr. Aoki and Thomas LeClerk both have certificates for beekeeping, paid by House Cusabo. The main beekeeper is our janitor, Bruce Sprenger. He looks after the hives here and also has his own at home. He's the expert. There are a few other members of staff who help take care of them, though I'd have to look up their names."

"Thank you. That would be great." Andi leaned back, ignoring Geena's inquisitive glance. "Is Mr. Sprenger here by any chance?"

"I'm afraid not, Detective Hayes. Bruce has been on sick leave for five days. He caught some nasty bug."

"Oh, I hope he's better soon." *Truth, but the blob doubts it, the scent of it heavy, cloying, distrust was such a terrible thing, worry was worse, both of it thick in the air, stifling, Andi wanted to get out, away, too cold to fly, no prey, a few more days, soon, the room was warm, cozy, not too bad, if only the blob would leave, always so noisy, disturbing everything, a nuisance, he needed him, though what for, he had forgotten, it couldn't be important, blob stuff never was, never.*

Andi felt George's hand on his elbow, gently guiding him out of the office. The place where Regina Miles had last time greeted them with so much disdain was now empty; only the computer remained like the last guardian still standing. He heard Dr. Blackton telling them goodbye, still caught in his worry. Something bright and quick came from Geena, curiosity, always fun, so easy to interpret. They left House Cusabo. Andi let George deal with dodging the news vans, too busy texting Evangeline.

Have you found pollen or honey?

He knew he was being cryptic and rude. The question mark followed by a thumbs-up from Evangeline told him it was okay, though. He then deleted the text, not wanting to be forced to come up with an explanation as to why he had thought this was something the coroner should be investigating. If Evangeline found anything, Andi was more than happy for her to have the recognition.

"Are we going back now?" Geena leaned forward between the seats in the front, her tone telling clearly how much she didn't want to get back to the precinct just yet. Andi's sentiment exactly. He glanced at George.

"Actually, I thought we should take another look at the bunker. Geena, you haven't been out there yet, and we were busy when we found the corpses. It's time to get a feel for the surroundings, don't you think? And we're already on the road."

Both Geena and Andi nodded frantically. Anything was better than being at the precinct at the moment.

15. THE MYSTERIES OF TRANSPORTATION

WHEN THEY reached Bloody Dick Swamp, George chose a better place to park his car than the last time before they got out. They all had sturdy enough shoes to be able to make the hike to the bunker without getting their feet wet. On their way, George realized the ground was a lot drier than on the day they had found Tyler. Then again, it hadn't rained for a few days, and the swamp wasn't a real swamp like some in the area but rather something that aspired to be one. Otherwise it would have been impossible for Cervill Senior to build the bunker in the first place. When they reached the clearing with the boulder, they saw it was still taped off. Closer inspection showed that the old trapdoor had been replaced by a new one with an impressive padlock barring people from entering.

"The killer definitely can't return here." Geena stared at the lock. "And he probably knows it by now."

"Probably." George turned around to leave the narrow space inside the boulder. Andi was standing under the angel oaks, staring south of where they had come from. "You think this is the way?" George said it for Geena's benefit. He already knew Andi had found the path the killer used. His partner nodded. His gaze was glazed over, his tone too even because he had to concentrate so hard to speak in complete sentences. Or what could pass as one.

"Good path, beneath the trees, mostly dry, broad enough for the stinking thing, he can come close, only has to carry them for a few yards, easy."

"It's kind of creepy when he gets in the zone." Geena appeared next to them. "But he's right, and I have to admit, I envy you for having such an intuitive partner." She brushed past them, following the barely there trail Andi had indicated. "I can see tracks. Broad, reminds me of a tank, just closer together."

George followed her, grabbing Andi's elbow to navigate him over the roots. "The ATVs for swamp land have extra broad wheels."

"Makes sense. Do we follow these?"

George looked at Andi. His partner was still at home, but barely. Before George could contemplate a good excuse for Andi staying back, he touched his hand.

"I'm fine. We need to follow the trail, see where it leads."

"You already know."

"We still need to see. Chain of evidence."

"Fucking damn." George kept Andi at his side, deciding to let Geena think what she wanted about them. No way would he let his partner fall.

The trail of the wheels was prominent where the ground was wet, harder to follow where rocks underneath made the ground dry faster. In any case, the ATV the killer used had to be high quality because the terrain was rough, even for something with broad wheels. After about half an hour they reached a forest road. A quick GPS track showed them it connected to an asphalt street about two miles farther out, which led back to Maybank Highway.

"Now we know how he comes and goes. Or came and went. Should I be worried that it seems to be so easy?" Geena stared at the forest road as if it had somehow insulted her.

"It comes with the territory. Even though Charleston is densely populated, there's all this land around us where people hardly ever go. I don't want to know how many crimes go undetected because nature helped destroy all evidence." It was a white lie. George had a vague idea how many crimes they never got to punish, and if Andi wanted, he could find most of the corpses hidden in the swamps and woods around Charleston. It just was no use and all in all better not to think about it too intensely.

"Let me take some pictures before we go back." Geena got her cellphone out and started documenting the road and part of the path. "We should ask CSI to make a cast of the tire or whatever this is." She gestured at an especially deep and clear groove just off the road.

George looked at Andi, who nodded slowly. "Good idea. I'm not sure if it will do any good because these tracks look pretty flawless, as if the tires are brand-new." He pointed at the sharp ridges and valleys in the mud. "All ATV tires for muddy ground are the same, and if we're lucky, CSI is going to find some small irregularities that will help us assign the vehicle to the killer. Probably. I have no clue how many ATVs are out there and how easily accessible they are."

"Well, we can at least try. Plus, it's standard procedure anyway. And I've seen cases cracked with less." Geena didn't sound too optimistic while she typed a short message to her contact at CSI before she shoved her cell into the back pocket of her jeans with more force than necessary. "Let's go back."

They marched in silence, Andi sometimes cocking his head as if he was seeing something interesting while Geena veered off the path now and then "just in case." When they reached the copse of angel oaks close to the bunker, Andi stopped.

"Someone's there," he whispered.

Geena, who had been only a few feet in front of them, stopped immediately, her hand reaching for her gun. Her entire body tensed, turning her from casual wanderer into predator in the blink of an eye. She looked back at George, motioning for him to go to her left. While he did so, he looked at Andi, trying to determine if the person in front of them was a threat. His partner shook his head subtly, indicating with his chin that he would stay on the path. They moved forward in a fan formation, Geena and George with their weapons drawn, because George thought it better to follow her lead instead of having to explain why he didn't see a reason to get his gun while approaching a trespasser at a serial killer site. Andi just kept walking, although silently. When they reached the edge of the copse, they took cover behind the two biggest angel oaks and looked into the clearing.

Geena relaxed behind her tree to their right. In the clearing stood a young woman who seemed to be in her twenties. She had her phone out and was taking pictures of the ground. George nodded at Geena, before they both stepped into the clearing, startling the young woman.

"Charleston PD, don't move!" George had his weapon trained on her, more out of habit than because he was worried about a potential threat. The young woman held up her hands, clutching her cell like a lifeline.

"I'm not doing anything wrong!"

"Which is about the most suspicious thing you could have said," Geena answered, stepping closer to her. "Identify yourself."

The girl huffed. "My name is Tina Whitewall. I'm Izzy Whitewall's big sister."

"Oh." Geena lowered her weapon the same time George did. "I guess I don't have to ask what you're doing here, then."

With an angry gesture that betrayed her agitation, Tina shoved a long dark brown strand of hair behind her right ear. "I wanted to see where she was buried for so long." The faint tremor in her voice squeezed George's heart. Her pain was like a sharp knife cutting through his professionalism.

"I'm not sure that's a good idea." He put his weapon back into its holster. "Would you mind answering some questions for us, though? We would have visited your family in the next few days anyway, so we might as well do it now."

Tina shrugged. "Why go to the trouble? You didn't want to hear what I had to say then, and I can't imagine it'd be different now."

George shared a look with Geena and Andi. They hadn't had the time to closely look at the protocols of Izzy's disappearance. Something for either Tobias or one of the beat officers Sandra had by now added to their task force. "I can assure you, we're listening now." He held his hand up in a soothing gesture. Tina watched him with narrowed eyes for a moment, clearly weighing whether to trust him. George decided to take a small risk.

"We already know Izzy was—different than the other victims."

Anger sparked in Tina's light green eyes. "Come on, say it. You think she was crazy."

George shook his head. "No. Not at all. Me and my partner"—he gestured to Andi—"have seen too many things to simply dismiss other… perceptions. And I'm sure it's the same for Agent Davis." He glanced at Geena, trying to convey with his eyes for her to play along. It wasn't necessary. Geena was an old warhorse.

"Yes. There certainly are things that never make it into the reports. Doesn't mean they're not real, though."

Tina relaxed the tiniest fraction. "My sister wasn't crazy, just sensitive. Our parents didn't understand and were spooked by the whole talking-to-people-that-aren't-there thing. I can't blame them. Sometimes it was tough for me as well. But sending her to that asylum? That was so, so wrong. Izzy had no business being there."

"I assume you visited her regularly?" George could see the love Tina had for her sister. It wasn't a hard guess.

"Of course."

"Did she ever mention anything strange? Was she afraid of something? Nervous?"

Tina sighed. "You're going to think she was completely off her rocker, but I can assure you, she was absolutely clear in the head. They didn't give her any medication either, because they had deemed her degree of schizophrenia so low, they hoped to be able to help her with various therapies. And Izzy was smart enough to let them believe that. It's not like they could have helped her anyway."

"You're saying her mind wasn't clouded by any kind of medicine."

"Yes."

"And what did she tell you about House Cusabo?"

Tina put her cell into her jeans pocket, started kneading her fingers. "After about three weeks, she started talking about the bees. They have bees there, for therapy, you know, and first I thought it was good, that it was helping her. But the things she said…." She rubbed her hands on her jeans, went back to the kneading.

"Yes?" George held his breath. Tina was like a ten-pound salmon hanging on a line designed for five-pound fish. The slightest disturbance and the line would snap.

"She said the bees are death. Cloaking the darkness dwelling in House Cusabo."

George shot Andi a look. Again, the bees.

"She thought someone in House Cusabo was killing people?"

Tina nodded. "Izzy had her own vocabulary when it came to her… other sense. I didn't always get it right, but I'm absolutely sure she was referring to an active killer. The problem was, what should I have done about it? I knew I couldn't say anything because then they would have medicated her for sure. And I was still a minor. There was no way I could have gotten her out of the clinic. I told her to lay low, to not draw attention, and she promised. When she vanished, I told the police about what she had said. They didn't even laugh. They just handed me to my parents and told them to take care of me because, clearly, I was upset by my sister's disappearance." Tina's shoulders slumped. "I abandoned her."

"No. You didn't." George was surprised to hear Andi talk. Usually, he stayed out when things got emotional. "You did what you could. It's not your fault the odds were stacked against you. And you're helping her now. By being brave enough to tell us this, you help her get justice. It's not what you wish for, but it's the best you can have."

Tina stared at Andi for a very long time. There was a shimmer in her eyes, telling George this young woman was more perceptive than was probably good for her. Finally, she nodded. "You're right. Thank you. And thank you for trying to find her killer. I want that bastard to pay."

"He will." George fished a card out of his wallet and handed it to her. "If you remember anything else, no matter how crazy you think it is, don't hesitate to call us. We're always willing to listen."

Tina took the card, turned it around in her fingers. "Can I have your number as well?" She looked directly at Andi. "I think I'd like to talk to you."

Andi nodded. He pulled out his own card, which Tina took. "Thank you." She glanced at George. "No offense."

"It's fine. He's the prettier one."

Tina snorted.

"I have pretty cards as well, you know?" Geena teased, an amused smile dancing on her lips.

"I'll take it. Just in case." Tina held her hand out.

"I feel so appreciated." Geena handed over her own card, winking at the young woman. "I think we need to get going. Do you need a ride?"

"No, thank you."

"Just one more thing." Andi was already stepping away from Tina, in the direction of their car. "How did you know where Izzy was found? I know the information about a serial killer was leaked, and that there was a connection to House Cusabo, but not where the bodies had been found."

George froze, as did Geena. He hadn't even thought about that. Meeting Tina here had just felt so natural.

Tina fidgeted. Then she took a deep breath. "Izzy said the dead were hiding from the apocalypse. It wasn't hard to deduce she was talking about a prepper bunker, and I may have overheard somewhere that a large number of CPD ATVs had been sent here."

"You're a smart woman, Tina. Be careful." Andi started walking.

"Don't we want to question her about how she managed to 'overhear' the dispatch of members of the police force?" Geena asked, hurrying after them.

George shook his head. "No. Shireen loves a good puzzle."

"She's going to kill you." Geena fell in step beside them.

"Nah. She's just going to sic her newbies on it. Besides, Tina was helpful, wasn't she?"

"By insinuating her sister was psychic? I'm not sure that's what I'd call helpful. Then again, it's probably right up *his* alley, isn't it?" She gestured at Andi. If her tone had in any way been threatening or malicious, George would have put her in her place. As it was, Geena sounded more intrigued than unbelieving.

"Let's just say we've seen our share of interesting witnesses, and Tina Whitewall doesn't make the top five." George wasn't sure if she managed the top ten. He knew his number one were silverfish, because their interpretation of the world relied on different aspects, while moths, for example, as useful as their perception of pheromones was, provided a rather one-dimensional picture of events. And he couldn't believe he was actually thinking along those lines without getting hysterical. Life with Andi did toughen one up.

"She said Izzy was treated for schizophrenia. The others were either bipolar, depressive, or suffered from PTSD. Perhaps finding out why the killer chose her could help to find him?" Andi's voice still had a monotone quality, meaning he was receiving. George made a point of walking closer to him, in case he tried to use a leg he didn't have. It rarely happened when he was still lucid enough to form entire sentences, but George liked to err on the side of caution.

"So far we assumed he chose his victims because of their specific mental illnesses. Perhaps he had another criterium we aren't aware of because it's not that obvious?"

"I love him. I'm going to take him with me when this case is done." Geena made grabby hands in Andi's direction.

George laughed and batted at her like she was a pesky fly. "He's all mine. Hands off."

"Fine. Be a spoilsport." She pouted. "Let's see if things have calmed down at the precinct. Perhaps Luke can adjust his profile of the killer. I'd also like to talk to Tina's parents, just to get their view on things. And we need to talk to Thomas LeClerk again. I'd leave him to you and take the parents if that's okay for you?"

"More than okay. You sure you don't want to go back to House Cusabo?" George didn't want Geena to think they were hogging the main suspects and leaving her to do the legwork, even if she had suggested it herself. Good relations between different agencies were all about the balance.

"To be honest, that house gives me the creeps. I gladly leave it to you. And sometimes cases are cracked wide-open by witnesses that were deemed unimportant. I'm counting on that."

"More power to you." They had reached the Escalade, and George unlocked it with his fob. "Let's see how things are at the precinct."

IT WAS the sixth circle of hell, as depicted in Dante's *Divine Comedy*. Or at least that's how George imagined it. Not that there were any flaming hot tombs around, but the atmosphere had a decidedly burning quality, and everybody was holed up at their desks, trying to not draw attention to themselves. George suspected the chief had been lying in wait for them, because their attempt at getting to their desks was foiled the moment they reached the bullpen.

"Donovan, Hayes, in here!"

Geena looked longingly at their desks but moved to accompany them. George gently shoved her away. "I admire your bravery. Or pity your stupidity. Can't say for sure. Run while you can."

"You're such a gentleman. Next round of coffee is on me."

"Deal."

Andi entered the chief's office first, not bothering to sit down. George remained standing as well, close enough to his partner to keep him from doing something stupid. The chief slammed the door shut, turning on them even before the echo of the bang faded.

"Do you have the killer yet?"

"Uh, no. Obviously not. We have a few suspects but no credible evidence yet." Two could play this game of being rude as fuck.

"Then hurry. The mayor is hounding me, and with this leak, the press is going to be all over us. More than already. And make no mistake, I have absolutely no qualms putting all the blame at your feet. In fact, it would be my pleasure." The malicious glint in Norris's eyes was all George needed to know that they had left civil far behind them. Next to him, Andi tensed, getting ready for a fight they couldn't engage in right now because they had a killer to catch. He put his arm on Andi's lower back, a gesture not missed by the chief, as evidenced by the narrowing of her eyes. He hoped she would choke on her own aspirations.

"You better not keep us from work, then. I doubt the killer is going to just walk into the precinct." He ushered Andi toward the door, keeping himself between his partner and the chief. It seemed the shorter their meetings got, the more unpleasant they became.

"Don't forget you're on a schedule!" the chief yelled after them when he closed the door. She always wanted to have the last word.

"Can we kill her now?" Andi's hands were balled into fists.

"I'd love to say yes, but you know they'd come looking for us immediately. Let's find Gelman."

"To kill him?"

"Tempting. We need him, though. Yet not enough to not make his life uncomfortable."

Andi sighed. "Too much hassle. I'm tired."

"We just do a quick check-in before we drive home. What do you think, vegetable lasagna and a round of meditation?"

"I'm in."

After a short chat with Geena and Luke, who promised to look at other possible triggers for the killer aside from the mental illnesses, and a check-in with Sandra and Tobias, who were waist-deep in in all the calls that had come in after Izzy Whitewall's disappearance and had nothing new to report, they headed home.

Even though he had been very adamant about not moving in with Andi, George spent a lot of time at his house. Enough to make the rent he paid for his apartment seem like a waste. Not a topic for the moment, though. Once they were done with this case and had their holiday, they could talk about it. George already knew Andi wouldn't be opposed to the idea; he just wasn't sure if he was ready to make this step. To him it meant embracing the responsibility he had taken on with Andi on an entirely new level. It meant he would have to look deeper into his feelings for his partner, unsure if he'd like the outcome. So far, Andi hadn't given any indication he was romantically interested in George, even though one could argue the fact that he had no problem having physical contact with him could be interpreted that way. The problem was the usual rules didn't apply to Andi. George knew he would have to outright ask him at one point, to cut through the tangle of everything that was between them, open and hidden, spoken and unspoken. It was so easy to just fall into this thing they had, let it grow around them and see where it led. Only George couldn't do that. He was too much of a control freak, and not ashamed to admit it. So there would be a talk with Andi, as soon as George had gathered enough courage.

After he had weighed the pros and cons to death.

For the moment it meant he dialed his brother Daniel's number when Andi went upstairs for a shower after their meal and the following meditation, which had calmed Andi down, but not done the same for George. Just thinking this state of agitation was what Andi considered low-grade made George even antsier. How could he take care of Andi if he was so easily distracted? And why was he thinking about this while they were neck-deep in a serial killer case? And—It was time to call his brother.

"Best older brother speaking." Daniel picked up after the third ring.

"Why are you so happy?"

"Just closed a case. An ugly one. Beer might be involved in the celebration of catching a true asshole." In the background, George heard somebody whistling. "Yeah, we got that fucker!" A cheer sounded through the speaker before Daniel was back. "What can I do for you, beloved little brother?"

"Uh, forget it. I'll call some other time." George didn't want to put a damper on Daniel's surely well-deserved party, and he also didn't want drunk advice from his brother. It tended to be even worse than his sober advice.

"Nooo, you can't call, say forget it, and be done! That's not fair."

"How many beers did you have already?"

"I'm on my first. The party just started. We're still at the office, doing the final reports."

Okay, first beer wasn't that bad. Perhaps he could give this a try.

"I need advice, Daniel. Serious advice," George warned his brother, giving him a chance to back out. He knew he would if he were celebrating the successful closure of a case.

"Now I'm curious. I have all night to party. I can spare a few minutes for my favorite brother."

"You're only saying this because Griffin ate the last piece of chocolate cake on Dad's birthday."

"Something you, my beloved younger brother, wouldn't have done!"

George decided not to argue that point. He would have totally done it given the chance. Which Daniel knew. Griff had simply beat him to it.

"Anyway, how can I help you on this very fine evening?"

"I really don't want to bring down your mood," George tried one last time.

"Honestly, George, nothing you could throw at me could bring my mood farther down than it had been during this wretched case."

"Fine. It's about Andi."

"Figured."

"Figured?" George couldn't believe his brother's nonchalance.

"Figured. These days, it's always about Andi if it's serious. I wonder why I didn't guess it from your tone. Must be the high from solving the case. Or the beer." George heard shuffling, a closing door, his brother no doubt going someplace where he could talk in private. "Why are you freaked out this time?"

"I'm not freaked out!"

Silence. Daniel didn't dignify this statement with an answer.

"Fine. I might be a tiny bit—agitated."

"Go on."

"What would you say if I told you I'm thinking about moving in with Andi?"

"That you should probably ask him first?"

"Ha-ha. Assume consent has been given."

"Then I'd say 'finally,' brother. You've been heading in that direction since you met him." Daniel sounded very matter-of-fact.

"You wouldn't think it strange? Or inappropriate? Or, I don't know, unadvisable?"

"George, you need to enlighten me. Do you want me to talk you out of it or reassure you it's a great idea?" If there was a hint of laughter in Daniel's voice, George chose to ignore it. Had to be the beer.

"I don't know! That's why I'm calling you. Because I can't think straight and it's driving me crazy!"

"Calm down! I'm going to be your voice of reason, okay?"

"I can't believe I'm saying this, but please."

"Love you too, bro. Love you too. Anyway, let's look at the facts. You've been drawn to Andi since the day you met him. He's like the flame to your moth, appealing to your protective nature. That's perfectly normal and to be expected. Since you still haven't told me what exactly his deal is, I have to assume his position in your partnership, but so far I haven't gotten the impression he's some damsel in distress. Whatever he brings to the table is good enough to strengthen your bond beyond your need to take care of him. Now tell me, are you sexually attracted to him?"

George hesitated. It was a complicated question. He never discriminated when it came to his partners in bed, but then again, that was just about scratching a biological itch. It had never involved a complicated, multilayered connection he couldn't even begin to grasp because every day he found something new, not to mention all the (tiny) variables out of his control. Objectively, Andi wasn't the type George would have gone for. He wasn't hung up on looks; it was more Andi's prickly nature, combined with the lack of care he had for his appearance. Before he met his partner, George had always thought it showed little self-respect, something he didn't want any part of. After getting to know Andi, he was now ashamed of his earlier assumption. Andi's appearance had nothing to do with lack of self-respect and everything to do with simply not having the energy for dealing with something so mundane and, ultimately, superfluous as appearances. It made George want to apologize to everybody he had judged in the past. When he thought of Andi, sex had become part of it some time ago, but never in a prominent role. George instinctively realized it was just a facet of what they were building. Whether he liked it or not, at the core of it would always be Andi's *geschenk*—it was the deciding factor, shaping everything and everybody in Andi's vicinity. George knew it was his job to make sure it didn't take over all the other parts, consuming Andi in the process. Sex with him would be—desirable, as part of the physical bond they were forming through constant touch. It wasn't the main prize, though.

"Uh, George? Are you still there?"

George startled from the maelstrom of thoughts he had been sucked into. "Oh, yeah, yeah. Still there. Just thinking about your question."

"If it takes that long, it's more complicated than I thought. You should probably talk to Mom."

"And tell her I'm seriously thinking about starting something with a colleague?"

"Brother, I hate to break this to you, but it seems to me, you *are* already in a relationship with Andi. No thinking about it. More like realizing it."

And just like that, Daniel (or the beer, George wasn't sure which one) had answered his question. Even if there hadn't been any sex yet, even if there wouldn't be any sex in the near future, or the future in general, he already had left the partnership part behind and was in a very serious relationship with Andi. Now all he had to do was find out if Andi knew it as well.

"Thank you, Daniel. You actually helped me here."

"Don't sound so surprised. I'm counselor material!"

"I wouldn't go that far. Enjoy your beer and have a good party."

"Thanks, bro. Will do. Take care of your man."

Daniel hung up. George stared at his cell for a few minutes, trying to get his thoughts in order.

"George, are you coming?" Andi called from upstairs. George felt a smile on his face.

"On my way!"

16. MAKING HEADWAY

ANDI WOKE up to the smell of coffee wafting through the air and the happy agitation of the silverfish in the kitchen. George was in a much better mood than the day before, where he had been all tension and stress. Andi hated it when George couldn't calm down. He was aware that he was adding to his partner's burden, and it irked him when he couldn't do anything about it. Knowing that they were both at capacity concerning their levels of stress didn't help him with his guilt.

Since nothing would come of his musings, Andi got up, took care of his morning routine, slipped into the fresh clothes George had laid out for him—gods bless him—and ventured down the stairs into the kitchen. George wasn't just in a better mood, he was—

A burst of colors, the scent fresh and warm and soothing, like being safe in the middle of the hive, like being cozy under the bark, inside the cocoon, there were green and red and yellow, bleeding into each other, contentment, George had decided something, it was good, a glimmer of orange, here and there, he was sure of himself, but not of something else, probably Andi, the cinnamon and lemon aroma of his determination enveloping Andi, like home, George was home in so many ways—

"Good morning, Andi. You look better." George put a mug of steaming tea on the kitchen island.

Peppermint and honey. Perfect to wake up. "Good morning to you too. It was a good night. You are happy." Andi had stopped some time ago changing his statements to questions when addressing his partner. George knew he could sense his emotions, up to a certain degree. No need for pretense. It was liberating for both of them.

"I am. I talked to Daniel yesterday and finally realized something." He placed a bowl with fresh fruit—strawberry, ripe and juicy, banana, still a little green but Andi would brave it, and pineapple, sweet and sour in one, what a marvel—in front of him. There were some walnuts and sunflower seeds sprinkled over it, to give things a crunchy aspect.

"You realized you know who our killer is?" Andi teased before he took the first spoonful. Flavor exploded on his tongue, and he moaned a bit. Even the unripe banana couldn't diminish the overall deliciousness.

"No. More important." George got his own bowl of fruit, together with a glass of his nasty green smoothie. "I'm spending a lot of time here, and I've been thinking about your offer of moving in."

Andi froze. Hope bloomed in his chest. There was a slither of shame as well, because he was so needy, because he was so glad, because he was burdening George when he should have let him walk away. Only Andi was too selfish to do that. "And?"

"And there's no reason for me to be wasting money on a place I rarely stay at." Again, the spike of orange, George was sure of himself but not of *Andi*. How laughable was that, as if he didn't know there was only one answer Andi would give?

"When are you moving in?"

Yellow and green and purple, relief and joy and happiness intertwining, the scent of earth and warmth and cinnamon, all flooding Andi's senses, George's reaction making him realize how much *he* had wanted it to happen, and wasn't that the strangest, how everything fit so perfectly while the pieces never revealed the whole picture?

"Well, a good portion of my clothes is already in the guest room. There are a few things I'd like to have here, like my recliner, but most of my furniture can go into storage. Unless there's something you want to have?"

"Your TV is bigger than mine. We could put mine into the bedroom and yours down here in the living room."

They both very carefully didn't address the singular of bedroom.

"And we need to talk rent. Of course, I'm paying you." George's tone brooked no argument. Silly man.

"We'll see."

There was a *look* before George went back to his fruit. The remaining breakfast went by in companionable silence.

When they arrived at the precinct, Geena was waiting for them at the entrance, her face grim. Andi didn't need the input of the spiders and silverfish to know something bad had happened. George picked up on it as well.

"I guess it's not a good morning?"

Geena shook her head. "Don't ask me how, but the press has gotten wind that Tyler 'found' the corpses. The chief is at home, trying to keep the vultures at bay. They have the nerve to camp out in front of the chief's house."

Andi immediately thought of Tyler and how he had to deal with those vultures on top of everything else. There was even a small hint of pity for the chief. Having the media in front of your home wasn't something he wished on anybody. He thought about calling Tyler but refrained when he realized the boy had been talking to him with his dad's cell. No need to risk the chief's wrath.

"There's nothing we can do at the moment except try to find the killer as fast as possible. That should divert their attention back to us." Geena went ahead into the building, going directly to the morgue. "Evangeline said she has something for us."

They followed her to Evangeline's office, where she was sitting behind her desk, staring at her PC while hacking away at the keyboard with two fingers because there were so many mounds of paper boxing it in, she couldn't put her elbows down on the desk to use all ten fingers. Not that she would have been any faster then. Evangeline's hands were made for cutting flesh, not hitting buttons on a keyboard.

"Ah. *Manuia le taeao*. I'll be done in a sec."

"Good morning, Evangeline." Andi watched her movements, tuning in to everything going on in the precinct. It was the usual hubbub, maybe a bit enhanced because of the news about Tyler. Luke Gelman was standing in front of their whiteboards, thinking hard, the cool scent of his concentration ripped by the acidic stink of the antifungal nail polish he still used. Sandra and Tobias were talking while wading through stacks of paper, the two beat officers who were helping them sitting at a desk that had been placed in a right angle to Sandra's. Most of the other detectives were at their desks, working or chatting, filling the air with aromas ranging from sweet and pleasant to sharp and disgusting, like a goulash of almost everything the blobs had to offer.

"*Faia*. If you'd be so kind to look at the screen." Evangeline pointed at the black surface on the wall. It flickered on, showing the picture of a mass with spikes and bubbles, something bizarre that would have been right at home in a horror movie.

"What are we looking at, Evangeline?" George stared at the *thing*.

"Ask your partner."

"Pollen." Andi squinted. It was magnified, but he was able to connect the spikes to something he knew—*Southern magnolia, they had blossomed so well last summer, so much food for the hive, the brood, the arthropods.*

"Yes. Magnolia grandiflora or Southern magnolia. I found it on the clothes of Marco Flores." Evangeline changed the picture on the screen to another blob. "Asclepias tuberosa, butterfly weed. Found on Lola Monarch." Another picture. "Rosa Carolina, Carolina rose, found on Carl Latimer. We're not done yet, but so far, we have found traces of pollen on each of the victims, sometimes pure, like in these three cases, sometimes mixed. Your hunch was spot-on, Andi."

Andi felt Geena's gaze drilling into him, her curiosity sharp and tangible in the air. George simply put his hand on Andi's lower back in silent praise and backup.

"Can you tell us which area the pollen is from?" The hope in George's voice was clear as day.

Evangeline sighed. "Yes, but it will take some time, and it's not something that will have much clout in court. We have to compare DNA samples to place the plants in a certain area. The bitch is, those are common plants, nothing rare or fancy you only see in a few spots. Every lawyer worth their salt will point this out. Sorry."

"Not your fault. Any idea how the pollen got there?" By his tone, Andi knew George already suspected the answer.

"The way the pollen is cramped together makes it highly likely it's from a beehive. So my guess is a beekeeper."

"They have bees at House Cusabo." Geena was still staring at Andi. "And Tina said her sister, Izzy, thought the bees were hiding death. She was *onto* something."

"Don't forget that in Greek mythology, bees were associated with the underworld and the souls of the dead," Evangeline chimed in. "Probably because the hives of wild bees are often found in cracks in rock walls or caves."

"If the killer sees bees as a connection to the underworld…." George trailed off. It was important information. Something they needed to add to their whiteboard and tell Luke about.

"Anything else, Evangeline?"

"*Leai.* I'll call you when I find something new."

"Thank you. This was great work." George waved at her, already on the way to the door.

"Thank Andi. He told me what to look for." She winked at Andi. "Don't worry. I'll make it look good in my report."

He nodded, conveying his gratitude with a look before he followed George upstairs, Geena directly behind them. In the bullpen, Luke was still standing in front of the whiteboards, his brows furrowed.

"I'm sorry, but I can't come up with anything that could lure the killer to the victims besides their mental illnesses," he said instead of a greeting.

"We can probably help you there. Evangeline said she found pollen on the victims—and the shape suggests it's from a beehive." George hung his jacket over the back of his desk chair. Luke turned to him.

"A beekeeper? The killer could be a beekeeper?"

Geena nodded.

"Bees are associated with the underworld...." Luke went back to staring at the whiteboard. Andi wasn't surprised he knew the Greek myths. Luke might not be his favorite person at the moment, but he was no idiot. After some pondering he opened a black marker and wrote *beekeeper* under the word *killer*. "It's a plausible theory. If the killer is a beekeeper and knows his lore, the bees might be the other thing connecting the victims. In what capacity remains to be seen, but it could be the link we've been looking for. Would make sense as well. If the killer is delusional, he might think the bees are leading him to the victims. Or pointing them out in a particular way."

"By buzzing differently?" Geena didn't sound convinced.

"Could be." Luke rubbed his eyes for a moment. "In Europe, during the witch trials, one proof of being in league with the devil was when flies sat down on your skin. All the inquisitors did was put the accused out in the open, waiting for the flies to sit down. With personal hygiene being what it was back then, they usually didn't have to wait too long until they could speak the death sentence."

"How sick. What if the flies settled on the inquisitor?"

"That, Geena, was proof how powerful the witch was—getting Satan's minions to overcome their fear of the holy and dare put their tiny legs on men of God."

"I hate the patriarchy." It was so heartfelt, Andi went to pat her on the back.

"I think everybody does. At least anybody with a compassionate bone in their bodies and a few brain cells to rub together." He started for his desk, but a sudden spike in George's stress levels had Andi turning to his partner before he reached his destination. "Seems like Timothy Cervill is off the hook."

Andi stepped around George's desk to look at his computer. The screen showed an email from Shireen, stating that she had found video proof of Timothy Cervill visiting a fetish bar on the outskirts of Walterboro about an hour and a half from Charleston on several occasions. One of them being the time of death of Marco Flores. She had video footage from the parking lot and the inside of the bar attached, complete with a time stamp. Andi had to admit he would have never pegged Cervill to be into public humiliation, which just showed what a bad idea it was to judge books by their covers. Even though kink wasn't Andi's cup of tea, he could appreciate the beauty of Timothy Cervill's submission, albeit in a theoretical capacity.

To him, the endless varieties of sexual games were like a language he didn't understand. He felt a connection to them, in a distant, non-involved way, because it was something blobs did to and with each other. For Andi, it was mostly meaningless because it didn't serve procreation, the only reason *they* did it. In an abstract way, Andi understood that this was something else he missed out on because of the *geschenk*, and only since he'd met George had he started to register this lack on a more primal level he could actually associate with himself. They made him uneasy, these feelings of lust that were, at the same time, more and less than the sense of belonging and safety he experienced with George daily and in growing intensity. It was too much, too complicated to ponder on top of everything else.

"Our pool of suspects is rapidly dwindling. Damn, he fit the bill so perfectly." Geena was looking over George's other shoulder. "I'm heading out to talk to Izzy's parents. You try to nail LeClerk. He's the last on our list." She glanced at the whiteboard, where Luke was helpfully erasing Timothy Cervill from the list.

George saluted in his chair. "Yes, ma'am."

She hit him on the shoulder, not gently either. "Be grateful I'm leaving the only remaining suspect to you."

"You just don't want to be the one to clear him and throw us back to square one." George was mainly teasing, with only a hint of wariness Andi understood too well. If LeClerk turned out to be innocent, they had nobody left on their list. With the media closing in and Tyler now in their sights, that simply wasn't an option. Andi sat down at his own PC to pull up the work schedule somebody at House Cusabo had sent them. Thomas LeClerk would be on shift starting at noon, which left him the entire morning to get his reports up-to-date and ponder the possible angles of the case.

Geena called Tina Whitewall's parents and left shortly after to talk to them. Luke was still standing in front of the whiteboard, his nervousness creating a stir among the silverfish. Andi didn't have the time or patience to deal with the man's bad conscience and hoped George would take over for him. His partner sighed. Yellow mixed with a muddy brown. Exasperation and wariness.

"Is there anything you haven't told us, Luke?"

"Concerning the case? No. I think we have all bases covered."

George just lifted a brow. Luke threw his hands in the air, the marker still clutched between his fingers.

"I'm sorry, okay? I know things are far from ideal, and I'm working hard to make it right, which would be easier if you wouldn't give me the feeling you're this close"—he indicated a hair's breadth with his thumb and forefinger—"to murdering me. I fucked up, because I misjudged the situation. I can't do more than apologize and try to correct my mistake."

Andi felt George's gaze on him. He looked up, conveying with his body language that he was way too exhausted to spare the energy to have emotions regarding Luke that went beyond a low-simmering anger he couldn't stop without using strength he desperately needed for other things—like staying awake.

"We get it, Luke. And we're not out for your blood. Too much hassle. We just want this done and over with. You gave us a choice between your way and ours, and we let ourselves be convinced, which is on us, I give you that. I don't mean to be cruel, but I'm sure you can see how it's hard for us to trust you at the moment. Let's try and focus on the case, put everything else on the back burner."

Luke's shoulders slumped. Andi could taste his disappointment in the air, sharp as his nail polish, unpleasant not just for the senses of the silverfish and spiders, but also for Andi on a level that went beyond pheromones and electric charges, into territory where these charges meant something more than just what the arthropods felt. They acquired a meaning Andi had never been good with, something he knew triggered a certain response in most socialized blobs, the urge to smooth things over, because discord in the clan meant fewer chances at survival. Back then, when humans had been little more than apes with attitude, the instinct was there, buried under civilization, another concept he had no use for;

still he caught the currents, he was part of the world of blobs, however fleeting. Sometimes he felt like he was sitting in a watercolor picture after somebody had tossed an entire glass of liquid over it, all the colors blurring, no shapes, no borders, no sense. He knew the colors, could even deduce their meaning, but it never meant anything to him beyond a theoretical concept. Luke's discomfort was like an itch Andi could never hope to scratch. He really hated his life sometimes.

George must have picked up on whatever Andi was broadcasting— he was sensitive like that—because he managed to send Luke away under the pretense of preparing for the interview with LeClerk.

17. SQUARE ONE?

THE DRIVE to House Cusabo was silent. They both needed time to think, time to recharge what energy they could get. Whatever would come of this interview, George was determined to call it a day afterward and head home. A nice hot bath was in order, perhaps after some workout to get rid of part of the tension. Andi had a very nice tub, more like a jacuzzi, which they could use together. Yes, a bath, some soothing tea, chamomile or lavender, a few hours of forgetting everything. Sounded heavenly.

"You're feeling—better, hopeful."

"What does that look like to you?"

"A mix of purple and indigo, some blue. All muted, not in a bad way. Not oppressed. Tastes like apples after the first frost, pinecones, and resin."

"Resin tastes good?" George steered the Escalade toward the gates of House Cusabo. Only one news van remained, as far as he could see from the distance. The others had probably gone to Chief Norris's house.

"It's…. not bad. The scent, mainly. An appealing combination."

"For you or them?"

Andi shuffled in his seat. He always did that when he didn't know the answer to something.

"I don't know. Hope is something good, so the taste must be good? Also, resin is antibacterial. Ants use it to keep their nests free of fungi and bacteria. It's positive, I guess."

"You won't see me eating pinecones anytime soon. Too crunchy, for one."

"I guess. The taste is linked to the colors and the emotion. I have no way of… of deciphering it. To them, you taste good and—"

"Wait a moment. We're in the car. How do you—"

"There's a spider under my seat, close to the back, must have gotten there yesterday, I think, plus some ants. Don't worry, they're almost dead. No food here."

"Do you know where they are? So we can throw them out?" George was already setting the blinker. He didn't want arthropods in his beautiful car. It was an arthropod-free zone. There had to be boundaries. He looked expectantly at Andi.

"The ants are in the trunk. I'll try to get the spider."

The gate to House Cusabo wasn't far, half a mile perhaps, but this couldn't wait. George got out, watched Andi climbing back to lay down flat on the back seat and reach under the passenger seat. After a short moment, he pulled it back out with a brownish spider half the size of his palm. George could clearly see the eyes and the black pattern on the back. He shuddered. Andi got up from the seat and crawled backward out of the car, holding the spider carefully. It sat there, on his palm, judging George with its eight eyes. Andi's eyes were glassy.

"Warm, air, too bright, don't forget, you have two legs, not eight, thump, thump, thump, fsss, don't move, high up, need to hide, crcht, click, click—"

The spider's mandibles moved in time with Andi's clicking sounds. This was a first, Andi dealing with a single arthropod in front of him, sucked into its senses. George quickly decided that he liked this even less than when his partner was buried under an avalanche of thousands of them. This felt personal, direct, not like a thin web with so many connections, it didn't matter when some ripped because there were always others to take their place. No, this reminded George of the dreams Andi sometimes had, when his subconscious was dragged into one arthropod mind. It was almost always a nightmare with the animal in question dying and Andi waking covered in sweat. The spider seemed to directly communicate with Andi, forcing him into an endless hall of mirrors, without the slightest chance to find the exit because he was the spider (was he was the spider? was he?) George could see it clearly, how Andi's legs twitched when the spider made a slight move, the barriers thinning, the frontiers vanishing, and at the heart of it all, George's greatest fear, that one day, Andi might decide it wasn't worth the fight, that staying in this other world was preferable to dealing with whatever madness humans could come up with.

He stepped forward, ignored the spider, suppressed his natural aversion, a reaction triggered by his lizard brain, not conscious thought, and put a hand on Andi's arm, the one with the spider. A shudder ran through his partner and the spider stirred, backtracking to Andi's fingertips, where it clung for a moment, dangling over the edge of the void, until it fell, down into the grass, where it scurried away. Andi let his hand fall to his side, his body stiff.

"Are you okay, Andi?"

"Huh? Yeah, yeah. The grass is so high. Difficult to maneuver but good to hide. She'll be fine."

"You know it's a she?"

"Full of eggs."

For a moment they both stared at the grass blades where the spider had vanished. Then George remembered his other blind passengers.

"Where did you say the ants were?"

After they had successfully gotten rid of all the uninvited passengers—there had been a short discussion about whether it was merciful to kill the ants quickly or let them die slowly without their nest—they drove up to House Cusabo. Killing the ants had won because even six-legged intruders in his precious car deserved mercy. This time they didn't go to see the director but asked directly for Thomas LeClerk. According to the schedule they had gotten, he would be starting work in fifteen minutes. The ever-friendly man at reception sent them to the locker room for employees, where they found LeClerk changing into his scrubs. His dark hair was in a messy bun with some strands dangling out. The quick glimpse George got before the man pulled on his shirt was enough to confirm he was probably strong enough to haul a victim down the stairs of the bunker. George didn't know much about work in a mental facility, but he assumed strength was an advantage in an environment where people weren't at their best.

"Detectives. Can I help you?"

Andi was standing slightly to George's left, his gaze absent, his posture relaxed. Whatever he was picking up, it wasn't alarming. Then again, he probably had to get attuned to the distorted images he was getting. After their first visit in House Cusabo, Andi had explained to him that dealing with an environment where so many drugs and physical instabilities mixed was like listening to an orchestra playing the same song but in different tempi, with some of the notes just off enough to grate on one's nerves. Intent on giving his partner the time he needed to adjust, George focused on Thomas LeClerk.

"Yes, actually, we think you can." He looked around. Two other people had entered the locker room, glancing at them curiously in passing. "Is there anywhere we can talk in private?"

"Of course. The weather is nice. Why don't we go into the garden?"

He led the way out of the locker room and down another long hallway. House Cusabo was like a labyrinth or a termite hill. Out in the garden, they strolled along a path laid with stone squares. LeClerk looked at him expectantly.

"Mr. LeClerk, we got the coroner's report on Kesha's death, and the math about her leaving House Cusabo, the missing person report on her, as well as her time of death, don't add up."

LeClerk stiffened a bit at that. If George hadn't been waiting for a reaction, he wouldn't have seen it. Andi remained relaxed. "According to the files we got from Dr. Blackton, Kesha left House Cusabo in January 2018 and was then reported missing in March of the same year. That report came from House Cusabo, or more precisely, you, because why should the clinic bother with somebody who wasn't a patient anymore? And we know somebody had kept her medicated because if she had gone cold turkey from the cocktail she was on, it would have been noticeable. Our IT specialist found slight discrepancies in the files documenting the incoming and outgoing medication. All this leads to the conclusion that somebody was helping her, and we think that somebody was you." George let the words hang in the air for a few moments, watching LeClerk's facial expression like a hawk. The man didn't look guilty or nervous. More resigned. He had been waiting for this.

"I loved her." It was a simple statement. One George had heard many times before, far too often from people who had just hurt or killed the person they supposedly loved. In fact, he had heard these words so often as an excuse for the most vicious and heinous crimes, he thought he would never be able to speak them in innocence to anybody. Or hear them said to him without being deeply suspicious. Sometimes his job really sucked.

"And?" He wanted the man to tell his story. With any luck, there would be holes in it they could use to convict him of mass murder.

LeClerk bent down to rip out a blade of fresh green grass. He started tying it into knots. "I assume you are well aware that patient/caretaker relationships are strictly forbidden?"

George nodded. Andi was staring in the direction where George thought the garden with the beehives was. He didn't pay LeClerk any attention, which meant the man probably wasn't their culprit. They were back to square one. Though perhaps LeClerk could shed some light on the case, possibly leading them to the killer.

"In the beginning, we tried to resist. Kesha was such a straight shooter. Going against any kind of rule was pretty much unthinkable for her. That's the military for you." A single tear rolled down LeClerk's cheek. If the man wasn't the world's greatest actor, he was off their list. His emotions rang true.

"Is that the reason she checked herself out of House Cusabo?"

"No, even though she had thought about it. But I convinced her to stay. I was even willing to put our relationship on hold. She was doing so well. She could have gone into outpatient care by the end of the year. That wasn't too long. She agreed to stay, and she refused to halt our relationship. Said it was the main reason she was doing so well. Which was BS, of course. It was her iron will and her stubbornness." He smiled bittersweetly. "We tried to keep it on the down-low, and things were looking good. Then suddenly, shortly after Christmas, she was getting anxious. I first thought there was a problem with her medication. It happens, you know, even if people are seemingly well-balanced."

"The medication wasn't the problem?"

"No. I kept a very close eye on her, discussed it openly. She knew her own body very well. After two weeks, she had me convinced. The main problem was that she couldn't tell me what was setting her off. A general feeling of unease, she called it. And of course, she investigated, because that's what a member of the Air Force does—grab the bull by the horns."

"What did she find out?"

LeClerk's shoulders sagged. "She never told me. In the middle of January, she was back to normal, well, not anxious anymore. She said she had her suspicions and that I was safe. Kesha was big about protecting me. Because of my job."

Looking at the deep lines around LeClerk's eyes and with the general air of exhaustion he radiated, George could easily understand why Kesha would have wanted to protect him. It reminded George too much of his own desire to take care of Andi to look at it too closely.

"And then she left."

"Then she left. We discussed it several times, heatedly, as you can imagine. In the end, I trusted her instincts. She was a trained fighter, a warrior. And in my job, the first thing you learn is how vast this world truly is, in a metaphysical way. I kept her medicated—cheating our computer system is way too easy—and everything seemed to calm down. She spent most of her time at my place, focusing on her therapy as if she were still in House Cusabo."

"Keeping up a schedule helps under stress." That George had learned from Daniel. The military was all about schedules and repetitive patterns. There was safety in dependency.

"It does." LeClerk threw the knotted grass blade away. "Second week of March, she grew restless again, said something was brewing. I believed her, but it was like watching a tornado sweep over a village. There's nothing you can do. I begged her to either leave the city or at least stay inside my apartment until things calmed down, whatever 'things' were, because she still didn't tell me. 'I refuse to live in fear,' she told me. And I get it, I do and I did." More tears were streaming down LeClerk's face now. He wiped at them halfheartedly. His grief was too great to care about appearances. "When she didn't come home the second day, I knew something had gone wrong. I reported her missing immediately and logged it in through House Cusabo, hoping that would force the police to be more thorough in their search. But it was already too late, wasn't it?"

George held LeClerk's gaze. The pain flaring behind the sheen of his tears forced him to be honest with this deeply wounded man. "It was. The killer doesn't seem to keep them for any length of time. He catches and kills them in quick succession. If it's any consolation, she didn't suffer. The traces of tranquilizer we found in the latest victim's blood suggest he drugs them out of their minds before he kills them. There is no pain involved as far as we can tell."

"Thank you." LeClerk rolled his head in a helpless gesture. "I guess that's all I could hope for."

They were silent for some time, gazing at the path and the different gardens around them.

"I need to start my shift. If there's nothing else?"

"No, no. You can go." George didn't know what else to say, to acknowledge the loss LeClerk had suffered. His pain was so real, George had the feeling he could grab it with both hands, like a wriggling worm with poisonous spikes digging into the flesh, leaving it raw and bleeding. Once LeClerk had vanished, George turned to Andi.

"I'd say he didn't do it."

"Probably not. His emotions were genuine, strong. It felt like drowning. I don't think the killer is capable of such deep emotions, especially for a victim."

"Which means all our suspects have gone poof. Damn."

"Yeah, damn." Andi started down the path. "Let's visit the bees. They are active today."

They could hear the buzzing before they reached the hives. The busy sound transported George immediately to lazy summer days spent in the garden at his parents' house, drinking cold lemonade and just letting time pass. A luxury he hadn't indulged in for a long time. Andi went to the first hive in the row, looking at it with his head cocked to the side.

"Anything interesting?"

"The queen is getting old. The entire swarm feels it. Makes them restless. The workers have already decided to hatch several new queens this season."

"I know they don't make conscious decisions...."

"Not in the way you'd define conscious. It's instinct. Knowing in the bones even though they have an exoskeleton." Andi sighed, clearly annoyed about his inability to explain something that was absolutely obvious to him. George put a hand on his shoulder.

"Hey, we've talked about this. I may not understand immediately, but I won't ever if you give up on me."

"It's a small miracle you haven't given up on me."

"I would never." George looked at Andi, the buzzing of the bees growing louder in the sudden silence between them, not awkward or shy or loaded, just silence, acknowledging *in their bones* what was true. Andi's eyes lit up.

"It's like a thousand minds in one, or one in a thousand, depends on how you want to see it, all tumbling thoughts and snippets of information, chaos if you're at the wrong distance, but when you step back or close enough, you see order, the patterns in the chaos, the overruling mind. It's so hard for blobs to imagine. I know there's studies on social insects, arguing it's all about the chemicals and the pheromones, forgetting that is all what blob brains are as well, that to be a mind you don't have to be trapped in a bowl of bone, you don't have to limit yourself to one body, two legs, two arms, you can have thousands, millions even, if you desire so, and every tiny bit makes you bigger, stronger, better, shows another facet you haven't seen before, adds to what is already a complicated picture with hundreds of angles, and you can get more and more and more, it never stops, with each one born you grow, and each death is a lesson learned, a memory gained, in an endless cycle, and even if the individual dies, the mind survives, forever carrying on, true death lies in forgetting, not with them, they never ever forget until the last one of them is gone."

"Wow. I think I get it better now. You say to you the hive is like one of these pictures, where lots of photos form a face or a city or whatever?"

"Yeah, like that. Each picture tells a story, and combined, there is an overlaying pattern. The queen is old. They need a new one."

"Only this hive?"

Andi concentrated. "No, the third one from the other side, they have the same situation."

"This sounds like something the beekeeper should be worrying about."

"Usually, they change the queens well before they die to keep the gene-pool fresh. There's a whole industry dedicated to breeding queens. It's bizarre, and not yielding the results they're hoping for. Worse, really."

"Isn't that always the case when humans interfere with the natural world?" George shook his head. They weren't militant vegans or anything, but seeing documentaries about how meat was produced—the whole process one of exploitation not only of the animals but of the workers, the land, the water, all resources that should be treated with the utmost respect—in addition to Andi's preference for a plant-based diet because of his *geschenk*, had made both of them almost completely vegetarian. Even before he'd met Andi, George had tried to only buy quality meat, and since he started cooking for his partner on a regular basis, his standards had only risen.

"I assume bees have similar problems to cattle?" George asked.

"Yes. Beekeepers use a lot of antibiotics to keep them healthy, which ultimately weakens them, and then there's the Varroa mite, a nasty little fucker which latches on to bees and their larvae, sucking them out and causing serious deformities in the young bees. It's all because humans always need more than they are given. There are studies showing that bees with a healthy social life, meaning lots of grooming, and more aggressive bees, have no problems with the mite because they bite them off their sisters. Bees that have been bred for maximum honey production and docility lack the grooming urge, as well as the aggressiveness that would compel them to kill the mites, aka the intruders. The solution is for the beekeeper to use ethanoic acid to kill the mites, which, of course, harms the bees as well. A clusterfuck."

"I can see that." George looked at the hives, which seemed so tranquil in the sun. "What's with these bees? Are they of the docile variety?"

"They're mixed. Somebody's trying to make them sturdier. There are a lot of dead mites in all the hives. You can see the bodies at the entrances."

"Because intruders must be terminated." The voice came from the entrance to the garden. George turned, spotting a man in a beekeeper suit. He had his hat and veil still down, and George was able to see his gruff face with a wild black beard and dark brown eyes. He was tall, a good six foot two, and burly, with a paunch pressing the white suit outward. The man extended his hand. "I'm Bruce Sprenger, one of the facility managers for House Cusabo and the main beekeeper."

"Nice to meet you." George shook his hand. "I'm Detective George Donovan, and this is my partner, Detective Andrew Hayes."

Andi shook Sprenger's hand as well.

"We're glad to see you're doing better. Last time we were here, Dr. Blackton told us you were sick?"

"Ah yes, nasty stomach bug. I haven't been ill in *ages*, and out of nowhere, *bam*." Sprenger shrugged, then patted his stomach. "Didn't do much to the old storing facility, though."

George chuckled politely, keeping an eye on Andi.

"Dr. Blackton told us there are several people here who tend to the bees and that they're used for therapeutic purposes." George smiled at the man, trying to radiate innocence. There was little chance Sprenger didn't know why they were there, not with all the ruckus in the media, but it couldn't hurt to try to get his take on things without him realizing they were poking around.

"Yes. Thomas helps the most, he's good with them, and some of the patients are reliable too. I also have two fellow members of my beekeeper's club who lend me a hand. Dr. Aoki doesn't shy away from the work either, though she's more interested in what the bees do for her patients." Sprenger shrugged again, the hat at the back of his neck swaying from side to side.

"I really can't imagine what therapy with bees would look like. Do you help with it?"

There it was, the spark of superiority, the chance of divulging wisdom to those less in the know. Most people fell prey to it, especially when a person of authority, also known as detective, was asking. Andi shuffled a bit closer, playing his part of interested servant of the public.

"It's a hassle, I can tell you. I sometimes have to help when Thomas isn't there, and just getting six people into the suits is trying. When the group has done it before, we go straight to the hives, but when there's newbies, there's an entire lecture about how to handle the bees, how to stay calm and everything. They never get much work done. That's my job, organizing it all. It's more about the patients getting a feel for other beings and, in reflection, themselves. Or so Dr. Aoki says. Personally, I think it's not worth it. There's always somebody who freaks, and it takes days for the bees to calm down. They don't like fear."

"No, that they don't," Andi murmured softly.

"Oh, you a beekeeper too?" Sprenger was definitely interested now. More than George would have thought.

"I was. Not enough time now. I have wild bees in my garden, though. In one of the trees."

George immediately knew which tree Andi meant. At the very back of the garden, where George never went because it was so wild. To reclaim it as a garden, they would have to bulldoze it completely. He did remember Andi had mentioned bees once, but with all the other things going on in their lives and all the arthropods constantly swarming Andi's senses, the bees had been nothing more than a footnote. They didn't cause trouble; therefore they weren't of interest.

"Wild bees. How absolutely wonderful. Your very own gatekeepers in your garden. I envy you. They always catch all the swarms, never let one settle where they want, even though we have so many great spots for bees on the premises." Sprenger's voice was full of longing.

"Gatekeepers?" George hadn't expected Sprenger to know about bees in mythology, an assumption he quietly chastised himself for. If there was one thing he had learned as a detective, judging people on sight was always a bad idea.

"They guide the dead to the other world. Fitting, I think. I'm looking forward to when they escort me."

Sprenger must have seen something in George's or Andi's expression, because he was quick to explain his cryptic words. "You see, we had this professor at one of our club meetings. We invite them from time to time, to keep up-to-date with all the innovations regarding beekeeping. It's usually technical stuff, how to select queens, the best materials for hives, legal questions. But this one time we had a professor for mythology over, and she talked about the history of beekeeping and the lore connected to them. It was such a success we invited her again for next month."

The conversation was veering into territory George wasn't sure what to make of. Andi, on the other hand, didn't seem to have that problem. Then again, he lived in a place nobody else had access to. "Such a fascinating topic. I have to admit, I only know the basics, never had time to dive too deep into it. And yes, they're excellent guides, knowing of the ways in the world. I think it's great your club is so open to all aspects of beekeeping."

George looked at his partner sharply. At times like these, he wondered how much Andi was going where his dialogue partner was leading and what was genuinely him. The archaic phrasing suggested the first, while what Andi had just told him about bees made George think it was the latter.

"We try our best. With all the toxins and climate change, keeping bees is becoming more and more of a challenge. Deepening our knowledge about them is such an important thing to do. As is building a network of like-minded people." Sprenger reached for his beekeeper hat and pulled it over his head, closing the veil with the zipper at the bottom. "It was nice talking to somebody who understands, so nice. But I have to start working now, see how the hives are doing. Spring is a busy time."

"We'll leave you to it, Mr. Sprenger. Thank you for your time." George turned back to the path they had come from. For today, they had seen enough of House Cusabo.

Back in the car, they shared a glance before George started the engine. "That was interesting."

"Yes. Another beekeeper." Andi stared at his hands. "He's also strong. And the scent was close. Of the smoke, I mean."

"Close enough to make you suspicious?"

"Yes. But when we talked to Thomas, he had traces of it on his skin as well. He must have worked with the bees recently. Not to forget the patients who help. It stands to reason they all use the same ingredients for the smoker. And Sprenger just mentioned members of his club giving him a hand. I don't know much about being in a club, but I could imagine they're likely to use similar ingredients for their smoke. Especially since they are 'like-minded.'"

"So potentially a whole club of suspects, some of whom have access to the bees here, meaning they have access to the patients as well. Do we know how strict House Cusabo is on keeping the patients in? If there are some who are free to leave now and then, we have to consider them as well. At least we have crossed Thomas off the list."

"Yes, *we* have." Andi rubbed his forehead with a tired sigh. "Because we can be reasonably sure it wasn't him."

"The old problem—we can't rule him out officially because we don't have evidence to back it up. On the contrary, his involvement with Kesha makes him suspicious." George felt as if somebody had dropped a lead weight on his shoulders. "And we suddenly have a bunch of other candidates—the members of that club. How many beekeepers are there who are close to Thomas and Sprenger in stature?"

"I don't know, and we need to find out. And we only assume the killer has to have ties to House Cusabo because some of the victims are from here, there's bees here, and because we had some likely candidates for the killer being from here as well. Emphasis on *had*."

"We have to check how long Sprenger has been working for House Cusabo. And who from his club has helped him. Also, it probably won't hurt to check all the current and former male patients who fit the bill height-wise. Sandra is going to kill us." Sandra Mescew was overseeing the beat officers and organizing the review of all the documents and tips and other paper trails they were getting. Asking her to check all male patients who had contact with the bees would make her roll her eyes. In a very specific way George didn't like. The woman could be scary as hell. George set out for the road back to James Island. Andi fished for his cell and started scrolling once he found it in his inner jacket pocket. How the man could place the thing in a different spot every time was another mystery about him. George was still contemplating buying Andi one of those cell halters for belts, but then he would be tempted to buy him a new belt as well, which would lead to another shopping spree where he'd have to remind himself that boundaries were important.

"Here it is. I'm glad Dr. Blackton gave us unrestricted access to the employee files. Bruce Sprenger, forty-three, started working for House Cusabo July 2015. That was the year Izzy Whitewall went missing."

"They already had the bees back then, didn't they? Otherwise, Izzy wouldn't have said the bees brought death." George started tapping the wheel to the rhythm of the song playing on the radio. Something about calling somebody by their name.

"Yes. We should find out when they started using them for therapy. If it coincides with the first deaths or is close to them, we might have another lead."

"I'll text Shireen. We're going home?"

"We're going home."

18. Who needs to talk anyway?

GEORGE WAS quiet on the way home. He had his thinking face on, the one that acted like a barrier, at least for Andi. He knew his partner's boundaries and did everything in his power to respect them. It was far too often he forced George to bend them for him when he was too lost in *them* to care about anything. Showing that he cared when he could was all Andi had to offer. The silence also gave him time to ponder the case. It was such a shame the arthropods couldn't give him a clearer picture of the killer. The thing with the beekeeper suit was a genius move, he had to give the killer that. Even if the man was clueless about Andi's talent and the whole thing probably had a metaphysical component for him, wearing the suit during the crime was great for avoiding evidence. No traces of skin or hair on the victims, just the pollen that could be from anywhere in Charleston. Andi still wondered if the killer's choice of victim could be something else besides the mental illnesses Gelman had stipulated as the deciding factor. Perhaps they had it all wrong and the man wasn't hung up about the bees. Perhaps he was simply a deadly genius who knew how to conceal his identity by wearing protective clothing during his kills and by choosing victims nobody would miss, and who, by chance, enjoyed working with bees. If Tyler hadn't followed his ghost friends, nobody would know about the bunker and the next victim could already be in the killer's sights. Perhaps it wasn't the bees at all. Perhaps they were just a means to an end, a byproduct. It would change the angle of their investigation, but neither the suspect pool—somebody who dealt with bees—nor the fact that all they could be sure of was the killer being male and strong enough to carry drugged people down into a bunker would change.

And until they found out where the killer picked up his victims, Andi wouldn't even dream of diving into the minds of his informants to find an event as specific as somebody being dragged into a vehicle against their will. Or willingly. They simply didn't know. The use of drugs before the kill suggested the killer didn't enjoy violence, he didn't want his victims to struggle, perhaps he didn't even want them to suffer. If he was simply giving in to his urge to kill but was a functioning member of society otherwise, not a psychopath, it could be he chose his targets with the thought that nobody would grieve them. Izzy Whitewall didn't fit that estimation, but she could have been a mistake. Most killers made them, though usually early in their careers. If only the smoke wasn't so cloying, Andi could find the man; he knew he could. Ending this case wasn't as important as solving it, but he would take anything at this point just to get it over with.

"Andi?"

"Huh? What? Sorry, I was thinking about the case." Andi blinked at George, who had parked the car in front of the house.

"I can see that. I wanted to know if you need some more time in here?"

Andi looked around. The car was nice, arthropod-free again, but no matter how soft the seats were, they weren't as wonderful as his own sofa in the living room. "No, no, I'm coming."

They both left the car. Andi opened the door while George made sure the Escalade was locked. He then sauntered over to Andi, his entire body a kaleidoscope of emotions, pheromones, chemicals, electrical charges. When Andi looked at George purely through the senses of the arthropods surrounding them, he was still the most attractive blob Andi had ever seen, gorgeously bright and soothing at the same time, a safe haven for him, a place where he could rest, and he needed to rest, his entire body screaming at him to let go, his muscles all too ready to go lax, his mind taut to the point of ripping, *them* just waiting for his walls to crumble. And George knew, George saw it because he held out his hand and guided Andi inside to the sofa, where they sat down, Andi as close to George as possible, tugging his legs under his ass, putting his head on George's shoulder, hearing, sensing, feeling his heartbeat, the familiar views of the resident arthropods taking over, shielding him some from what was going on outside and in his head, and George's breathing was so soothing, relaxing. Andi was ready to sleep, to slip under the blanket of darkness that promised peace, temporary peace. He closed his eyes.

When he opened them again, it was to his head resting comfortably on one of the pillows, a blanket thrown over his legs, and the scent of baking potatoes in the oven. There was garlic too, a feast in the making. Andi sat up a little groggily. He was now at an age where naps during the day were welcome but left his system wonky.

"Ah, I was about to wake you up. Dinner is ready." George was standing in the doorway to the kitchen, radiating calm, the tense lines around his eyes softened. Andi glanced at the clock above the fireplace, an antique from his gran, all gold and glass and gleaming. Six thirty. He had slept for over two hours. No wonder his legs were jelly. He followed George into the kitchen, where his partner prepared two plates with perfectly crisp potato chips—baked in olive oil because that was the healthy option—and generous dollops of lean curd with garlic and fresh herbs. A feast indeed.

After they had eaten and cleaned the kitchen—the mere idea of leaving food for their tiny roommates had George sweating—they went upstairs, George walking behind Andi because apparently, he didn't trust him on the stairs, which was sweet and a bit patronizing and exactly what Andi needed, even if he wasn't in any danger of falling down, not today at least. In front of Andi's room, they stopped, Andi reaching for the handle, looking at his partner.

"How about a bath?" He could have added that filling the ginormous tub was a waste for just one person or that they could take turns or whatever, but it wasn't necessary. They both wanted closeness, to not be apart just yet, perhaps never again. The electricity surrounding George sparked; his pheromones conveyed his happiness.

Andi led the way to the tub, started the water, while George rummaged through the drawer under the sink until he found the lavender bathing salt. He had bought it recently—until then, Andi had put in the water whatever he could find, usually very old bubble baths and salts from his gran, who had loved a good soak. George had spent one Sunday afternoon to sort through it all and then had, very politely, very worried, asked, as if Andi were made of glass, if those bathing substances held any meaning to him because they needed to go, immediately. While saying this, he had held a two-pound bag of hardened rosemary and sage bathing salt in front of him as if it were about to explode any minute. All of Gran's bathing salts had hardened, but Andi had a hammer, so it wasn't a problem. Luckily for George's mental well-being, Andi held no special connection to his gran's toiletries. That was reserved for other things, like her room, which still remained the same, unchanged, like his love for her, even though her scents and her impressions on the arthropods were starting to fade, too much time gone since she'd last been there. The bathing salts, old soap bars, bottles with foaming gels and milky liquids were disposed of and replaced by George's things. He had taken Andi with him to the small shop where he bought his vegan, ecological, plastic-free toiletries, but the wall of scents had taken Andi out within seconds, and so he had waited in the car while George took care of yet another thing for him. In hindsight, the good thing about Gran's stuff had been that it had lost most of its scent.

Now the very politically and ecologically correct bathing salt went into the water, the soft, unobtrusive aroma reminding Andi why high-quality stuff was worth the money most of the time. He started undressing because he wasn't shy about his body. Unlike with most teenagers, Andi's build had never been a problem for him. He didn't compare himself to the jocks running around bare-chested to impress the girls with their muscle mass. At that age, Andi had had completely different worries, and his reputation as the resident freak you better not mess with had spared him any and all comments that might have impacted him. Then again, probably not. He already knew that blob bodies were imperfect, kind of useless, the hard bits inside instead of outside protecting the squishy parts, no wings, only two legs, how could anybody get anywhere with only two legs, it was a mystery, lungs instead of spiracles, what a stupid concept, two sacks of bloody tissue instead of elegant tubes steering oxygen into the body, only one measly brain, consisting of 2 percent of the entire body's weight but using up 20 percent of the oxygen, and not even reaching into the legs, instead of making up 80 percent of the body, as it was with some spiders, no connection to a bigger mind, all alone, it was a miracle blobs were functioning at all.

Andi knew his body could be described as wiry, leaning dangerously into underweight, his sinewy muscles from all the running around adding some mass to what would otherwise just be a sack filled with bones. Compared to him, George's body was a study in what blobs deemed perfection, his muscles trained, not to the point where it was too much, but well enough to do the job, to make women and men drool, his movements sleek, graceful from running, no sharp angles on him; everything about him screamed healthy, hale, fit. Andi's opposite in everything, dark where Andi was pale, round where Andi was bony, full of energy where Andi felt he was drained to the core. All these were mere observations for Andi, nothing that worried him or made him insecure. Bodies were the way they were. George had no problem getting naked in front of his partner either, his happiness saturating the air far more than the bathing salt did.

They stepped into the tub, the water warm and soothing, the lavender salt making it feel as if they were in southern France. Or how Andi imagined southern France to be when the lavender was in full bloom. George got into the water at the other side of the tub, writhing a bit until he found a position he liked. Andi could feel sudden tension mixing with his calmness, knew it wasn't just the case resurfacing as it did in Andi's mind when he least expected or wanted it, but something else, something about them. He might be emotionally challenged, but he wasn't an idiot.

"You want to talk about something." He also didn't beat around the bush.

George lifted his right hand from the water, tiny droplets splashing back in, the *pitsch*, *pitsch* so sweet, not like the atmosphere, heavy with *something*.

"I'm not sure if this is the right time, Andi. Hell, I'm not even sure what I want to talk about exactly because so much of it is nonverbal." George was frustrated. It was a scraping greenish yellow front and center in Andi's senses.

"We're in a bathtub, the water is hot, neither of us can go anywhere in a hurry. Seems perfect to me."

George grinned, genuinely amused. "I sometimes forget you're not like other people. You're right. Okay, here it comes. I know we are close. I know me moving in with you is more than just two friends saving money. I know what we have goes beyond friendship. The point is…. The point is there's so much to talk about, and not everything can and should be talked about, and Daniel said I should be open, but sometimes it's hard to read you, which makes being open difficult."

"Because you're afraid of saying something that'll hurt me?"

"That too, among other things."

Andi leaned forward to put his hand on George's knee. The tub was so big, he couldn't reach farther without bending over. His partner's skin was wet and warm, and the touch sparked in the minds of the silverfish, comfort and warmth for Andi, protectiveness and adoration mixed with lust for George.

"George, you see me. You know my secret, and you haven't run screaming for the hills. No, you try to make my life better, to help me, you're enraged on my behalf for the unfairness of it all. There is nothing, I repeat, *nothing*, you could say to me that would make me abandon you."

Slowly, oh so very slowly, George lifted his right hand to put it on Andi's. The spark intensified, making Andi almost dizzy. "I think I love you, Andi. I don't know what kind of love it is, not yet, but the things I feel for you, around you—they are too deep to remain invisible."

It was all Andi's selfish heart had hoped for, all he knew he shouldn't want because binding George to him was unfair, sentencing him to be Andi's caretaker, even though he could leave at any time, technically, but he was too conscientious, Andi knew it, just like he knew he couldn't let George go, just like he knew that George *needed* him to not let him go, it was all such a complicated mess, like his bond to the arthropods, out of his control, driven by instinct, and so he said what needed to be said, for the sake of honesty and full disclosure, for his own sake, so when everything went to pieces, nobody, not even he himself, could say he hadn't warned George.

"And why should they? I think I love you too, George. Though I don't know how much of it is my dependency on you and what is tied up in the *geschenk*. You know I'm a mess. I've never had a relationship. My libido is generally low because I usually don't have the energy to waste. I have no clue what goes into the making of a functioning relationship, let alone a good one. I don't dare to talk about perfect, because perfect is impossible, we both know that. Being with me is trying. It's not just all the issues I pose, it's how people are going to view you, our relationship, us. You're not only with a man, a white man at that. You're also with the crazy guy, the one without friends who keeps everybody at arm's length."

George leaned forward as well, took both of Andi's hands in his.

"I know. And I'm not going to lie to both of us by saying it won't ever be a problem. There will be times when I'll resent what we are, what society sees in us. What I do know is that being with you is going to be one hell of a ride and that I'd regret it to my dying day if I didn't take this chance. Also, I have already decided to petition to stay in Charleston as soon as Chief Norris is gone."

Andi stared at him, drinking in the beauty, inside, outside, chemically, that was George Donovan. "Why didn't you tell me?" He knew George hadn't wanted him to worry about that as well, but he liked hearing it from him. George grinned knowingly.

"Didn't want to worry you."

"That's something I'd love to worry about."

"I don't think it will be a problem with the chief gone. Charleston isn't exactly teeming with detectives, and we make a great team, have numerous solves under our belts. What's not to approve of?"

"Anybody who rejects such a perfect proposal would be an idiot." Andi grinned. He felt so light inside, he thought he might be able to fly. Not right now, though, because the hot water was also making him tired. George tugged at his hand.

"Come here."

With a sigh, Andi turned in the tub until his back was snuggled against George's chest, his head once again close to his partner's (boyfriend's? lover's?) heart. The most perfect place in the world. Andi closed his eyes.

"I'll take care of the sloshed water later." George kissed his temple, soft, unhurried, like he had a right to do it, which he had, and it felt perfect, two pieces finally slotting into place.

19. Intensification

Waking up with Andi snuggled against his back was nice, George decided. After their bath and that first tentative kiss, going to the same bed had been the logical conclusion of their evening. With Andi so close, George's sleep had been even better than if he'd been in his room. It was another sign telling him that things were going in the right direction. He always slept worst in his apartment, too far away from Andi to be there for him should anything happen. His sleep was leaps better when he was in the guest room, on the same floor, with his and Andi's door ajar, but a certain tension remained because there was still distance to be covered. Now, with Andi's warmth seeping into him, George had slept better than ever before in his life. He finally understood how great his need to protect Andi truly was, giving him peace in their otherwise troubled times. This was where he belonged, where he was meant to be. He turned to his partner, looked at his face. Andi was connected; George had learned to read those signs as well, the difference between a dream—which rarely occurred—and Andi piggybacking on a single arthropod's senses during his sleep. It was definitely creepier when he was awake. George still shuddered inwardly when he thought about the spider in his car. At least when Andi's eyes were closed, the part of George that protected his sanity—or what was left of it anyway—could pretend it was just a lively dream. It wasn't. It usually was a death experience, plain and simple, but the human mind was capable of many things, and lying to itself was one of the greatest achievements humankind had ever made, at least in George's opinion. It allowed him to calmly reach out and sling his arm around Andi, close his eyes as well, and concentrate on his partner's breathing, which was too flat, too quick, to be restful. He tried to match it, his adrenaline spiking, evident in the quickening of his heartbeat hammering in his ears. He envisioned the castle, the strong stones withstanding the raging sea, keeping it away from the inhabitants, offering protection in an environment that was woefully void of it. George lost himself in the image, the crashing of the waves synchronized with his and Andi's breathing; the walls stood strong, and the rooms within remained dry, untouched. And then he felt it.

A tug at his mind, so weak, barely there, he almost didn't believe he'd felt it. It came again, stronger, more desperate. He turned toward it, kept his mind on the waves and the stones, the steady in and out washing through his thoughts, emptying them of meaning, until there was only the tug left. It felt like pincers in his soul; it *was* pincers in his soul, small, crowned by eight eyes, *another spider*, the castle and the waves, they were overlayed by branches, crisscrossing in front of his sight, as if he were looking at the stones from behind it, far behind because the branches were huge, or was he just smaller? He felt something else, Andi, he would recognize him everywhere, he knew it; the crashing got louder, he felt water on his skin, dripping down the net; there was a net; the spider retreated a bit; Andi was wrapped around him, in him, not letting go, clinging to the castle while the spider clung to the net; three images, only one his own, blurring into one, and George knew he had to keep his mind strong and clear because he was just getting the echoes of Andi's daily life, glimpses so weak they didn't really count even if they threatened to drag him under just like the waves would do if he fell; there was some type of lizard, Komodo, he thought, that swam through the spume, always in danger of being smashed onto the rocks; they had to do it to feed; he needed to concentrate; Andi wanted to come back, to the castle, the stones, in and out; George started breathing more deeply, changing the rhythm, forcing Andi out of his pace and into George's, yanking him back bit by bit, not letting go while the branches faded; the pincers let go of his soul, the spider went back to the recesses of the net, waiting for prey, and Andi was with him, groaning, burying his head into George's chest, inhaling him like he was a cat and George catnip.

"Thank you."

"You're welcome. It's easier when I'm already in the same bed with you."

"It is. Please, let's keep it that way."

"Always." George pressed the second kiss in their relationship on Andi's head. It was as far from anything sexual as the first had been—they weren't ready for that, not by a long shot, and to his own surprise, George was content to wait. He'd never been one to not scratch an itch when it occurred, but for Andi he was willing to wait. And he did have two healthy hands. He stroked Andi's back until his partner straightened.

"I know you want to go running. I'm fine now. I'll take care of breakfast."

George lifted a brow.

"You know you want to go. You need to process, as do I. And I do have the recipe for that awful green slosh you like to drink. I can make it, promise."

This time, George went for Andi's lips. Soft, with a bit of stubble, rasping against his own, tasting of Andi and sleep and garlic. Perfection.

AFTER THEIR breakfast—Andi did get the spinach-kale smoothie right, much to George's surprise—they went to the precinct to discuss what Thomas LeClerk had told them with Geena and perhaps Gelman and to explain to Sandra and Tobias why they now had to go through the patient lists of House Cusabo to find out who of the male patients went to bee therapy and could be a potential suspect. Fun times. On the drive, they talked briefly about Andi's suggestion that the bees might not have the same significance for the killer as they had for the victims and for them, that the man was perhaps simply pragmatic, seeking his victims for their accessibility, not for anything else, though the fact that they all had some kind of mental problem spoke against that part of the theory. Still, George kept it in the back of his head. Just because one part of an explanation didn't fit didn't mean the rest wasn't accurate. He did agree with Andi that even if the beekeeper suit was just for safety reasons—to keep evidence contained—it didn't change the direction they had to go, just the significance of part of the puzzle pieces.

Geena was already waiting for them, together with Gelman.

"Good morning, George, Andi. How did your meeting with LeClerk go?" She sounded chipper, while Gelman looked as if some coffee directly into the vein would be advisable. Tobias and Sandra weren't at their desk, probably getting their morning shot of caffeine in the common room.

"Good morning, Geena, Luke. It was—interesting." George went to his desk to put his jacket over the back of his chair. Andi held on to his herbal tea from Starbucks and managed to thump into his chair without any spillage. Oh, glorious day. "He admitted to having been in a relationship with her, providing her with the medication she needed, and that he reported her missing in the name of House Cusabo because he had hoped that would spur the police into action."

"You don't sound like he's our killer. Why don't you sound like he's our killer?" A certain manic desperation crawled into Geena's voice.

George steeled himself. This time, Andi wasn't completely sure of LeClerk's innocence because he couldn't identify the killer clearly, but the man's feelings for Kesha Raport had been convincing to George from an outside perspective and to Andi on a chemical basis. If he was the killer, their assessment of his personality was completely wrong, which did happen, even to experienced profilers, but not often. Still, no harm done making sure. He turned to Luke.

"How convinced are you that your estimate of the killer is correct?"

Luke scratched his chin. "Reasonably convinced. You know as well as I do that profiling is more like the weather forecast than basic mathematics, where two plus two doesn't always equal four, but the whole pattern is a textbook classic, down to the statistical deviation in victim selection and the tweaks in the MO, namely switching from the belt to the rope. We can't be sure of his motivation, but he's an escalating serial killer, most probably a psychopath, though it could be he's a man on a mission, some religious zealot or the like. I'm still leaning toward psychopath because the methodical way in which he kills makes it unlikely for him to have any feelings."

"You read up on that?" It wasn't a dig; George was glad Luke was taking the case so seriously. The IA agent seemed to get it.

"Yes. I wanted to be sure. This is not something I want to make a mistake on."

"If you're convinced the killer has to be a psychopath, then LeClerk is out. He was clearly shaken by Kesha's death. He told us she was worried about something going on in House Cusabo and that she wanted to protect him."

"And she didn't tell him from what." Geena sounded so dejected, George felt the urge to pat her on the back. He could relate to her misery. He felt it too.

"No, she didn't. How do you know?"

"Because I read her file and saw myself in her. I wouldn't have involved somebody I perceived as vulnerable either."

"Vulnerable as in civilian?" Andi took a sip from his tea, his eyes trained on Geena.

"Yes, why do you ask?"

"Because I've been wondering why she didn't go to the director of House Cusabo. We know she knew something, yet she decided to go into hiding and not drag anybody else into it. LeClerk says she was perfectly medicated, that her coping strategies worked, that she was of sound mind, and that he trusted her instincts. None of this sounds like a terrified victim to me. She was ready for a fight."

George turned toward the whiteboard. "Tina said her sister knew something as well. She was just a teenager, though. She probably was frightened."

"And they both ended up dead, just like the other victims." Geena huffed. "It's an interesting thought but doesn't really help at this point."

"It tells us something about the killer." Andi had a ballpen in his hands, and the tea stood next to his keyboard, an accident waiting to happen.

"What?" Geena was confused, but George thought he knew what Andi was hinting at. He made the three steps to Andi's desk and placed the tea far from the keyboard. Crisis averted.

"Kesha might have lost a leg, but she was a trained member of the Air Force, battle hardened, secure in her abilities and mentally stable. How did the killer manage to subdue her? And Izzy. She was a frightened teenager, seeing ghosts everywhere."

George froze for a moment, afraid either Geena or Gelman would pick up on Andi not meaning this as a figure of speech. Luckily for him, both were too intrigued where Andi's reasoning was going to look too closely at his words.

"Same question, how did the killer subdue her? Both would have been highly suspicious of anybody coming close to them. So how did he do it? We know he uses tranquilizers, and we deduced from his entire MO that he likely drugs his victims before he kidnaps them. Assuming neither Kesha nor Izzy knew who the killer was, just that something deadly was going on, who would have had the opportunity to get close enough to them to drug them, aside from the staff at House Cusabo or another patient?"

"Which brings us right back to LeClerk, who you say is unlikely to be the killer." Geena tugged at her short hair. "I hate this case!"

"We met another beekeeper at House Cusabo yesterday, Bruce Sprenger, one of the facility managers. He started working there the same year Izzy Whitewall was killed." George took one of the pens to write the name on the whiteboard, a little to the side. He wasn't sure what to make of Sprenger yet.

"Is he a potential candidate?" Geena stared at the name with burning intensity.

"He's tall and strong enough. He tends bees. He fits the bill just like every other male over five eight with more than a hundred and sixty pounds who keeps bees. Plus, he told us a few of the members of his beekeeper club help him with the bees at House Cusabo. I thought to ask Tobias and Sandra to look into this club, see if there are any other likely candidates." George sighed.

"A good idea. We haven't looked at all the staff from House Cusabo because we assumed it had to be somebody who was already there when the first kills happened." Gelman stared at the whiteboard. "Which is a logical and necessary step to get a starting point in the investigation. But now that we've ruled out the suspects who had been there and who could have had a motive, I think we need to change the parameters. Do we know how long Sprenger has lived in the area? Or any of the other staff who have come to House Cusabo after TJ Ross and Celia Murdoch were killed? What about the other beekeepers? Who helped to start the bees at House Cusabo?"

"We'll have to ask Shireen to find out." Geena was already turning. "I'll go talk to her. And I'll tell her to give the lists to Sandra."

"And ask her if she can find anything about Kesha after she left House Cusabo. I know she already looked, but perhaps there's something she didn't find...." George saw the look Geena threw him and winced. It was nothing compared to what Shireen would do when he doubted her like that. "We will—"

"Hayes, Donovan, my office." Chief Norris's voice was like a bucket of ice water to George's discomfort under Geena's glare. This time she turned and left in a hurry, the traitor. Andi got up from behind his PC. Gelman made a motion to follow, but George stopped him with a shake of his head. Whatever fresh hell this was, Luke would probably be useless, again.

They made it into her office where this time she slammed the door behind George with so much force, the glass in the upper part clinked dangerously, before she stormed to her desk and thumped her fist on the gleaming surface.

"You've gone too far!" she barked. "It's one thing that you defy me at every step, try to undermine my standing in this precinct, but to involve my son is such a low point. I'm not going to stand for it a second longer!"

George glanced at Andi, who was standing right next to him, his posture more relaxed than George suspected he was. "What do you mean, involving Tyler?"

"Don't say his name! You don't get to say my son's name after the hell you brought on my family's head!"

Another glance at Andi, who shrugged almost imperceptibly. "With all due respect, Chief, you'll have to spell it out, because my partner and I have no clue what you're talking about."

She stared at them with pure hatred in her eyes. "Not only have you talked to my son behind my back—oh yes, I know about your calls—you also told the press he was the one who found the corpses! I will have your badges for that, believe me. And nothing, not even a flawless solving statistic, is going to save you this time."

"You think we did what?" George was so angry, he heard his voice rising several notches. If he'd needed any more proof that Norris was getting unhinged, this was it. The sheer audacity to doubt their integrity in such a way. And given how worked up she was, she clearly believed her own fabrications. This woman was a danger to herself and the precinct, and George was ready to go into a showdown here and now, and to hell with Gelman and all his well-thought plans. George had had enough. He made a step toward the desk, an intimidation tactic he had seen his mother use countless times, never getting close enough to make it look like assault but hinting at what you could and would do. Norris actually flinched and angled back from the desk, changing direction as soon as she realized what she had just done. Too late. George had detected weakness. He was ready to pounce.

This time it was Andi who prevented him from doing something stupid he would likely regret later on by touching his wrist.

"It's because she wants to believe it, don't you, Chief? Because you want to get rid of us so badly, you're grabbing at straws. Unless you have proof, Chief Norris, undeniable proof pointing straight at my partner and me, I suggest you keep your accusations to yourself. It looks bad if the chief doesn't trust her two best detectives, doesn't it? Especially since they were the ones to find her missing son in the first place. Just imagine the story the press would make out of *that*."

Both George and Norris stared at Andi with wide eyes. The chief's cheeks were pumping like she was preparing to let loose, but not a sound came out of her mouth. George knew how she felt. Andi usually used his grumpiness as his shield, making everybody believe he was nothing but an introverted detective with a serious lack of social skills. Every now and then, though, he would say things like what he did just now, reminding everybody that there was a lot more to him than just a prickly outside. A mind like a steel trap, for one. He had pointed out her motive, had called her out on her lack of proof, had reminded her of her place, and threatened her none too subtly. All in an atmosphere that had left volatile behind a long time ago. Andi's calm interjection helped George to get his own temper back under control.

"We're leaving. Unless there's anything relevant for the case, I'd suggest it's better we don't see each other for a while." He followed Andi out of the office, leaving a stunned and still fuming chief behind. Getting away from her presence was like stepping into fresh air, the relief instantaneous.

"We need to solve this case so we can finally get rid of her," Andi whispered, but George understood him just fine.

"My thoughts exactly. Thank you for keeping your cool. This could have gotten ugly quickly."

"Don't get me wrong. I'd have loved to see you fight it out with her, but we have more pressing concerns, like a killer on the loose and no suspects or too many suspects, depending on how you view recent developments."

They reached their desks, where George woke his PC. He saw the email notification the same moment Andi's cell beeped. They both stared at their respective screens, taking in the information Shireen had dug up for them.

With the new parameters, she had found two men working at House Cusabo who had lived in the area since before the first murder had taken place. Marcus Kespers, fifty-eight, worked as a cook in the kitchen and had been employed at a hospital in the same position before he came to House Cusabo in 2014. Zane Werner, thirty-three, who was a night guard at House Cusabo, had worked at a retirement home and had changed employers in 2019. Shireen had attached pictures she had found, showing they both fit the physical requirements for the killer. Only Marcus Kespers was a member of the local beekeeper club, but Zane Werner could still be helping with them at House Cusabo, something George and Andi would find out once they got there. Perhaps it was as Andi had said and the killer only used the beekeeper suit for pragmatic reasons, which would make Werner a suspect even if he didn't have anything to do with the bees, as long as he had access to the equipment. Shireen had also found out that Sprenger had moved to Charleston in November 2013, after TJ Ross and Celia Murdoch had been killed, which made him the least likely of the three candidates, though cars were a thing and Spartanburg wasn't too far from Charleston to make it completely implausible for him to have killed there before he moved.

George looked at Andi, who was already putting on his jacket. Geena came from the direction of the bathrooms, and her eyes lit up when she saw they were getting ready to move. "Shireen found something?"

Andi nodded.

"I'm amazed how quick she is. I'd love to steal her when I leave." She winked.

"Don't you dare. Shireen is ours," George grumbled.

"I assume you're going to follow that lead?"

"Yeah. Do you want to come?" It was the polite thing to ask, and Geena hadn't been as much of a hindrance as George had feared at the beginning, so he was feeling generous. His temporary colleague shook her head.

"I'd love to, but I've got a meeting with my boss in fifteen minutes. She's on her way to Norfolk and has decided to spare me a few minutes of her time to harass me." Geena's tone made clear the harassment wasn't as bad as the words suggested.

"Lucky you. Have fun." George followed Andi toward the exit.

They were on the road to House Cusabo, both of them deep in thought, when Andi's cell started ringing. He dug it out from the left front pocket of his jeans, making a distressed sound when he checked the caller ID. George watched from the corner of his eye as Andi swiped across the screen.

"Tyler, buddy, how are you?"

George felt his brows raise to his hairline. Just what they needed, more forbidden contact with the chief's son. Theoretically, Andi should end the call immediately, after telling Tyler to never contact him again. Practically, neither of them had the heart to cut off the lonely boy like that. When Tyler started speaking, George was glad Andi had answered. The boy's voice was hushed, nervous, close to being frightened.

"Andi? The ghosts—they are acting strange. I don't like it."

"What are they doing, Tyler?" Andi sounded so calm when George could see from the tension in his shoulders he was anything but.

"They're all here, swarming like ants before a storm. I've seen it on TV. All nervous. And they're older. Some of them look… disgusting."

"Are you sure it's the same ghosts? Your friends?" George gave his best to sound as reassuring as possible. He didn't like the disgusting comment in the least.

"Yes, I can still recognize them. It's… I don't know the word. They vibrate the same way?"

"Don't bother with semantics, Tyler. You say they are the same ghosts, we believe you." Andi, in his no-nonsense way. "Are they just acting weird, or are they trying to communicate? What about Izzy? She seems to be the most stable."

"They're changing, and they don't make any sense. They say the end is coming, that it's all culminating. Some of them are flickering, bones and *pieces*. Izzy is there, but she's not talking, just flitting around. I think she's looking for something. Andi, I'm afraid."

Andi and George shared a look before Andi started talking again. "I understand, Tyler. Okay, here's what you're going to do. You find your dad. I assume he's with you?"

"Yes. He's in his studio."

"You go find your dad right now and you stay with him. Ask him to make you a hot chocolate, give you some cookies. Things that help distract you. Are the news vans still at your house?"

"Most of them are gone. Only two left, and they have gone down the road after Mother threatened them." The sound of rustling clothes and tentative steps came through the speaker.

"Good. You don't want to give them a show. Are you at the studio yet?"

"No, I have to go through the kitchen—no, Izzy, Andi says to go to my dad. Don't—why are you doing this? Stop, Izzy. Muriel, stop!" The panic in Tyler's voice was rising, and his harsh breathing came over the phone, invaded the inside of the Escalade, made all of George's hair stand on end. The boy was in trouble, and there was nothing they could do. Only he was already looking for the next exit to turn the car around and drive to Tyler's home, the chief and her hatred be damned. The boy needed help.

"What are they doing, Tyler?" Andi, still calm, though he held his cell with an iron grip, his knuckles white.

"They won't let me through. They're blocking the kitchen door. I can't get through."

"Are they saying why?"

"*Danger, the end. All comes to an end.*" Tyler's voice had now the same eerie quality George knew from Andi when he got in too deep with his tiny informants. It didn't bode well. George tapped the button on his steering wheel that connected him to his cell and called Luke. Whatever was going on, they needed help.

"Tyler, if they don't want you to go outside, don't do it. Calm down. Take a deep breath. Don't focus on how they look or what they're saying. Focus on the intent. Let go and let them have control. See what they see."

George shuddered. Andi's world, boiled down to a few words, so simple yet holding inside them so much pain and suffering, an entire world, no, worlds, completely different from what other people perceived, and he was asking a boy of fourteen years to trust in that otherness and give himself to it. Only somebody who lived the same paralyzing reality could ask this of a child in such a calm tone.

For what seemed like eternity but was only two rings on Gelman's phone, who still hadn't picked up, there was silence. Then, "There's somebody in the house. Dad is on the floor, he's not moving. I need to run."

A clattering sound, no doubt Tyler letting go of the cell, the only connection they had to him. Footsteps, quickly fading, the bang of a door closing. Nothing.

"George? What is it?"

20. Crawlers and Ghosts

"George?" Luke's voice was tinny in the deafening silence surrounding them. Andi hadn't ended his call with Tyler, still hoping the boy would perhaps come back and pick it up, though the chances were slim to nonexistent. George cleared his throat.

"Luke, tell the chief something is going on at her house. Tyler called us, said somebody had broken in. Also inform Forard to get his team ready. We might need them. We're on the way to the chief's house, ETA fifteen minutes."

"We're coming." Luke ended the call.

George was all determination, his lips pressed into a thin line, his hands gripping the steering wheel so hard, Andi feared it would break. While George drove as if the hounds of hell were on their heels, Andi checked his weapon, knowing he would probably need it. He could feel them in the air, Tyler's words, no, the ghosts' words: *things are coming to an end.* Arthropods had no concept of things like endings and beginnings, just of being and not being, a great difference Andi wholly understood but couldn't explain. It was something you had to experience, and if you weren't an arthropod or didn't have a *geschenk*, you would never know. Arthropods also had a sense for pressure, a pressure Andi was feeling now, a pressure that never meant anything good. *They* didn't know what it meant; it was just there, a change not interesting to them, while for Andi it carried a world of meaning. The anticipation of something bad, things he couldn't prevent, only react to. He hated it.

George briefly placed his hand on Andi's thigh, which had been bouncing on the seat. He couldn't do more, not with the speed he was driving at, but they were at a long stretch of road, close to the chief's house.

"We're going to save him. We will." It was a declaration, an affirmation they both knew could be as true as it could be untrue. Until they found Tyler, there was no way of telling what would happen.

They passed the two news vans on their way to the house, and Andi lowered the windows to get a better feel for what was going on, opening himself to the arthropods of the area.

Blood and pain and despair, he could feel it all, not so bad, tasty, panic, the small blob running, the huge blob following, wreathed in that damn smoke, making it so hard for Andi to know who it was, though he did know, it was the bad blob, the killer, the one they were looking for, chaos, the air sharp with panic, the small blob hiding, not good enough, the big blob coming, sonic, loud and shrill, disturbing everything; was this happening now, or had it come to pass, too close to the present to be a memory, not for them, memories were for blobs, they stored information, had imprints on their minds of things that left an impact, more sonic, the rhythmic kind Andi had learned to associate with motorized vehicles, damn, so it was the past, recent enough to still be fresh, no, fading already, ten minutes were an eternity for some of them, so much time, or so little, it was the context that made it significant, they were running out of it, definitely, how had the smokey blob found Tyler anyway, oh yes, the media, what was the media, no concept, no way to translate, it was bad enough from their world to his, but vice versa was a nightmare, impossible. Tyler was gone, the small blob, they needed to find him, there was another blob, Tyler's dad, unconscious, the electric field said he was hale, just not present, his heart steady, whump, whump, *no place to lay the eggs, the car came to a halt, he needed to get out, needed to be ready—*

Andi felt George's hand on his wrist, steadying him, bringing him back enough to be present without losing the connection. He led the way around the house to the studio where they found Aloys Norris unconscious on the ground with a huge lump on the back of his head, the hair matted by blood, but not too much; head wounds tended to bleed, he was fine, though he would have a terrible headache when he woke, the weapon lay next to him, a baseball bat; it was always a baseball bat; they were so handy, easy to carry, with so much destructive potential, Aloys Norris could attest to that. George was already on the phone calling an ambulance, trying to shake Tyler's father awake. He wouldn't wake up, not any time soon; his body needed time to heal. Andi felt it in the way the cells fired, the chemicals brewing, he was slipping, dragged into *their* world, he could feel it.

Another vehicle, Luke and the chief storming into the house, the chief screaming her husband's name, holstering her weapon as she went down on her knees next to him, George telling her the ambulance was on the way.

"Where's Tyler?" The question hung in the air. Gelman was staring at him, wanting to know. He needed to talk, complete sentences, only it was so hard, he was receiving fully again, knowing time was of the essence, they needed to follow the vehicle, outside, through the swamp, it was unusual enough he could find it, echoes of the path the killer was taking flooding Andi.

"ATV. Killer on ATV with Tyler. Need to follow."

Luke turned toward the chief. "Do you have an ATV?"

Norris shook her head, her face a mask of worry. She didn't look like a threat anymore, how funny was that, not at all, her son was missing.

"Our neighbors just bought two. They should be home."

Luke left, and Andi followed his trail to the next house, the ambulance thundered down the street, the neighbors were there, handing over the keys, Andi went toward the door, George followed, the first responders entered, went through the house to the studio, the chief told them to take care of her husband, went after George; they ran to the neighbors, got onto the ATVs, a double roar. Andi held on to George, a blob behind a blob, the other ATV, Gelman and Norris, not important, they needed to follow the trail, into Bloody Dick Swamp, toward the forest, the ground was wet, not treacherous, though, once George saw the trail, it was easy to follow, all Andi had to do was not to fall off and keep his senses sharp.

They reached the tree line, went into the forest. The ground got harder, the swamp receding, until they reached a forest street, small, not often used. They left the trees, and George steered the ATV along the pebbled street, following the direction Andi had pointed out, left, deeper into the wilderness. Gelman was fumbling with his cell, probably informing Forard to follow his GPS. The chief was driving, and they were going as fast as possible. The trace was there, luckily for them, the stinking ATV made an impression on the arthropods. The fork that came, Andi had no trouble indicating the right direction. Deeper they went, until the road just vanished, there one moment, then gone, seemingly swallowed by the giant trees with their writhing roots, standing too thick, the ground too gnarly for even the ATVs. There was one standing at the side of the road, almost in the ditch, as if it had been parked in a hurry, the scent of smoke lifting. Andi could detect nuances. He didn't know the killer, hadn't met him personally yet, only an echo of him. Yes, he'd seen glimpses, drugs and chemicals and sickness, not of the body. House Cusabo, it was here, in parts; they had been right about that at least. George parked the ATV, got down, helped Andi, the chief stopping behind them. Andi turned toward where the trees grew thickest and started to walk, quickly, quickly, the scent was hanging in the air, thinning, intruder, intruder, they were intruding, where was the other one? He had to find them, had to find Tyler.

GEORGE WAS holding Andi's right shoulder, stabilizing him while he led them through the trees, following a trail only he could see. Behind him, Gelman and Chief Norris were trying to keep up, both of them not as fit as would have been desirable. A brief flash of smugness was quickly overridden by his worry for Tyler. The boy had been missing for almost two hours now, and there was a lot that could happen to a victim in two hours. If their killer stuck to his usual MO—and George had no doubt it was their killer, even if they still didn't know who he was and how he'd found Tyler; the press probably, those useless hounds—there was still some time, but George wasn't banking on it. They had taken his lair from him, had driven him out, had increased the pressure, which could be enough for some internal switch to flip and make it all worse. It always got worse with serial killers. An escalating curve.

"Close, we're close, they're down, in the earth, not so deep, not like the other place, Tyler is awake, fuck, it's somebody from House Cusabo. I think I've seen him once, briefly, can see him now, so clear he's there, waiting, Tyler is moving, we're almost there, slow down, slow down, *whump, whump, whump*, something's wrong, the scent, it doesn't match, so confusing, *krth, krth, krth, thump, thump, crch*...."

Andi had stopped, facing slightly to their left, where George spotted a clearing where the angel oaks formed a sort of wobbly circle. He could see that the brush was disturbed, the brambles trampled.

"Andi? Where is Tyler?" George could hear Gelman and the chief approaching them.

"Under, they're under the earth. Only one entrance, just the trapdoor." He kept staring in the direction of the clearing.

Gelman came to a halt next to George, looking in the same direction. "There's another bunker?"

"Apparently not like the one where we found the victims. Tyler and somebody from House Cusabo are down there."

"How do you— No, forget it. It's not important at the moment." Chief Norris drew her weapon.

"No, we can't just barge in." Gelman held her back by grabbing the sleeve of her jacket. When she rounded on him, her eyes small, angry slits, he lifted both hands in a placating gesture. "We can't. We don't know what we're going to find down there. We don't know if there are other exits, where exactly Tyler is, or if the killer has a weapon, which is likely. The way things have been escalating for him in the last week, he'll probably kill Tyler the moment he realizes we found him. He's *not* going to listen to reason. You know that."

For a long moment, Chief Norris kept her weapon trained on Gelman. Then, with a frustrated huff, she lowered it. "What do you suggest?"

"One tunnel, not long, a room at the end, one mattress, Tyler is on it, killer is *thump, thump, thump*, upset, sharp, expecting, only one entrance, just this hole, Tyler is all wrong, smells of tranquilizer, but it's not right, wrong chemicals, knife, aggression, acid, *thump, stomp, roomps*, too much—" Andi collapsed, and George barely caught him. He managed to get his partner to the ground without hurting him. When he looked up from where he was kneeling beside Andi, holding his head in his lap, Gelman and the chief were staring at him with wide eyes.

"What he just said—is that true?" Norris's voice was shaking.

George sighed. So much for keeping everything secret. He had always known this was bound to happen, that one day, Andi would be found out. It was inevitable. George had just hoped it wouldn't be the chief and a psychologist from IA who would hold Andi's—and George's—fate in their hands. All this had to wait, though, because Tyler was still down there with a serial killer who had shed the last of his control.

"Yes. Apparently, the killer is pacing the room. He's agitated, waiting for something. If I had to guess, it's for whatever he has given Tyler to work, and it doesn't."

Chief Norris put a hand to her mouth, a little whimper escaping her. "Tyler is immune to a certain group of agents. Like his grandfather."

"Which is his luck, because the killer can't do whatever he's planning as long as Tyler is awake. Profiling was right—he can't look his victims in the eyes, needs them to be unconscious. This buys us time. We need a plan, quickly."

George looked down at Andi, whose breathing had gone shallow. His skin was clammy and cold, his eyes closed. Every instinct inside of him screamed to get his partner, the man he loved, somewhere safe, where he could keep him warm and guide him back to the human world. He also knew Andi would hate him if he didn't save Tyler first.

"Forard is on the way. How long will it take him to get here?"

Gelman got out his cell and stared at it. "Too long, I'm afraid. I texted him after you called me. He was in Charleston, luckily close to the precinct, but still, he has to get the team ready, they have to drive out here, following our GPS, and then they have to hike the last two miles. I don't want to bet Tyler's life on them arriving in time. And even if they were already here, the situation doesn't change. Only one entrance, one tunnel, one room. The killer has all the time in the world to kill Tyler as soon as he realizes we're here. Sorry, Chief."

Norris was shaking her head. "There has to be something we can do." She sounded so desperate, so vulnerable, George felt some of his resentment for her melting away.

"I'd say we take a look around. See if we can't find a way to get inside without the killer noticing."

Neither Gelman nor Norris looked hopeful, but they both started approaching the clearing. George had just put Andi's head on a piece of moss that looked a little bit more comfortable than the rest of the ground, when he heard it. A deep, vibrating hum invading the clearing. Hastily he got up and ran toward Gelman and the chief, who were standing stock-still, staring at the other side of the clearing, where a dark cloud was moving toward them, sounding like thunder rolling down the hills.

"What the fuck?" Gelman's mouth was hanging open.

George was still trying to make sense of what was going on, when two things happened at once. The bees—for it was bees, thousands of them—descended on the trapdoor George could see just beneath the bramble, and a frightened scream tore from the ground.

"Tyler!" Chief Norris was making a few steps toward the trapdoor, which was now covered in bees. The ones who hadn't landed yet were like a curtain keeping them away. Another scream resounded.

"That's not Tyler. That's the killer." Gelman was holding the chief back.

George turned to look where Andi was slumped on the ground like a bundle of rags. He detected faint movement on his clothes and skin— arthropods, a lot of them, covering his partner like a blanket, scurrying over his face, sliding under his clothes, cocooning him in. Whatever was going on here, he needed to be with his partner.

So he went.

ANDI WAS down in the bunker or hole, yes, it was more a hole than a bunker, nothing sophisticated, just for emergencies, Tyler on the mattress, a thin thing crawling with mites, the boy was wrong, his body oozing pheromones, busy rejecting the drug the killer had given him, that was good, it gave them time, but for what, there was no other way in, Tyler was trapped, he couldn't leave through the ground, there were so many little tunnels, it would be easy to slip away, crawling and skittering, quickly, quickly, to safety, away from the nasty blob with the knife, reeking of despair and crazy, he couldn't take Tyler with him, needed to help him, what could he do, he was out on the moss, his body cooling rapidly, future nourishment for the forest. Tyler was down there, George, George walking around, searching, the chief, Gelman, the trees, earth in the hole, fungi, rotting leaves, a warm breeze, promising better times, soil crumbling under heavy steps, the bees, in a tight bundle, walking across the honeycombs, feeding the queen, so many bees. If only they knew how much they were needed out there, how desperate he was for help; he was safe inside their midst, nothing could touch him here in the hive. No, he couldn't stay, Tyler was too young, who was Tyler, why was he important? The bees were getting nervous, waking, preparing to fly out; they felt the call, his call. How was that possible, why did it matter, as long as they came. He needed them desperately, but they were not enough, too far away. He had to be quick, chitin rubbing, breaking, no longer alone, he was never alone, never, they were always there, the ground breaking open, worms coming up, pill bugs and centipedes, swarming the hole where Tyler was. He still knew about Tyler, something from the other world, the one where he was a single unit with two arms and legs, not this skittering, scrambling, floating mass of thousands of bodies, limbs, minds. He had a mind, he was Andi, not a bee queen, not a hive, not hundreds of centipedes; there were more and more of them, ants, some bugs, the bees were flying now, coming to the clearing, they were all coming because Andi needed them. He wasn't just a guest anymore, he was more and less, pleading, asking, demanding, and they heeded his call, whatever it was he was calling, overwhelming, like a tidal wave, filling the hole. The huge blob was screaming in panic, spiders were dropping into his hair, several fat dung beetles who had mated in the soil above the hole were slithering down his neck, making him scream again, then run for the tunnel, leaving Tyler alone, the knife on the ground. The first bees had found their way in, through the cracks in the trapdoor, coming for the blob, stinging him in the face, his hands, scrambling under his shirt, stinging, stinging; he was squealing now, the pheromones all over the place, a sweet perfume, cloying the air, his body reacting to the poison, swelling. More bees were coming; the blob tried to reach the trapdoor, managed to get a foot on the first step, sting, sting, another scream, garbled, his throat swelling shut, the blob swaying, clawing at the walls of the tunnel, finding no traction, falling down, a heavy thud killing hundreds of centipedes and pill bugs and spiders and bugs, but he was down, wheezing, trying to get air into his lungs, the bees all over him now, attacking his neck and nostrils, his eyes, entering his mouth when he tried to shout again, stinging there as well, because Andi knew how to kill a man, knew why he was panting, could interpret what the change in his oxygen levels meant, and dead was dead. This blob had killed so many, it was only just; what did that even mean? He was getting rid of an intruder, an enemy, a threat; threats had to be dealt with, the hive had to be protected, the nest. The blob was dead, the *thump, thump, thump* silenced, the change in him evident for the arthropods even though they didn't know yet what it meant, not before certain chemical reactions emanated the smell the scavengers would react to, but Andi knew. Crying, somebody was crying, Tyler, in the room, on the mattress, pressing himself against the wall. Andi couldn't soothe him, he wouldn't understand; something was with him, no, somebody, a disturbance in the electric field, too weak to be noticed by anybody but the moths and pill bugs, they were sensitive to it, them, ghosts, crawlers of another kind, not his crawlers, though, no connection, just their presence, of no use, not food nor help nor information. Yelling, not in the hole, above ground, two blobs arguing, the bees obscuring the trapdoor, a cold body lying a few feet away, another blob bent over it. George, that blob was George; he was holding Andi's hand and talking to him, begging him to come back, that it was over, it was over. How did George know? The other blobs, he knew them as well, the chief and Gelman, no way they didn't know now; he'd always known it would happen. The agitation was subsiding, the earth-dwelling arthropods retreating through the tunnels and nooks and crannies they had come through, the bees making their way back to the hives. The queen was safe, Andi was safe, he was grateful, and they didn't understand, had no concept for blob ideas. The waves, he heard the waves, gently rolling, his breathing matching them automatically, a thin shaft of warmth piercing his skin where George was holding him, guiding him back, he needed to come back, it was all done.

Andi was tired.

WHEN ANDI finally opened his eyes, George almost didn't hear the arrival of Forard and his team. He looked down at his partner, whose skin was slowly gaining some color back. His hands weren't as clammy as before, and the cold sweat on his forehead was drying. Forard appeared next to them, not commenting on Andi on the ground or the hum of the bees in the air or anything else.

"What's the situation, Hayes?"

George wanted to protest that Andi was too exhausted to do anything right now, even if it was just talking, but Andi made a face, lifted his head, grabbed George's hand harder, and started to speak.

"Perp is dead, anaphylactic shock after being stung by bees. Tyler is still in the room where he left him. Give it a few more minutes, then you can go in. Nobody else in there, knife on the ground halfway to the room with Tyler. Wait till the bees are all gone."

Then he sunk back on the ground with a soft groan. "My head is killing me."

Automatically George found the small packet of Tylenol in his pocket, his emergency kit for situations like this. He unscrewed the lid and Andi swallowed it all, the amount exactly what a grown person was allowed to take in one go.

Forard nodded at them before he turned to his men, barking his orders.

"Surround the trapdoor. Wait for the bees to leave. Then we go in."

Shuffling and the cracking of twigs indicated several men and women getting in position. George didn't really care what was happening. Andi had said Tyler was safe, which meant he could start worrying about Andi's well-being. His partner was still too cold to the touch, even though he seemed to be getting some circulation back. What he needed now was a warm, soft bed to lie in, hot soup waiting for him when he woke up, and a huge bucket to throw up into. How he was supposed to get Andi out of the forest and back to civilization he didn't know. They had come here by foot, the trees for the final distance too dense for a vehicle.

"Is he all right?" Gelman appeared, seemingly out of nowhere, and would have startled George if anything could have still startled him on this day.

"He's going to have a migraine, and he's too cold. I need to get him out of here."

"I think the SWAT team drove up to the place where we parked the ATVs before they had to abandon their trucks. It should be doable. And I have keys for one of them. Shall we go?"

George stared at Gelman, full of suspicion. "What's your angle?" He knew he sounded aggressive, but he also felt entitled to it after everything that had gone down the last few weeks. In the background, they heard the SWAT team opening the trapdoor and Chief Norris's voice, calling for Tyler. The answer was faint, though clear. "I'm here, Mom. I'm fine."

"My angle is to get Detective Hayes out of here. Once we have him at his home, we can talk about the rest. And don't look at me like that. I'm no threat to you. I swear."

George was conflicted. He looked down at Andi, who had his eyes closed and was still holding his hand. His partner groaned. "I don't care what happens next. I need a bed."

That cinched it. George tugged Andi to a sitting position, got up himself, and then, with the help of Gelman, hoisted Andi to his feet. They kept him between them when they started the careful journey over roots and stones, brambles and branches.

Reaching the SWAT trucks seemed to take an eternity, during which Andi had to throw up twice. The second time, not much was coming up anymore, Andi's body wracked by violent convulsions. George held his partner, ignoring the worried looks Gelman was directing at him. This was normal as far as he was concerned, and he needed some time to adjust to the new situation. He knew Gelman was coming with them to talk about what had happened in the clearing. Only a fool would assume otherwise. The question was, how should George handle it? There was no denying what Andi was capable of, not after he had led them to Tyler without even once straying from his path. The thing with the bees was new. Until now Andi had never let on that he was able to control his tiny informants. George was sure his partner would have mentioned it, so it had to have been a surprise for him as well. Though when he thought about it, it made sense. Why should a connection as intense as the *geschenk* only work in one direction?

They stepped through another row of oaks onto the dirt road where the SWAT trucks were parked behind the ATVs they had used. It took Gelman a moment to find the one he had the keys for before they were on their way back to Charleston.

"I assume we drive to Detective Hayes's home?" Gelman found George's eyes in the rearview mirror.

"Your assumption is correct." George had Andi's head in his lap, stroking the sweaty, dirty-blond hair. Andi was on the verge of falling asleep, wincing occasionally when the truck found a bump in the road. He would need some more Tylenol until he could get his well-earned rest.

As soon as Gelman pulled up in front of Andi's house, George was out the back door, leaning back in to get Andi. Gelman came around to help him, and George gave him the keys to the house. He picked Andi up in a fireman's carry—even though his partner was slim, he wasn't exactly a feather—and followed Gelman into the house. In Andi's bedroom, he carefully laid him on the bed, took off his damp clothes, managed to get him into the new pajamas he had bought for him only three weeks ago, and coaxed Andi into swallowing another dose of Tylenol with some water. Then he tucked Andi in, shut the blinds, placed the bucket next to his bed, while marveling the entire time how normal these things had become for him in less than a year. Once he was sure Andi had fallen asleep, he left his room, leaving the door cracked open so he would hear him should he need anything. Gelman was standing in the hall, with a soft expression in his eyes.

"You're taking good care of him."

"Nobody ever has."

Gelman raised his hands, the gesture a bit helpless. "Let's talk."

"Yeah, let's talk." George brushed past Gelman down the stairs into the kitchen. He knew he wouldn't like what was going to be said and felt entitled to a coffee while battling it out with a representative of IA. At least it was a good exercise, preparing him for the inevitable confrontation with the chief. George started making the coffee, listening with one ear as Gelman sat down at the kitchen isle. Only yesterday it had been Andi sitting there, watching as George made dinner for them both. The atmosphere had been so tranquil then, so perfectly domestic, nothing like the crackling tension he was experiencing now. George was willing to postpone their discussion until the coffee was done, but it seemed Gelman had different ideas.

"Detective Donovan, George, first of all, I want to assure you that you have nothing to fear from me or IA. If anything, I'm your ally. I know it's hard to believe at the moment, but please let me explain."

"It seems to me I can't stop you no matter what." George knew he was being rude. He didn't care. He was standing in his partner's, his lover's kitchen, said lover in bed out cold, which put all the responsibility of keeping Andi safe firmly on George's shoulders. How he hated that Andi couldn't be here to be part of this talk. But that wasn't possible, not after all he had gone through during this case, and time was of the essence. George couldn't afford to wait until Andi got better. It would give Gelman and the chief too great an opportunity to corner them. So he looked at Gelman expectantly. At least the man had the decency to squirm a bit.

"I have a confession to make, George. I wasn't entirely open with you and Andi."

"In what way?" George was intent on not giving anything away until he knew more about Gelman's angle. It was a trick his mother had taught him. If you're on uncertain ground, let the enemy do the talking. Contrary to what Gelman had said, George wasn't yet convinced he wasn't an enemy.

"Like Andi, I'm not what I seem to be." Gelman started tapping his fingers on the counter of the kitchen island. That got George's attention.

"You're like him?"

"No. No. I'm—" Gelman huffed. "I pretend to be from IA, but in reality, I work for a branch of the law that doesn't exist officially."

"Meaning?" George's thoughts were spinning so fast, he almost felt smoke coming out of his ears.

"We don't even have a name, just calling ourselves the Office. Our job is to find people like Andi and either try to convince them to work for the government or protect them from being detected."

George's thoughts came to a screeching halt. Out of all the things he had expected, some secret government operation was the last one on his list. "You're doing what?"

"Looking out for people like Andi. And Tyler, apparently. Though Tyler's talent is quite common, while Andi—he's absolutely unique. I've never come across somebody like him."

"You're telling me there's more people like Tyler? So many you think him talking to ghosts is common?"

Luke didn't seem to be surprised in the least that George knew about Tyler's gift. "Uh, I might have phrased that wrong. People with… talents are rare, very, very rare. As far as we know, and the Office was founded in the 1970s, only one in half a million people is born with an additional gift that can't be explained rationally. Many of those who are born with such a talent never realize, because it's either too weak to have an impact on their life or they never experience the kind of traumatic event it takes to awaken it. Of those, about a third can't cope and commit suicide. Roughly another third hides it successfully from their environment, taking the secret to their grave. The remaining third start using their gift actively, either for good or bad, becoming mediums or going into some form of law enforcement. Apart from them, there's another, miniscule group. We're talking about roughly one in five million here. Their talent is active from birth and grows in strength the older they become. It's typically passed on within a family, like with Tyler. Or Andi. With Tyler, we know his grandfather, Chief Norris's father, had the ability to not only see ghosts but communicate with them up to a certain extent. He even worked with law enforcement on occasion. Was only called into the really bad cases because he was such an asshole. We looked at Andi's family closely and have come to the conclusion that it has to be the German side of his family tree where his gift originates. Unfortunately, the German authorities are either not aware of the potential those with special talents pose, or they're greedy, protecting what they think is theirs. Anyway, we couldn't find out much about Andi's mother's family except that they're from Bavaria and live in a remote part of it."

George couldn't suppress his grin. That sounded exactly like Andi's *Oma*. "I don't know much about the family, but from what Andi has told me, they're tight-knit. I'd be surprised if the German authorities knew anything about them."

"Well, that's one mystery solved, then." Gelman accepted the mug George held out to him. "Where was I? Ah yes, the Office. Over the years, the specialists at the Office have come up with ways to find the people who have turned to law enforcement by going over cases. There are certain signs a trained eye can see."

"I understand." George did understand. He just wasn't sure if he should be relieved or even more on alert. As far as he could see, this could go both ways. "When I contacted IA, you saw Andi's case files and realized something wasn't as it should be." Knowing it was basically his fault that this ominous Office had set its sights on Andi was something George would examine later, when he was alone.

Gelman cleared his throat. "No. We've been watching Andi for a while. Actually, Chief Renard knew about the Office and was in contact with us. He kept an eye on Andi, protected him, and kept us in the loop. When he retired, he assured us he had impressed on his successor how important it was to leave Andi alone and that it was best to not approach him. Seeing as the chief's father was… special himself, we didn't expect any trouble from her. If we had known Chief Norris would take Chief Renard's words as a challenge, we would have taken measures."

"You can do that? What would these measures have been?" George took a sip of his coffee.

"We would have either installed another chief or approached Andi to change precincts. Whatever was easier."

"Instead, he got me as a partner."

"Which is a very lucky, very fortunate coincidence. I don't have to tell you how taxing a talent can be. You already know very well."

"I do. And Andi calls it his *geschenk*. That's German for gift."

"I'm not sure if I'd want a gift like that."

George snorted. "Believe me, you don't. Andi doesn't want it either. But he's got it, it's not going away, and he has to deal with it. End of story."

"He has you now." Gelman's tone implied he was trying to convey something without using actual words.

"I'm sorry, Luke. I had a few trying weeks and one hell of a day. If you want me to get something, you have to spell it out for me."

Gelman chuckled. "Have I ever told you how much I like your bluntness?"

"No. I usually try to hide it. It's not good for my career."

"Speaking of which…. Well, you asked me to not beat around the bush."

"I stand by that."

"Another thing the Office does is providing the people with talent with somebody who looks out for them. Either as a partner in the field or some mentor who protects them from other authorities who don't know about us. Sometimes, we give them both. You are already taking care of Andi. Perfectly, I might add. If I hadn't known what to look for, you could have fooled me."

"I can't not take care of him. You've seen today how bad it can get."

"That I have. Which brings me to the part I've been trying to imply. Now, how do you feel about officially becoming Andi's caretaker? It's probably not the direction you had in mind for your career, but I can assure you that for all the doors closing on you when you decide to accept my offer, better doors are going to open. And I don't mean in the philosophical sense."

"You don't have to bribe me. In case you haven't noticed, Andi and I have a very deep relationship. We've decided that I'm going to move in with him. It's all very new. I honestly don't know where it's going to lead, but even if we were just partners on the force, I could never leave him. Not with what I know about him. He needs me."

"So you're no longer planning to leave Charleston in two years?"

"Fuck no. I talked about it with Andi recently. Initially I wanted to have it all wrapped up before I told him so he wouldn't have to worry about my petition to stay here going through. I expected it to be difficult because of Chief Norris's hate for us, but then we had a serious talk, and it just came up naturally."

"Don't worry about her." Gelman waved his hand. "I'm going to have a discussion with her as soon as we're done here. You're willing to stay with Andi, become his caretaker?"

"I already am. There's no changing that. And I highly doubt he would let somebody else in. He's like a cactus. Or a hedgehog."

"I've noticed. Fine. I'll inform headquarters to get the necessary papers ready. You will get a raise of course, and extensive rights, including access to highly confidential databases. Your rank won't change officially—we want to keep everything on the down-low—but you will have all the right phone numbers and names to move freely."

George narrowed his eyes. He had been playing the game too long to be glamoured by some pretty words. "What's the catch?"

"Catch?" Gelman did have the gall to look innocent.

"I'm not stupid, Luke. What you're offering sounds too good to be true for two simple detectives who are working in a precinct in Charleston."

"Uhm, you might be working cases in some other states. Charleston would still be your home base, and we would only call you if we really needed you. Like when a serial killer is on the loose. You'd be contacted by the Office and sent where you're needed, which means you'll be working not only with other precincts, but also the FBI, the CIA on occasion, and even the different branches of military investigation. You've gotten along well with Agent Davis, so you shouldn't have too many problems."

"She's sensible. And doesn't have a fragile male ego. Made it easy to work with her. What you're describing is a wide field. I have to talk to Andi about it. And to be honest, I have no idea what he's going to say. Not a year ago, he thought nobody knew about his *geschenk*. I can't say how he's going to deal with suddenly realizing that he wasn't as alone as he thought."

"If it's any help or consolation, we've never come across a talent like his. All the others we found so far are spiritual, for lack of a better word. Seeing ghosts, reading auras, scrying objects and persons. A connection with insects—that's new."

"Arthropods," George said automatically. "It's arthropods."

"There's a difference?"

"A huge one. To put it in layman's terms, arthropods are all animals with segmented legs, including insects, arachnids, crustaceans, and Armadillidiidae. Then there's the worms and slugs, invertebrates which Andi can also sense for some reason, even though they aren't arthropods."

"Oh." Gelman looked a bit overwhelmed. "That's a lot of creatures."

"Yep. Billions. Now, what happens if Andi decides he doesn't want to work for your office? You just said it yourself, he's unique. I know what governmental bodies are capable of doing with uniqueness."

"Your worries are understandable but unjustified. I'm not going to tell you we're such good people we would never dream of doing something unethical for the sake of the state, because we both know I'd be lying through my teeth. No, the reason we're going to leave you alone should Andi wish so is experience. When the Office started, it tried to force people with talent to work for them. As the agents back then learned very quickly and very painfully, stressing people whose senses are wide-open inevitably leads to disaster. And after what I've seen Andi do today, I wouldn't dream of forcing him to do anything. Death by anaphylactic shock is at the very bottom of my list of ways how I wish to die."

George stared at Gelman with narrowed eyes. He believed the man up to a certain point. It made no sense to force Andi openly when they could come up with other, more subtle ways. It was only a matter of when, not if, because having a resource like Andi at the tip of your fingers was too much of a temptation, as George very well knew. It would be up to him to shield Andi from the politics involved with working for a secret government agency and to get the best deal for both of them out of it. Until he had spoken with Andi, he didn't want to make any decisions, so that discussion had to wait. A change of topic was in order.

"Speaking of anaphylactic shock, what are you going to do about the report we have to write?"

Gelman shrugged. "I've thought about it, and it's probably best to state there was a wild bee's nest close by. The animals were disturbed when the killer brought Tyler to the bunker, and when the four of us arrived, it triggered them to attack. I'm sure we can come up with some official-sounding BS about bees sensing drugs, which explains why they attacked Sprenger."

"It's not BS. They are able to sense all kinds of chemicals, and some do make them aggressive. There's scientific proof for that." George thought about all the things he had learned about bees in the past weeks. They truly were amazing animals.

"Even better. It means we only have to manipulate the evidence a bit so the killer has traces of one of those chemicals on him. Splendid. And because he's dead, there won't be a trial, which means we can bury the report, claiming it is confidential because we don't want the memory of his victims sullied. I love it when things resolve themselves so smoothly."

"Lucky you." George got up. "I don't want to be rude, Luke, but can I ask you to leave now? I need a shower in a bad way, and then I have to cook some soup for when Andi wakes up."

Gelman immediately got up. "That's absolutely no problem, George. As I said, Andi is our priority, and you as his caretaker have the last say in practically everything concerning him."

George decided to take that with a grain of salt. He wouldn't rely on Gelman's pretty words until he had seen proof of their truthfulness.

After he had seen the man out, George looked in on Andi, who was sound asleep. The shower was hot and wonderful on his sore muscles, and cooking the chicken soup from scratch was soothing. He and Andi had a lot to talk about once his partner was awake.

21. A Future, Bright and Clear

It WAS already getting dark when Andi finally tramped down the stairs. He looked like death warmed over twice, lacking his usual grace, which meant he should technically still be in bed. It was no doubt hunger that had driven him out, which was no wonder since he had lost everything in his stomach in the woods. The soup was ready, and George had two bowls on the kitchen island before his partner entered the kitchen.

"Hey, you hungry?"

Andi homed in on the bowl of soup like a heat-seeking missile, and his stomach gave a loud grumble. With a smile George watched as Andi started carefully taking small portions of the soup with his spoon. Another thing George had learned from Andi—never overtax your stomach after throwing up. Small sips and bites were the way to fulfillment. He dedicated his focus on his own bowl, savoring the rich flavor. Adding a bit of ginger root to the broth had been an excellent idea. Once his stomach was pleasantly filled, George leaned back to watch Andi finish his food.

"What did Gelman want?" Andi didn't look up from the soup, navigating the last sips to his mouth.

"A lot. Apparently, he's part of a secret government organization calling itself the Office, who work with people with talents. Like Tyler. Like you."

"What?" Andi looked up from his food.

"It gets better." George knew he sounded grim. "It seems your old chief, Renard, knew about the Office and told them about you. It's the reason he protected you the entire time. He didn't know exactly what you were capable of, but he recognized the signs. When I put in the complaint about Chief Norris, they sent Gelman to help you. Well, at least that's how he told the story."

"You don't believe him?"

"It's not about believing. What he told me is far too crazy to not be real. It's about trust. He offered us a new job, so to speak. You as a secret weapon the Office can send everywhere in the States, and me as your caretaker. We're talking a raise and far-reaching authority here. We'd still be based in Charleston."

"You think they're going to exploit us?" Andi was done eating and looked at him with furrowed brows. George knew his partner was not only relying on the words George said or even his body language but also his pheromones, which apparently showed his agitation more clearly than he was comfortable with. He sighed.

"They certainly will. A talent like yours? They won't be able to resist temptation."

"But—"

"But I think we can control it to a certain extent, if you want that. If not, we can try to wiggle out of it."

"Which probably won't work." Andi started stroking the edge of his bowl with his fingertips. Without a word, George took it from him to refill it.

"Thank you."

"Always."

"I guess wiggling out of it isn't our best bet." Andi took the spoon to stir the soup. "Can we use it to our advantage? I mean, more money and somebody up there knowing why my cases go the way they do doesn't sound so bad."

"It doesn't, no. And yes, we can use it to our advantage. Gelman did say that backing out was an option, but I'm sure they'll find ways to make us cooperate."

"Then let's cooperate and take all the candy they offer. It's probably for the best. It'll free up some of our time if we don't have to fabricate plausible evidence and clues anymore."

"Sounds good."

Andi furrowed his brow over the bowl. "You don't sound happy." He lifted his gaze. "You're unsure, afraid, nervous, glad, I think because everything went okay, and still a little angry." The last was said with a slight pitch, indicating a question. It reminded George that even if Andi was able to read his moods accurately, he couldn't always put things into context. Communication was still important.

"I'm not entirely sure what to make of Gelman and the Office, and I'm surely going to fret about it for some time until we have some experience with them. As for the rest—this case has taken a lot out of us, Andi."

His partner looked down into his bowl, where the remaining soup was going cold. "You mean them coming to me?"

"I mean the bees swarming to you and sitting on you. I mean the spider interacting with you as if you were one being. I mean several hives and countless wood-dwelling arthropods coming to the rescue and killing a killer. I'm not exactly surprised because I always wondered if the *geschenk* only works in one direction, which it obviously doesn't. I'm worried, though. Back in the woods, you were out, Andi. All clammy and cold, almost like a corpse yourself. What happened exactly, and what can I do to make it less scary in the future?" George hadn't planned on unleashing his full worries on Andi while his partner was still suffering the aftereffects of close proximity with his tiny informants, but somehow, his mouth hadn't gotten the memo.

Andi inhaled deeply. "I'm not exactly sure what happened. I mean, I've been overwhelmed before. The situation in the bunker wasn't my first encounter with a feeding frenzy. It never affected me so badly." He lifted his hand to stop George from saying something. Andi really did know him too well. "I thought it was because I still hadn't recuperated from the Portius/Miller/McHill case. Which was a valid assumption. And the bees—well, bees have always been special. More so than wasps or ants or other social insects. I think it's because they are domesticated. Anyway, the incident at House Cusabo with them wasn't scary. At least not in hindsight. And in the woods…." Andi closed his eyes. "I was at my very limit, physically and psychically. Too wide-open to have any control left. Which is usually the space where new developments occur."

George grabbed his bowl so hard, he felt the blood being pressed back from his fingers. "I should have told Norris we couldn't take the case and to hell with the consequences." He was getting ready to lunge into a full rant about everything he should have done differently—and there were a lot of things he could think of—when he felt Andi's hand on his, soothing, reassuring, sucking the tension away, letting the blood return to his fingers.

"It was a decision we made together, and I don't regret it. If we hadn't taken the case, Tyler would now probably be dead. That alone is reason enough to be glad how things turned out. And if it hadn't happened during this case, it would have happened with the next or the one after. You know it, George. The *geschenk* can't be stopped. At least now with Luke, we have something tangible, somebody to rely on, even if he's only helping us for his own gain. Barely a year ago, I was all alone. I had nobody and was headed straight for a mental breakdown. Then I got you, and now we have this ominous Office as well. For the first time, I don't feel completely isolated, George. Of course I would prefer if the *geschenk* would slow down so I get some time to breathe, but for the first time in very long, I have hope. What I felt with them, it was overwhelming, too much, and yet not enough. I will have to explore it, experiment to find the boundaries of what I can do. With you by my side, I'm willing to take the risk. Which is a lot more than I would have done before I met you. So no regrets. No self-reprimanding. We look forward, not back."

George stared at Andi. "Thank you. I needed to hear that." He took both bowls to put them in the dishwasher. "Do you want to go back to bed or nap on the sofa for a bit?"

"Are you going to watch a game?"

"Yes."

"Then the sofa." Andi got up. "I love cuddling with you."

George felt a broad smile tugging on his lips. Whatever the future might bring, now, at this very moment, they had a comfy sofa, some gripping college sport on TV, and each other. Life could be a lot worse.

It was the afternoon of their second day at home after Tyler had been found. The boy had briefly called and talked to Andi on the phone, telling him that from now on he would see every creepy crawler as a tiny hero and that he was trying to talk his parents into getting him bees. Andi was on the sofa, dozing while watching the history channel, some documentary about the Celts, while George was busy preparing their dinner. Kneading the dough for rigatoni left his mind free to ponder everything that had happened the past two days. He still didn't know how Luke had managed to get them four days of leave, and he had the strong suspicion it was to show them how well the Office would take care of them should they decide to work for them. It also meant George and Andi had gotten a first taste of how long the Office's arm was, even if it was in a small way. As Andi had accurately pointed out, working with the Office was inevitable. All they had to do was make sure it happened on their terms. Even though they were both curious concerning the details of their case— Geena had apparently led the raid of Zane Werner's house, one of the two new suspects Shireen had dug up before everything went sideways, and had found plenty of evidence there—they had asked to be left alone until they returned to the precinct. Because the killer was dead, getting their reports done wasn't as pressing as with other cases, which allowed them to get the rest they so desperately needed. Work would wait.

When the doorbell rang, George put the dough on a plate to rest. They weren't expecting anybody, and Andi was still a bit woozy, so whoever it was wouldn't make it across the threshold. Or so he thought until he saw Chief Norris standing there, her face a forced mask of indifference, her eyes displaying so many emotions George didn't even try to decipher them.

"Chief Norris."

"Detective Donovan. May I come in?"

George hesitated. Like with Gelman, the talk with Norris had to happen and soon, but George wasn't keen on it being at this very moment. The chief had obviously picked up on his inner conflict because she held up one hand.

"I'm not here to make a scene or anything. We need to talk, and there's a few things I have to say to both of you. Please?"

George stepped back to let her inside. "Come in."

He led the chief to the living room, where Andi was now sitting upright, the TV switched off.

"Chief Norris."

"Detective Hayes. I hope you're feeling better?"

It was literally the first time the chief had ever inquired about their well-being. Hearing the words was a little shock for George. The chief must have seen something in his expression because a wry smile flickered over her face. "I am capable of being civil, Detective Donovan."

"I never doubted it."

An uncomfortable silence settled between them, Andi on the couch, the chief and George standing a few feet apart, like a triangle of doom. George cleared his throat. "May I offer you something to drink? Tea, perhaps? I still have some chamomile left, or I could brew you something spicier, with cinnamon and cardamom?"

"No, thank you. As I said, there are some things I have to say, and if it's okay with you, I'd like to get it over with."

"Fair enough." Andi leaned back on the pillows, the bags under his eyes not as bad as they had been in the morning. "Begin."

Chief Norris started pacing in front of them, her hands clasped behind her back. "First of all, I want to thank you for saving Tyler. Both of you. I know he would be dead if it weren't for you."

George nodded. "It's our job, and Tyler is a wonderful boy. You're lucky to have such a great son."

"I know. I'm just afraid I don't show him how much I love him nearly often enough."

"He knows you love him. What he needs is for you to accept him the way he his." Andi's tone was soft, contradicting the sharp meaning of his words.

Norris made a strange sound between a laugh and a sob. Her eyes were glistening. "That's the other thing I need you to understand, though Agent Gelman has hinted you know already. My father—he was like Tyler. Like you, Detective Hayes. In fact, the reason I've been making your life hell is because you remind me of him. Every time I look at you, I see the grumpy man who had no love for anybody, who kept to himself, was always right and acted as if the world owed him something. The way you shut others out, ignore authority, and just generally do whatever you want, it's like he's back, haunting me."

George looked at Andi, who didn't seem surprised by this outburst. His partner just sighed. "Let me guess. He never let you close, never told you he loved you, just wanted you to function and not make any hassle because he was always busy, always preoccupied with things you couldn't grasp? It's a shitty thing to do to a kid. And I'm not going to tell you what he did was right, because it wasn't. All I can say to you is that he was even more miserable than you. Gelman told us that he was born with his talent, just like Tyler, and that these things get stronger with the years. If Tyler is any indication, your father must have lived with thousands of ghosts constantly vying for his attention. Being dragged in so many different directions, something has to give. Being sociable takes the most effort and energy, so it goes first. Simple math."

Norris's shoulders sagged. "Is it like that for you? I don't even know what exactly your… talent is."

Andi looked at George, silently asking him for advice. George shrugged. The chief already knew something, and with a son who talked to ghosts, they might as well tell her what Andi could do. A smile flitted over Andi's lips. George basked in the knowledge how much his partner, his lover, trusted him.

"I refer to my talent as *geschenk*, that's what my *Oma* called it. I have it from her. As for what I can do, I'm connected to all the arthropods within a half-mile radius, and I can expand that radius if I wish so. I can't stop it. The images are always there, which is the main reason I come across as grumpy. Balancing the different ways I sense the world takes up so much energy, I have none left for politeness. Some days, I don't even have enough to feed myself."

Chief Norris wiped her eyes. "Sounds a lot like my father. He was always… somewhere else. And knowing there were others in the room with us, even if I couldn't see them, even if they weren't a threat to me…. It was creepy and hurtful because these other people seemed to be so much more important than me."

"They weren't. They were just more persistent. I honestly don't know how it is with ghosts, though from what I've learned from Tyler they show varying degrees of understanding, just like living people, which means your father was probably never able to get a moment of silence. And from painful experience I can tell you that's bound to make you—unlovable."

George stepped to Andi to put a hand on his shoulder. "You're not unlovable. You do your best."

Andi looked up at George with a weak smile. "I wasn't talking about myself. I meant my *Oma*." He turned his gaze back to Chief Norris. "My *Oma* had it too, the *geschenk*. We're not supposed to speak ill of the dead, but she wouldn't mind, because she never minded anything in her life. She was a nasty old bitch who took pleasure in other people's misery because she herself was miserable all the time. Not that it stopped her from using her *geschenk* in any way she saw fit. I hate her to this day, though I have to admit I'm beginning to understand how a great deal of her unpleasantness was coping mechanisms. I'm not so different from her, and I'm not saying it's okay. All I'm saying is that the human mind can bear only so much till it fractures. Friendliness and morals are fragile things. They tend to break first."

The chief stared at Andi with her mouth hanging open. "That's actually the most accurate description of my father I've ever heard." She slumped down on the armchair next to her. For a moment, silence reigned, not yet uncomfortable but on the way. Before George could no longer suppress the need to lighten the mood, the chief started talking again. "I'm going to be honest with you, Hayes, Donovan. I have no idea how I'm going to be able to cope with all this madness. Actually talking to you, knowing what's going on, helps me to understand better, but years of ingrained hatred are hard to shake, as you can imagine." When George opened his mouth to answer, she held up her hand. "As I said, Gelman has already talked to me about you and Tyler, and he has made it very clear who is expendable and who is not. He has offered me another precinct, and I seriously considered it."

"But you didn't take the offer. Why?" George thought he knew. Better to hear it from the chief, though.

"Tyler. Moving again wouldn't be good for him, and, well, he can't stop talking about you, Hayes. I've never seen my son so happy, so carefree. Because he now has somebody who believes him. I can't take that away from him."

"It's not about believing." Andi leaned his head against George's thigh. He did that a lot, seeking contact. George didn't mind in the least. "Don't get me wrong, finding somebody who believes you is great. Finding somebody who *knows*? That's close to impossible."

George felt the muscles in his neck tensing. On a deeper level he understood that Andi wasn't slighting him, that his words were a statement of facts, not a complaint. It still tore at his pride, while at the same time his heart bled for his partner and lover. Imagining the loneliness Andi had to endure, the feeling of being cut off from the rest of the world because of something he had no control over—it was devastating. As if he had read his thoughts, more likely the change in his pheromones, Andi took George's hand in his. Chief Norris watched, not commenting. Instead, she straightened in her seat.

"I can't promise you roses from now on, Detectives. There will certainly be times when I wish nothing more than to strangle you slowly and vice versa. What I will promise you, though, and not just because you saved Tyler and Gelman has threatened me in no uncertain terms, is to give my best to be open from now on and to have your back like I should have from the beginning."

She started to rise, and Andi did so as well, taking George with him. Andi actually smiled. "That's all we're asking. And I promise to try and keep in mind where you're coming from."

The chief lifted a brow. "No promises of changing your ways?" George couldn't believe it. There was a hint of amusement in her voice. Was she really trying to make a joke? It seemed so, because she relaxed a bit more.

"I think everybody here knows that would be impossible. Lenience is all I can offer." He held out his hand. Norris took it.

"I'll take it." She offered George her hand as well. After they shook, she turned toward the front door. "I also wouldn't mind if you spent some time with Tyler. If that's okay for you?"

"Gladly. He's a good kid." Andi slumped back onto the sofa. The interaction had probably drained him.

George escorted the chief out of the house before he went back to his dough. It was time to have a meal.

22. Happy Endings Everywhere

"Ooh, look what the cat dragged in!" Geena strode toward Andi and George with a big grin on her face when they entered the bullpen. Their four days of rest were up, and there were reports that needed to be written. Andi was also curious what Geena had found at Zane Werner's house. They still didn't know what had made Werner kill all those people.

"Geena, so nice to see you again." George made a face while hugging her.

She turned to Andi, spread her arms, and started grinning like a loon when he shied away from her. "Just kidding. I'd never dream of touching you, Hayes. You're not my type." She winked.

"You're evil." There wasn't much heat behind his words because he was still mellow from their free time.

"I get to be. You caught the killer without me, which wasn't very gentlemanly of you."

"We're sorry, Geena. I'm sure the meeting with your supervisor was worth it." George marched toward their desks, nodding at all the colleagues shouting their congratulations at them. Tobias and Sandra got up from their desks to greet them, clapping his back and following him through the bullpen.

"Asshole." Geena overtook George before they reached the desks with the whiteboards. "I did get to snoop through Werner's house, though, so I'm willing to forgive you." She beamed at them like somebody had told her she could have all the cake in the world.

George cocked his head. "Why do I have the feeling you have exciting news?"

"Because I do!" Geena stepped aside, making a broad gesture at the whiteboards. They looked a lot more organized, with neat arrows pointing between tidy lines of names, dates, and locations.

"You changed the whiteboard!" George tried for indignant, not fooling anybody. Andi could feel his happiness thrumming in the air, sparkling yellow and turquoise, smelling of apples and strawberries.

"Sorry, not sorry. I had to. It was chaos anyway." Geena motioned for them to get in front of the whiteboards. "So, we had some loose ends, some questions we couldn't answer. At his house, I found Zane Werner's diaries. Yes, you heard right: the man wrote every day, and what can I say? Suddenly it all makes sense. Terrible sense, but sense."

"Stop teasing us, Geena. Start talking." George was reading the whiteboards, just like Andi. And just like Andi he couldn't make full sense of them, as evidenced by the fluctuations in his pheromones. He was mildly annoyed, though not stressed because he knew they would get the explanation now. Next to them, Tobias and Sandra were grinning like loons. Sandra even went so far as to bump Andi with her elbow, but she let Geena do the talking.

"Fine. You're taking all the fun out of it." Geena grabbed a black marker to use as a pointer. "Let's start at the beginning. Zane Werner moved to Charleston in 2018 and started working at House Cusabo in 2019, the year Lori Heller, Ben Los Santos, Joshua Baluyot, and a Joe Doe were killed. We initially ruled him out because while possible, driving down from Spartanburg, where he'd been living before, for the killing of TJ, Celia, and the others who came before 2019 seemed unlikely. As his diaries revealed, he had lived in Charleston before, as a child, and his neighbor was no other than TJ. Shireen didn't find Werner because back then he lived with his mother, who had taken on her maiden name. Zane missed his father and took on his last name as soon as he turned eighteen and could legally do so. He then spent time in Spartanburg, where he saw TJ regularly. Apparently, they were friends, both working for the same construction company.

"And here's the bomb. Werner had been obsessed with bees from a young age. We don't know why he wasn't a member of the same beekeeper club as Bruce Sprenger and Marcus Kespers, but there were twenty hives in the garden of his house and countless books on bees and beekeeping inside. He mentions quite early on, while he and TJ still lived in Charleston, that the bees wanted to 'lead TJ to the safety of eternal rest' and that he hesitated to listen to them because he didn't want to hurt his friend."

"Oh man." George whistled. "Gelman's second guess was right—religiously motivated but no psychopath. Explains the tranquilizer."

Geena nodded. "It gets better. TJ was sent to House Cusabo in 2011 to treat his bipolarity. Zane visited him regularly, though under his mother's last name, which is one reason why Shireen didn't find him on the guest lists, the other being that they only started having them in digitalized form at the end of 2012. Otherwise he would have gotten on our suspect radar a lot sooner. He wrote in his diary the bee queen told him to use the other name. I can't tell from his writing if this is him preparing to become a killer or if he was simply paranoid at the time. That's one for the pros to untangle. In December 2012, Werner mentions Celia, saying he doesn't think she's good for TJ and that he was going to try and talk him out of her."

"He shared this estimate with Reuben McDonald." George hummed.

"Yes. From then on, the entries get more frenzied, cursing Celia and TJ's stubbornness, rambling about the bees, how he has to do something. Then at the beginning of May, shortly before TJ went missing, Werner writes he doesn't want to harm his friend but sees no other way now that he's found the secret chamber."

"Secret chamber? The bunker?" George pointed at the word on the whiteboard.

"Yes. He didn't dig the chamber where he buried the bodies, and I'm afraid who did it is going to stay a secret. Perhaps somebody who wanted to take over the bunker and then thought better of it? We'll probably never know." She shrugged. "It's the least interesting part of the story anyway. Shireen checked, and on the day TJ vanished, Zane visited him. It was six hours before TJ was last seen in House Cusabo. Zane came back through a hole in the fence. He met TJ outside, gave him a soda laced with diazepam, and transported him to the bunker. There he cut off his pinkie toe as 'proof for the bee queen,' choked TJ with a belt he found at Goodwill, and buried him in the chamber. After that, the entries in his diary are a mixture of guilt and elation, showing clearly how he slips into killer mode."

"TJ was his trigger."

"Yes, his first kill. It took him till September to come to the conclusion that killing the people 'walking the edge' was his mission in life. Then he took Celia, offed her the same way he did TJ but left the belt with her because it was 'too clumsy.' There's several entries describing how he finally settled on the manila rope and also how he found his next victim."

"What about the beekeeper suit?" Andi really wanted to know if it had been part of Werner's delusion, or if it had been calculation.

"As it turns out, both you and Luke were right. Werner described it as his armor, given to him by the bee queen, but also describes explicitly how the armor prevents him from leaving evidence behind."

"He was off his rocker and present at the same time. Fascinating." George tapped his thigh in a lazy rhythm.

"Yeah. As for Izzy Whitewall, Werner writes about her that she's a danger to his mission because she 'sees the bees for what they are.' Tina was right. Her sister had found something out, which made her the next victim. Kesha found something out as well. Werner rants about her poking her nose in his business and that he couldn't get a hold of her."

"How did he manage in the end?" Again George, his upper body slightly bent forward to not miss a thing.

"He stole the keys to LeClerk's apartment during one of his shifts, made a copy and then broke into LeClerk's apartment when both he and Kesha were gone, laced the water he knew she preferred with tranquilizer, and waited till she came home and drank it. It was risky, considering she was living with LeClerk, but he did it anyway to be able to carry on with his mission. Werner does mention how he checked LeClerk's schedule to be sure Kesha would be alone." Geena sighed. "According to his diaries, she was too close to finding him out."

They all were silent for a moment, thinking of the woman who almost caught the madman.

"Anyway, after he killed Marco Flores, he started writing that he should kill at least six people this year. He realized the bunker had been found three days after you searched for Tyler. And we were right about that as well. He never went inside the bunker in between kills, but he hiked there often to be close to the souls he had 'freed.' After it was obvious he couldn't stash his victims there anymore, the entries get frenzied. He was looking for a new place, mentioning the bunker he took Tyler to, but dismissing it as too small. Not appropriate. Then it was revealed that Tyler had found the bodies, and he became obsessed with him. Wrote that the boy was like Izzy, seeing through the veil, whatever that meant. His conclusion was that when he killed Tyler, he could go on with his mission, like it had been after he ended Izzy."

"And he might have been successful." George groaned.

"He wasn't, though. He made a mistake and you caught him. Killed him. Same difference." Geena smiled with a hint of sorrow in her eyes. "There's twenty-six victims we couldn't save, but if he hadn't been stopped, how many more would have died?"

"Thankfully, we'll never find out." George stared at the whiteboard. "It all makes a horrific kind of sense, in hindsight. I'm just glad it's over."

Andi stroked his back. The conclusion of a case always opened up a sense of limbo. As stressed as they had been with this one, the feeling was even stronger. Like falling after the rope you've been clutching too tightly crumbles and vanishes beneath your fingers. Luckily, Andi knew what would bring back a sense of balance.

"Let's write our reports."

They all groaned in unison. "I hate you, Hayes." Sandra hit him on his upper arm. It hurt because that woman didn't pull her punches. "After all the paperwork Tobias and I had to wade through for this case, I'd say it's only fair if you wrote our reports as well."

Tobias perked up. "I second that. Very strongly."

"Forget it." George pushed the two detectives in the general direction of their desks. "See it as the fitting conclusion of your truly remarkable work." He turned serious. "Really, thank you. Without you two, we wouldn't have been able to pull this off."

"You could show your appreciation by buying us another round of donuts." Tobias winked. "Believe a seasoned detective, sugar goes a long way toward making report-writing bearable."

"I'll keep that in mind. Now get on with the writing." George made a shooing motion, and Sandra and Tobias went off to their desks.

Andi watched their retreating backs for a moment, felt their contentment about a case they could close. It was a sentiment Andi shared fully.

IN THE afternoon, they drove out to Fenwick Hills to visit Tyler. Chief Norris had asked them to do so after they had finished their reports, saying they could take the rest of the day off. Geena had to finish some additional writing for the FBI, and they agreed to meet later for celebratory pizza at Da Tosto's with the entire team, including the two beat officers who had done a lot of the leg work.

Tyler's father greeted them happily. He couldn't stop expressing his gratitude until Tyler told him he wanted to talk to Andi and George alone. Aloys Norris winked at Andi conspiratorially before he went back to his studio. Andi and George followed Tyler to the front yard and out onto the street. After a ten-minute walk, Tyler stopped at the small hill from where they had first seen the copse. Andi put a hand on the boy's shoulder.

"How are you, Tyler?"

"I'm good. Mom told me about Grandpa."

Andi felt George tensing beside him. "Was it bad?" his partner asked.

Tyler shook his head. "It wasn't pleasant, but it explains a lot. She knows but doesn't want to. I'm just not sure if that's better than what Dad does, not knowing and trying to humor me, or worse or the same."

"You will see. I'm sure there'll be times when you prefer your mother's take on things and others when you'll turn to your father." Andi wasn't sure if his words were true. His own father had never tried to understand Andi. He didn't want to discourage the boy. There was enough of that in his future, as Andi well knew.

"I guess." Tyler stared down into the copse. "I asked Mom if you could come today because they're ready."

"The ghosts?" George stepped a little closer, putting his hand on Tyler's other shoulder.

"Yes. They want to go home. It's time."

"And you wanted to share it with us?" Andi was curious.

"No. They wanted you to be there. They know what you did. And Izzy says you can sense them?"

"Only as electrical disturbances. Not like you do."

"Still, you know. Sometimes knowing is all we have. All they have." Tyler lifted his hands, putting them on Andi's and George's. "They look like children again. Izzy says being a child means being free of the chains the grown-up world forces on us. She says it's the greatest freedom—not understanding what makes no sense anyway."

"Don't we all want that?" George sighed.

"They're getting all light. The sun is shining through them." Tyler's voice turned into a monotone. For the first time Andi understood why it freaked George out so much when he did it—knowing Tyler wasn't fully present anymore, instead making room for something completely different, was disturbing. "Thank you for stopping him, thank you for saving Tyler, thank you for bringing us peace. Tell Tina to stop worrying and start living. I don't regret anything. I love her. Thomas, he needs protection. Tell him I want him to be happy. Thank you, thank you, thank you."

Tyler stood absolutely still for a moment. Then he shook himself like a kitten that had gotten wet. "That's it. They're gone."

"Are you sad?" Andi squeezed the boy's shoulder.

"A bit. They were great company. Better than most living people I know."

"I can relate. Nevertheless, we have to deal with this world, whether we like it or not." Andi winked at George, taking the sting out of his words. He knew his partner was worried about him deciding to not come back one day. It was tempting, Andi wouldn't deny it. But in George he had found a strong reason to keep his ties to reality.

They brought Tyler home, talked to Aloys for a bit, before they went back to Charleston to meet their team at the pizza place.

"AND I say, anchovies have no place on a pizza. Actually, they have no place in a kitchen." Geena mock shuddered. "Disgusting salty little things."

"Says the woman who has pineapple on her pizza." Andi looked up from his spaghetti aglio e olio. George noted with some satisfaction that his partner had already eaten the small salad George had insisted on ordering for him. In his opinion, there could never be enough greens on a plate. He was the first to admit, though, that no salad could hold a candle to the fresh bread Da Tosto's served with their salads. Still warm, crunchy without being dry, the middle perfectly moist. It had successfully tempted him to let his rules about carbohydrates lay by the wayside for this evening.

"George? What's your take on this?" Geena prodded him with the back end of her fork.

"Yeah, George, tell her we can't believe we worked with somebody who eats pineapple on a pizza!" Tobias stuffed another bite of bread into his mouth while Andi was busy twirling noodles around his fork. Sandra made a face at the mention of pineapples, and the two beat officers snickered. They were young, in their early twenties, and George remembered too well what he had considered perfectly edible food at that age. Sometimes, getting older wasn't only bad.

"Well, at least pineapple is a fruit and therefore healthy." George lifted a brow. Andi pretended to stab him with his knife.

"Everything has to be healthy with you."

"Works for him, obviously." Geena speared a piece of soggy pineapple on her fork, pointed at George in a gesture of triumph before putting it in her mouth. "This is probably the best pizza I've ever eaten."

"It's because of the stone oven. An electric oven just doesn't get the temperature right." Tobias gestured at the center of the restaurant, where a huge pizza oven with brightly burning logs allowed the guests to see how their pizzas baked within minutes.

"If you say so." Geena cut off another piece of pizza. "I'm still glad I'm going home to Virginia tomorrow. This case sucked." She looked at them. "Not the colleagues, obviously, just the case."

"That's serial killers for you." George shrugged. "I'm not sure if the worst thing about this case was the number of victims or the fact that Werner killed them because of something he himself suffered from. He might not have been depressive or bipolar, but he certainly was delusional."

"To be honest, I'm glad he wasn't doing it for fun. I once had a case where a psychopath drove knives into his victims and filmed their faces because he wanted to capture the essence of pain. At least Werner thought he was helping them, twisted as it was." Geena stared at her plate, where only a small triangle was left.

"It's part of our job, unfortunately, that we see the worst humankind has to offer." George offered Andi a piece of his pizza with artichokes and dried tomatoes. Andi took it, pushing his plate with the pasta in George's direction.

"I know you probably don't want to hear it, but you two are really cute together." Geena lifted her glass of soda in a toast. "It was my pleasure working with you. You've been the first detectives in a long time that weren't territorial assholes." She swiveled her glass in the direction of Sandra, Tobias, and the beat officers. "The same applies to you."

"Likewise." George lifted his glass, saw Andi and the others doing the same. "Working with other agencies is rarely fun, and honestly, we were worried how things would play out with you. Our dynamic isn't easy to accept."

"Amen to that." Geena grinned. Sandra just shook her head, and Tobias rolled his eyes. "Your big bonus was the complete absence of maliciousness and arrogance. I could sense you weren't doing things to keep me out. You simply had problems adjusting to another dynamic where there's three instead of you two."

"They're not team players, these two." Tobias contemplated a forkful of lasagna before he stuffed it into his mouth.

"We did our best," George protested mildly. He didn't say more because Tobias was right. Andi was the very definition of a single player, and while George had always understood that working with a team was usually the way forward, he had to admit, at least to himself, that doing things Andi's way was a lot better than constantly minding other people's sensitivities. He tried the spaghetti. It was as good as the pizza.

"Thank you for being understanding." Andi managed a smile for Geena. "Even if you like fruit on your pizza."

She laughed. "Do you know what the absolute best is? Pizza with Nutella. We have this restaurant in my hometown where they serve it as dessert. It's absolutely delicious."

"It would be worth a try if George hadn't put a ban on Nutella. Too much sugar *and* palm oil. It's practically evil incarnated."

"Hey. I'm just being conscious of our planet's future! And your weight."

"Uh, George, I hate to break this to you, but Andi could definitely do with a little more fat." Sandra indicated Andi's form with the last piece of crust in her hand.

"More weight, yes, gaining it from pure sugar laced with palm oil, no." George crossed his arms in front of his chest. This was where he drew the line.

"If you ever want pizza with Nutella, come visit me. I'll hook you up." Geena's bad impersonation of a dealer had Andi laughing.

"I'll keep it in mind."

The rest of the evening went by in the same vein, with playful banter and tiramisu for them all. When it was time to say goodbye to Geena, George actually felt a twinge of sadness. She had been a wonderful partner. They hugged, even Andi allowed the physical contact, promised to keep in touch, which George had every intention to do, because having friends in other agencies was a wise move, and then watched as Geena drove away in her rented car. She would be catching a flight early in the morning and not getting much sleep.

After they had bid Tobias, Sandra, and the two beat officers a goodnight, George drove back to Andi's house, where they brushed their teeth, changed into their pajamas, and went to bed. Andi's back was snuggled close to George's front, his lover's dirty-blond hair tickling his chin. George drew lazy circles on Andi's right hip, trying to ignore how prominent the hip bone was.

"Stop worrying. I'm here. I'm fine. We caught the killer. We can take a break."

"You know worrying is my default state?"

"Yes. Stop it." Andi's voice was already drowsy with sleep.

George pressed a kiss to his temple, getting a satisfied sigh in return.

"Good night, George."

"Good night, Andi."

Only a few moments later, George heard Andi's breathing evening out. Automatically, he matched his rhythm, feeling Andi's heartbeat in his palm when he put his hand on his partner's chest.

Whump, whump, whump. Steady, strong, victorious. Andi was here, their breath flowing in sync, in and out, the waves washing onto the shore, skittering back into the ocean, taking with them the stress, the pain, the worry.

George knew there was more to come; the beach was huge, expanding farther than the eye could see. But right here, right now?

There was peace.

George closed his eyes, sinking beneath the waves.

Keep reading for an exclusive excerpt from
In His Sights,
the first book in the Second Sight series
by K.C. Wells

CHAPTER 1

Boston, MA. Tuesday May 15, 2018

DETECTIVE GARY Mitchell took one look at the naked dead man lying facedown on the bed and his day officially went to shit.

Aw Christ, not another one.

The bedroom was an eerie carbon copy of the previous crime scenes. A small bottle sat on the nightstand, and Gary didn't need to see the label to know it contained GHB. On the bed beside the body were a tangle of red rope and a pair of handcuffs. He glanced at the rug, and sure enough, there was the soiled condom. Gary returned his attention to the deceased, noting the marks on the wrists and ankles, just like the previous victims.

This one struggled too. At least until the drugs kicked in. It was all supposition until the autopsy, but Gary saw no reason why the killer would change his MO. It hadn't gotten him caught so far, right? Why change a winning formula? The thought made Gary's blood run cold.

But what made his heart sink was the bloodstain on the corner of the white sheet that covered the guy's lower back.

"We've already taken photos of the scene." Detective Riley Watson picked up the condom with his nitrile-covered hand and dropped it into an evidence bag, then sealed it. He scowled. "God, I wanna catch this bastard." He scribbled on the label, noting the time.

Gary didn't respond. There was no need. They all wanted that.

Detective Lewis Stevens stood next to Del Maddox, the medical examiner. Lewis stared at the sheet, then raised his gaze to meet Gary's. "Wonder what it's gonna be this time?"

"Maybe he's obliged us by signing his handiwork," Del muttered. He pulled back the sheet with care and sighed. "Here we go again."

A letter *X* was carved into the victim's lower back.

"Done before death occurred, like the others?" Gary inquired. The amount of blood pointed to that conclusion.

Del nodded. "Looks like he used the same implement too."

Lewis grimaced. "Jesus. I hoped we'd seen the last of this guy."

"You and me both." Riley peered at him. "I bet it's days like this that make you sorry you ever left Vice. Chelmsford PD get a lot of these kinda cases?"

Lewis shook his head. "Never saw anything like this."

"Give it time," Del observed. "You've only been in Homicide for what, four years? Wait till you've been at it for as long as I have." He gazed at the deceased, and Gary noted the compassionate glance. "He could be my age."

"Can we save the chat for later and concentrate on doing our jobs?" Gary's stomach roiled, and a rock had taken up residence in his chest.

Lewis was silent, but his scowl said plenty. Riley gave a respectful nod and withdrew to talk to the uniform boys.

Del glanced at the nightstand. "Thoughtful of the killer to leave the drug. Now I know what to look for in the tox screen. Except if he's anything like the previous victims, there'll be a whole cocktail of drugs inside him." He addressed Gary. "How many of these guys do we have so far?"

"He's number five." Another one to add to the board. *Any more and we'll need another board.* Gary couldn't suppress his shiver.

Del pursed his lips. "So, five letters now. Anyone succeeded in making a word from the previous four?"

"None that make any sense."

"The killer's probably a Scrabble player with a list of obscure words." Both Gary and Lewis gaped at him. Del pushed out another sigh. "Sorry, guys. I'm as gutted as you are, but humor is my default when I don't want to think about a maniac being out there." He gestured to the body. "Help me roll him so I can take a look at the front."

The three men gently rolled the body with a care that was almost reverential. The man's wide staring eyes threatened to unravel Gary's self-control, and he had to force himself to shut off his emotions and look at the body objectively. The victim was maybe in his mid to late forties, with a salt-and-pepper beard and dark brown hair tinged with silver at the temples. A handsome man who'd clearly kept himself in good shape.

I hope you didn't suffer. Except Gary knew it was a false hope. The knowledge that he'd been cut before death and the bruising on the guy's wrists and ankles were grim indicators to the contrary.

Del gestured to his assistants who were standing to one side, maintaining a respectful silence. "Okay, boys." They lifted the corpse and placed it in an open body bag. Gary watched as they zipped it closed, obliterating his view of that staring face. They hoisted the bag onto a stretcher before carrying it out of the apartment. Riley bagged up the cuffs, rope, and bottle and handed them to one of the assistants, along with the bag containing the condom, to accompany the body to the morgue.

Del stripped off his gloves. "I'll get onto this one first thing tomorrow morning." He peered at Gary. "I'll see you there?"

Gary nodded. He knew Lewis wouldn't attend. He'd barfed at his first autopsy, and that was the last time he'd visited the morgue.

Del followed his assistants to the front door. The police officer let them through before reattaching the yellow tape that barred entrance to those neighbors who tried to get a glimpse. The officer was polite but firm, and the rubberneckers soon gave up.

Gary's hackles rose. *Yeah, someone is dead. You can read all about it in the media tomorrow.* Christ, number four had made the headlines before the ink was dry on Gary's report. He breathed deeply. His energies were best directed to the case.

Riley came over. "The victim's name was Marius Eisler, age forty-five." Gary's stomach clenched, but he pushed down hard on the momentary flash of nausea that always accompanied a surge of grief.

Keep focused.

Riley continued. "The body was discovered at twenty-three-hundred hours by the guy from the apartment next door, one Billy Raymond. He had a key. He said Marius had a habit of working late and not eating properly, so Billy regularly dropped by with food. He didn't see anyone. Uniforms have questioned everyone on this floor, but no one saw our man."

"Too much to hope there are cameras?" Gary asked.

Riley snorted. "Sure, they have cameras in the hallway downstairs, but they don't work. The neighbors said there were always guys coming and going."

Lewis rolled his eyes. "Another queer? Now *there's* a surprise." Riley fired him a disgusted glance.

Gary didn't bother reining in his glare. "I'm going to pretend I didn't hear you say that. Now why don't you go speak with Sergeant Michaels? See what else you can learn about the victim, the building…."

Lewis's brow furrowed, but he went without a word.

Gary breathed a little easier. He didn't need Lewis's shit right then. He scanned the bedroom. "No sign of a cell phone?"

Riley shook his head. "Just like the others. We've searched the whole apartment." He gazed at the rumpled sheets on the bed. "I'll bag these too." Riley glanced toward the door with a distant stare. "This was one talented guy. Did you see his paintings?"

Gary hadn't seen a thing. He'd been in too much of a rush to prove that nagging feeling in his gut wrong.

One look at the blood on the sheet had confirmed his fears.

"Our killer's not in any hurry, is he? Five bodies in two years." Riley's shoulders slumped. "I really thought he was done. Nothing since December."

Gary had hoped the same thing. "What worries me is those letters. How many bodies are there going to be before whatever it is he's spelling out begins to make sense and we get a lead?" Because so far they'd had precious few of those.

He walked into the living room, leaving Riley to remove the sheets from the bed, and paused to get a feel for the place. The heavily varnished wooden floor and oak furniture gave the apartment an elegant appearance. It wasn't cluttered, and judging by the size of the windows, Gary imagined it would be a light, airy room in the daylight. Every inch of available wall space was taken up with paintings of men. Some of the models were clothed, but most were nude or seminude, and all of them were good-looking. An easel stood by the window, a table next to it on which sat an open box filled with squeezed tubes of oil paint. A glass jar filled with dirty liquid held three long thin paintbrushes, and there was a palette covered with blobs of paint, a layer of clear wrap laid over it. A couple of rags smeared with colors sat beside the palette, and the odor of turpentine lingered in the air.

Gary went closer to look at the canvas sitting on the easel. It was a detailed study of a middle-aged man, clothed, sitting in a wide armchair, the same chair that stood beside the comfy-looking couch. The artist had yet to work on the clothing; the model's shirt was blocked in solid colors, shades of dark and light.

And now he'll never get to finish it.

Riley joined him. "According to the neighbor, this is how the victim earned his living. I googled him. Pretty well-known artist. I'll see what else I can find out tomorrow." He inclined his head toward the door. "The CSIs are here to dust and document the scene."

Beside him, Sergeant Rob Michaels cleared his throat. "I'll secure the scene once all the evidence has been removed."

"Thanks, Rob."

Lewis came over to them. "I don't think there's anything else we can do here."

Gary had to agree. The day had almost ended, and he was in dire need of sleep. "I'll see you both in the morning. You can write your reports then." He bade a good-night to Rob, and once the officer at the door had let him out, he hurried along the hallway to the stairs, stripping off his gloves and stuffing them into the pocket of his jacket. Some doors were open, and residents peered out as he passed.

Gary paid them no mind. He was too busy thinking about their victim. *Please, God, let us catch him. Don't let there be a number six.*

GARY LET himself into his apartment and bolted the door behind him. The silence that greeted him held none of its usual comfort.

He knew why. All the way home, his head had been filled with thoughts of Brad. No, even before that. Memories of his late brother had suffocated him all day, to the point where he'd struggled to maintain his focus.

He'd have been forty-five today. The same age as Marius Eisler. It had taken every ounce of effort not to react when Riley had revealed the victim's age.

Gary trudged into the kitchen and peered into the fridge, not that he wanted anything. The neatly stacked microwave meals, bottles of iced tea and water, and foil-wrapped lump of cheese made the fridge's interior appear as minimalist as his apartment.

Despite his fatigue he wasn't ready for bed yet. Gary filled the kettle, then opened a cabinet to remove the box of chamomile tea. Its fragrance always soothed him, and right then he was in need of soothing.

When are we going to get a break? He loathed the hollowed-out feeling that pervaded each time he confronted their lack of success. The killer was either blessed with unholy luck or phenomenal planning skills. *How can he slip by unnoticed? Surely* someone *must have seen him.*

If they had, they had yet to come forward.

Sure, the police had the guy's DNA, thanks to the condoms, but he wasn't in the files. He left no prints, a fiber here and there, and appeared to have chosen victims who had a steady stream of male visitors. Lieutenant Travers had already intimated that the chief was making noises about bringing in more men. The shit had hit the fan after the discovery of victim number three, Geoff Berg, when some bright journalist had worked out all the victims were gay men.

Worked out, my ass. Someone leaked it.

The headlines had screamed Killer Targets Gay Men! for a couple of weeks, but as the months passed and no more bodies turned up, things quieted down. Thank God the letters had remained confidential. They had one tool left for weeding out the crank confessors. But that didn't relieve the resulting pressure Gary and his team found themselves under once news had gotten out.

The kettle whistled and he turned off the gas. As he poured water onto the tea bag, his phone pinged, and he glanced at the screen.

Still coming Sunday?

What the hell was his mom doing awake at this hour? Except he knew that was a stupid question. She'd been a poor sleeper for the past twenty-three years. As usual, cold fingers traced a path around his heart at the prospect of the monthly ritual of Sunday lunch. He hated himself for even thinking like that. Seeing his parents shouldn't be a burden, shouldn't fill him with apprehension.

But it did. And he knew he'd go, because not to would be unthinkable. Unforgivable.

He typed with his thumbs. *Sure.* There was no reply, but that was typical of his mom. Her texts were always succinct and infrequent.

Gary took his tea and went into his bedroom. He placed the cup on the nightstand. The closet door stood ajar, and Gary moved toward it without thinking. He stepped into the closet and headed for the built-in drawers. He paused, his hand on the knob, his heart racing.

Will it help?

He ignored the quiet inner voice. He opened the drawer and removed the folded sweater, inhaling as he held it close. Whatever scent it had possessed had long since disappeared.

Gary returned to his bed and sat in the center, pillows stuffed behind him. He buried his face in the soft yarn.

I'll find him, Brad. I promise. I haven't forgotten about you.

The reminder was etched onto Gary's skin.

CHAPTER 2

I PICKED up the red pen and walked over to the wall. "Goodbye, Marius," I intoned as I crossed out his face. Where the two thick strokes met, they obliterated his mouth. "Pity I couldn't have done that when you were alive." Anything not to have to listen to him drone on about his painting.

The four photos to Marius's left bore the same red cross. I gazed at the image on the right, enjoying the tingle that started in my chest, then spread outward. My stomach fluttered. Waiting was murder.

I grinned at my own joke. I had time to enjoy the intoxication a while longer, to bask in the radiant, fierce joy that had accompanied each death.

Marius's departure had been particularly delicious.

Once he'd gotten over his initial surprise—like the rest of them—he clearly relished the prospect of getting me in his bed. He wasn't on his guard. Why would he be? He knew me, after all. So easy to slip the Rohypnol into his glass and watch as he drifted into unconsciousness. And when he awoke, bewildered to discover he was naked, bound, and gagged, he'd pulled against his bonds. The sharp scratch as I administered the ketamine only added to his befuddled state.

I saw him resign himself to the act that was to follow. It was almost a pity to disillusion him.

Almost.

I waited until I'd filled him to the hilt before leaning forward to whisper in his ear.

Enjoy it. This is your last fuck. Because when I come?
You die.

And there it was, the ultimate thrill. Not penetrating that tight hole, not driving myself deep into him—that was an act to be *suffered*, not enjoyed. Even carving into his flesh brought merely a trickle of expectation. No, the anticipation of taking his life, of knowing he was unable to struggle against his bonds... *that* aroused me to the point of ejaculation.

I shivered. There would be time enough to dwell on Marius. The elation was still overwhelming. Another one gone.

I was in no hurry. My days had taken on a familiar pattern.

Erase one of those sluts from the planet.
Watch the news.
Add more names to the list.
Cross off the names of those who'd eliminated themselves.
Lay the groundwork for the next one.
Wash, rinse, repeat....

Only seventeen more to go. Seventeen men, out of a field rich with possibilities. The world would be all the better for the loss of those twenty-two souls. I'd have preferred a total of twenty-six, but it wouldn't fit.

Then again....

I might change my mind when I reach twenty-two. There are plenty of men to choose from, after all. And why stop if I'm getting away with it?

I gazed at the photo that took center stage, framed with bare wall, the images of my victims—actual and potential—kept at a distance so as not to taint it with their presence. Men like them had tainted him enough.

They're going to pay for what they did. And I've got nothing but time.

My gaze alighted on the image I'd already picked out. A definite possibility. My only difficulty?

I'd waited five months between victims, and it had been torture. It didn't matter that it had been the shortest time span thus far. I didn't think I could wait that long again. Not while the heightened emotions of the kill lingered still. Not with all those faces staring at me from the wall.

Not with *his* face gazing at me. His voice in my head.

"I'm doing this for you," I whispered. "To avenge you."

I had another motive too, one that suffocated me, haunted me, but I knew of one way to assuage that emotion.

I smiled at the image I'd selected. A handsome face with bright eyes and a firm jaw.

"You're next."

CHAPTER 3

DEL ARCHED his eyebrows as Gary walked into the morgue. "I thought I'd have seen you earlier than this. You're three hours late." He gestured to the sewn-up Y-incision. "Or did you stop by to complement me on my needlework?"

"I'm here for the edited highlights."

Marius Eisler lay on his back, the Y-incision the only visible evidence of the autopsy. Gary had watched Del at work on a couple of occasions and knew the reinforced thick twine that closed Del's cuts concealed the heavy-duty, leak-proof plastic bag containing the organs, hidden from sight in the empty chest cavity.

"Body fluids have already gone to Toxicology, but we know what I'm looking for."

"Your initial findings?" Gary knew better than to ask for more than that: it would be a while before the full autopsy report was finalized.

"As you correctly surmised, the letter was carved into the skin prior to death." Del's gaze bored into him. "And we know this how?"

"By the wound. Prior to death, the heart is working and blood is sent there. It has a different color, and the wound is significantly bloodier. After death, it's paler, more… withered, and there's less blood."

Del smiled. "Full marks, Detective. Good to know you've been listening. Although I'd expect nothing less from one of Boston's finest homicide detectives."

"I know there was a condom, but—"

"But you assume nothing, which is how it should be," Del interjected. "And yes, penetrative sex took place prior to death."

"Can you tell if it was nonconsensual?" The bruising on Marius's wrists and ankles appeared darker against the pale skin.

"Hard to tell." Del frowned. "Who's to say rough sex isn't consensual? There's some abrasion, some internal bruising, but nonrough sex can create some injury. What *you* want to know is if there was an overabundance of injury. There wasn't. As for the body fluids, I'll test for GHB, Rohypnol, ketamine, and barbiturates, although we found no GHB in the previous victims." His gaze flickered to the body on his table. "This one likes his routines." He frowned again. "So why does he leave the GHB at the scene? He doesn't leave any trace of the other drugs he uses. Is it some kind of message?"

Gary glanced at the table before meeting Del's gaze. "I'll be sure to ask him—once I catch the bastard."

"Where have you been?" Lewis demanded as soon as Gary walked into their office space.

Gary came to a halt. "One of us had to go talk to Del. Did *you* want to do it?" As if he didn't know the answer to that one.

"Okay, so I had a weak stomach that one time," Lewis countered. His mouth went down at the corners. "Travers wants to see us all, ASAP. Riley's already in there."

Aw crap.

Gary had a feeling a ton of shit was about to roll downhill, aimed right at him.

Without a word, he followed Lewis to the lieutenant's corner office. Riley sat facing Travers's desk, its surface invisible to the eye, hidden beneath an explosion of paper, folders, and coffee cups. Gary gave it a cursory glance before meeting Travers's stern gaze.

"It may look like the aftermath of a robbery, but trust me, it's organized chaos. I know where everything is, and I can lay my hand on anything in seconds."

Gary held up his hands. "Hey, I didn't say a word." He knew better.

"Your expression said enough." Travers pointed to the empty chairs next to Riley. "Sit." No sooner had Gary's ass touched the worn leather seat than Travers launched into his controlled rant. "So now we've got five bodies, and we're no closer to discovering who's trying to wipe out Boston's entire gay population." As usual, Travers didn't raise his voice. He didn't need to. His clipped tone was sharper than a razor, honed by years of practice.

"Hey, we don't know—"

Travers cut Riley off. "He's killed five. Who knows when he'll stop?" He picked up the folded newspaper from the top of a pile of others and tossed it at Gary. "We made ink again. Only now it's worse. The press has gotten hold of the stuff about the bondage gear. Great. That's just great." He squeezed the words through his teeth.

"I know you're pissed," Gary said, "but—"

"Pissed?" Travers glared at Gary. "I'm not pissed. Trust me, when I reach pissed, you'll know about it. The only thing saving your asses right now is that it hasn't gotten out yet about his little calling card. We've already had three guys stroll in here to confess to the killings, and Lord knows, that's only the start."

He sounded as weary as Gary felt, and Gary was bone tired. He'd slept little the previous night. Every time he closed his eyes, two men's faces swam there: Marius, staring at him before they'd zipped him into the body bag, and Brad.

Except Brad was never far from Gary's mind. There were occasions when he'd realize with a hot flood of remorse that he hadn't thought about Brad for a couple of days.

That was when the sweater would come out of the closet.

"We're exploring every avenue," Gary ventured. "We've pulled all the records—"

"I know what you're doing. I've read the reports." Travers scraped his fingers through his graying hair. The lines around his eyes seemed deeper than usual. "You're in here because the chief feels we can be doing more."

"Hey, if the chief has any suggestions, let's hear 'em." Gary folded his arms, his jaw stiff, a dull pain pulsing through his temple.

Travers mimicked his stance. "Actually? He has one. There's a psychic who's worked with NYPD and Chicago PD."

What the fuck?

Gary gaped at him. "You're kidding."

"Nope, not even close. Chief says this guy's gotten results. So he thinks we should bring him on board. Guy by the name of Dan Porter."

Lewis snorted. "Hey, we could give my grandmother a call. She reads stuff in tea leaves. Or there's this woman who claims she can tell the future from dropping asparagus onto the floor and looking at the patterns it makes when it falls. Maybe *she* can find our killer. Want me to go to the store for a shit-ton of asparagus?"

Travers glared at him. "I'll try to remember not to repeat your suggestions the next time I get called into the chief's office." He sat in his chair, elbows on the desk, his fingers steepled, his gaze locked on Gary. "I know how it sounds." His low, earnest voice was clearly an attempt at mollification. "I was as incredulous as you, but I've done some checking. Dan Porter appears to be a genuine psychic."

"Is there such a thing?" Lewis retorted.

Travers ignored him. "His results aren't flukes, that's for damn sure. I don't claim to know how he does it, but he's helped cops solve crimes. And *that* came from the chief. He's been in contact with NYPD and Chicago to make sure the reports were accurate." Travers sagged in his chair. "All I'm saying is, maybe we should talk to the guy. It can't hurt, right?"

Gary struggled to breathe evenly, his stomach clenched. "No. We are *not* resorting to mumbo jumbo, voodoo, or any other new age happy crap."

Beside him, Lewis nodded. "The chief may go in for all that hogwash, but come *on*. We're the professionals here. We know how to catch this guy, and it's by good old-fashioned detecting."

Gary had to fight hard not to stare at Lewis. *Well fuck, we agree on something.*

Travers's face hardened. "Then get out there and detect. I don't want you coming in here and telling me victim number six has just shown up." He stood, reached for a coffee cup, and went over to the pot that sat in the corner.

Apparently they were done.

XENIA MELZER was born and raised in a small village in the South of Bavaria. As one of nature's true chocoholics, she's always in search of the perfect chocolate experience. So far, she's had about a dozen truly remarkable ones. Despite having been in close proximity to the mountains all her life, she has never understood why so many people think snow sports are fun. There are neither chocolate nor horses involved and it's cold by definition, so where's the sense? She does not like beer either and has never been to the Oktoberfest—no quality chocolate there.

Even though her mind is preoccupied with various stories most of the time, Xenia has managed to get through school and university with surprisingly good grades. Right after school she met her one true love who showed her that reality is capable of producing some truly amazing love stories itself.

While she was having her two children, she started writing down the most persistent stories in her head as a way of relieving mommy-related stress symptoms. As it turned out, the stress relief has now become a source of the same, albeit a positive one.

When she's not writing, she translates other authors' manuscripts to German, enjoys riding and running, spending time with her kids, and dancing with her husband.

Website: www.xeniamelzer.com

Email: info@xeniamelzer.com

Follow me on BookBub

THERE IS NO CRIME WITHOUT WITNESSES

ARTHROPODA

AN
ANDI HAYES
MYSTERY

An Andi Hayes Murder Mystery

Detective George Donovan doesn't plan to stay in Charleston long. Skeptical and by-the-book, he's on the fast track to the top, and he won't let anything derail his career. Especially not Andrew Hayes, his grumpy, awkward new partner—and not the chief's secret order to find out how said partner solves even the most difficult cases.

George and Andi can't agree on anything except their mutual dislike, but when three dead girls turn up at a storage unit, they must put their differences aside before the suspected trafficking ring claims another victim.

There is no crime without witnesses. Andi knows George suspects his always-right "hunches" point to corruption, but he doesn't care. All that matters is catching a killer... and keeping his secret. But with leads on this sprawling conspiracy drying up, he has no choice. He just can't let his partner find out how he's getting the information.

Andi's on the verge of losing his life, his mind, and his career. He could take George down with him...

If the violent criminals who are always one step ahead don't get to them first.

www.dsppublications.com

THERE IS NO CRIME WITHOUT WITNESSES

ERUCA

AN
ANDI HAYES
MYSTERY

XENIA MELZER

An Andi Hayes Murder Mystery

There is no crime without witnesses

When Detective George Donovan and his eccentric partner, Detective Andi Hayes, need a break from their gruesome job, a hike seems like just the thing.

Unfortunately, the job catches up with them when they find three dead men in a lake.

When the promising clues dry up, George and Andi turn once more to Andi's "gift"—but this time things aren't so easy. Andi's mysterious talents are growing stronger, making it harder to block out the barrage of information and taking a toll on his physical and mental health. The cryptic clues his informants offer are even more bizarre than the case itself. And the more they discover about the victims, the more uncomfortable the investigation becomes.

Torn between catching a killer and serving justice, between George's career and Andi's sanity, the detectives have their work cut out for them if they're going to solve these murders.

www.dsppublications.com

CASTO

GODS OF WAR

XENIA MELZER

Gods of War: Book I

All is fair in love and war. Renaldo has lived happily by that proverb his entire life. But he has finally met his match, and he's about to discover how unfair love and war can be.

When demigod and warlord Lord Renaldo takes a beautiful stranger captive during an ambush, he is delighted to have found a distraction that will keep him entertained during the upcoming siege. Little does he know, Casto is keeping more than just one secret from him. Slowly, Renaldo gets sucked into a turbulent roller-coaster relationship with his mysterious prisoner, one that begins with hatred and soon spirals into a whirlwind of conflicting emotions. And when it seems that things can get no worse, an old enemy stirs right in the heart of his home.

Determined to keep Casto by his side, Renaldo has to find a balance between the capricious young man and his own destiny as a ruler and god to his people.

www.dreamspinnerpress.com

A DOM
AND
HIS
WRITER

XENIA
MELZER

CLUB WHISPER

A Club Whisper Novel

Life is perfect for Richard and Dean. Richard is a wealthy and successful businessman who also owns a BDSM club, and Dean is a best-selling author and sub to Richard. They're young, happy, and in love. The future is bright....

Until tragedy strikes and an accident claims Dean's beloved sister. Dean finds himself the guardian of a three-month-old infant, and soon he's trading in his leather fetish gear for diapers and drool bibs. But little Emily is all that remains of his family, so how can he abandon her?

It's not what Richard signed up for. As much as he tries to be supportive, he never wanted kids and misses having his partner to himself. Suddenly the life he imagined for them is gone, and he's not sure their relationship can survive the upheaval. But fate isn't through with Dean, and when misfortune strikes again, will he be able to turn to the man he loves? A final crisis will determine if they can pull together as a family or must face facts and part ways.

www.dreamspinnerpress.com

For more
great fiction
from

DSP PUBLICATIONS

visit us online.
WWW.DSPPUBLICATIONS.COM

www.ingramcontent.com/pod-product-compliance
Lightning Source LLC
Chambersburg PA
CBHW051639260626
47170CB00004B/1246